RAVE REVIEWS FOR EVELYN ROGERS!

DEVIL IN THE DARK
"Woven with suspense and an evocative flair
for the darkly dramatic, this is a perfect read."
—*Romantic Times*

THE LONER (SECRET FIRES)
"An enjoyable story and a must for those
who have been following the McBride saga!"
—*Romantic Times*

SECOND OPINION
"This plot sizzles with originality. Poignant tenderness
skillfully peppered with passionate sensuality
assures readers of fabulous entertainment."
—*Rendezvous*

GOLDEN MAN
"A sexy sensual story you won't ever forget. When it comes to
finding a perfect hero, this book has it all. Fantastic! Five Bells!"
—*Bell, Book and Candle*

WICKED
HOLT Medallion Finalist for Paranormal Romance!
"Evelyn Rogers brings this charming story of a man too wicked to
be good and a woman too good to be good to life."
—*Romantic Times*

DEVILISH THOUGHTS

Images flashed through her mind ... weeks of watching him work shirtless in the sun, trickles of sweat running down his face, his chest, his spine ... the sideways looks he cast her when he thought she wasn't looking ... the coldness of her wedding night memories ... the heat of his hands searching her body for injury.

Oh, yes, she thought with a strange kind of joy, let the devil himself take the warnings of danger, and take, too, her own vows for a solitary life. She had fallen in more ways than one, but she felt no regret.

She let her gaze trail down him, to his unfastened shirt, his tight trousers, his long legs with their powerful thighs. She had to force her eyes back to his face.

"If I am frightened, only you can make it go away," she said, then again in a fervent whisper, "Make the fear go away."

She wrapped her hands in the fullness of his shirt and held on tight as he touched her lips with his tongue.

"There is no turning back," he whispered against her opening mouth.

•

EVELYN ROGERS

The GROTTO

LOVE SPELL BOOKS NEW YORK CITY

A LOVE SPELL® BOOK

May 2002

Published by

Dorchester Publishing Co., Inc.
276 Fifth Avenue
New York, NY 10001

ISBN 0-505-52479-1

The name "Love Spell" and its logo are trademarks of Dorchester Publishing Co., Inc.

Printed in the United States of America.

Visit us on the web at www.dorchesterpub.com.

For Dr. Laurence Barker,
who showed me the riches of Italy.

And for Andrew Lawrence Rogers,
the newest hero in the family.

The GROTTO

Prologue

Within the hour, Conte Pietro Donati would begin the business of impregnating his wife.

He chuckled as he staggered along the path beside the night-shadowed Grand Canal. His luck had been abominable lately, but an heir would change all that. And there was only one way to get the brat. He would give his contessa what she deserved.

His wine-heavy blood pulsed at the thought. Stroking the small, jagged scar at the corner of his mouth, he thought of the Villa Falcone. An old anger ate through his lust and drunkenness. Oh yes, she would get what was coming to her.

And so would he.

The moon peeked from behind a cloud, casting a glow across the wall of mist-shrouded palazzos lining one side of the walkway. As if frightened, it hid once again, useless in the starless night sky. Pale and undependable was the moon, like the contessa. Both moon and woman made his way treacherous, he thought, one leaving him in darkness, the other driving him to drink and whores.

And to the gambling tables. It was because of her that he, Pietro Donati, last of an old and powerful family, was dangerously close to destitution. She was American, this wealthy woman, this *cagna* he'd taken as his wife. More than five years married, and still she did not understand how to satisfy him. His loins tightened. Tonight she would learn. He would get her with child.

A sigh of satisfaction mixed with anticipation shook him, strengthening into a sense of power. His contessa was wealthy no longer. He had long ago used up her funds. But he'd scarcely used her ivory-white body, not in the ways he preferred. Such was the reason for her barren state. Her fear of pain, of bondage, must end. She would pay for her years of scorn.

It was her duty to submit to whatever he wanted; even his beloved mother, weak though she was, had given her life in the attempt to bear him a brother. Again he fingered the scar. Caterina might look weak, but she was not. She should give him a dozen sons, if that was what he chose.

Concentrating on what he would do to her, he

slipped on a patch of wet stone but managed to right himself. Another chuckle. First he had to get home.

Clutching his cloak around himself, he lurched through the dark, each step as determined as a night of revelry would allow. The curse that had darkened his days and nights would lift with the coming dawn. Within the hour the contessa would know the man she had vowed to obey, know him as well as the two signorinas with whom he had passed the long night.

His lips twisted into a smile. They had been young, a third his age, and he had instructed them in the ways of lovemaking. In truth, rare honesty made him admit, they had also instructed him.

Tonight he was invincible. Had the whores not told him so? Even the Conte—Pietro always thought of his late father as the Conte—would be smiling his blessing down on his only son, a blessing he had never given when he was alive.

Waves from a boat passing silently along the canal lapped close to his feet, splashing water onto the narrow stone walkway. Again he slipped, then righted himself, held his squat body erect. The thought of bedding Caterina set feathers tickling his loins, and his blood pumped faster. Months had passed since she had last submitted to him. With her long legs and full lips, she was not without her allures. For whom did she save them?

3

He did not begrudge her her private pleasures. It was the way of the nobility. As long as she was discreet, as long as she spread those legs for him. As long as she put those lips where they could serve him as he deserved.

The whores had done just that, without his orders. So would his wife.

Footsteps sounded along the stones behind him. He glanced over his shoulder but saw only shadows cast by the flickering lantern on a dockside post. He wiped the moisture from his brow. The evening was cool, even in early June. He had no reason to perspire.

Again the footsteps. A sudden fear tore at him, sharp as the talons of a falcon. For no reason. He did not own the walkway; other revelers would be about. This was Venice, after all, a city devoted to late-night celebration.

And if the darkness hid a thief? What harm could such a scoundrel do him? His purse lay limp and empty in his pocket, the jewels that once adorned his fingers gone to pay his debts. He had reached the depths of his aristocratic world, a fact that on this cloudy night he could at last admit.

From this lowly position, he had only one direction he could go. Belatedly he would prove his father's prophecy wrong. He was not a wastrel, nor, as the late conte had sneered more than once, a mistake.

4

Righteousness masked his fear, and his short stride quickened. He would give up drink, abandon whores, devote himself to his duties as a conte . . . at least until his contessa was with child. Until then, he would not waste his seed on whores.

A curious exhilaration shot through him. Tonight he was invincible, was he not?

"Come forward," he shouted toward the somber sky, letting the sound drift down upon the shadows of the night. "Do not skulk in the dark."

The words echoed across the water, bounced against the high walls beside him, reverberated in the balconies overlooking the canal.

Slowing, he dared glance behind him. The shadows coalesced into the shape of a man, tall, lean, purposeful, the slope of his shoulders, the tilt of his head far too familiar for the conte to ignore. He blinked, looked away, then stared once again at the apparition. It was a man, most certainly, and not a ghost.

But the man . . . He was more than just a man. He was . . .

The conte's heart stopped and his blood ran cold. It couldn't be. He was staring at a lie. He licked his lips. Too much wine, that was the problem. He was right to give it up.

He gripped his head, trying to clear his mind. But the image and the fear it brought buzzed crazily inside him, the feathers in his loins turned to swarming bees.

"Who goes there?" he shouted, and in the answering silence he repeated the words, adding, "You are dead."

He must get away, reach the palazzo, where he could think. Quickening his step once again, he paid no mind to the slick stones, to the instability of his gait. When the worn sole of his shoe skidded on a shallow sheen of water, he pitched forward, helpless, arms flailing for support, his cloak floating like a dark cloud around him as he fell.

His head struck the edge of the walkway. Scarcely feeling the pain, he slipped beneath the surface of the canal, the lapping waves closing over him as if he had never been. His clothes—too many clothes—absorbed the dark water, dragged him into the murky depths. Deeper he sank, ever deeper, barely conscious, headed for the gates of Hell. If the air for which he instinctively gasped proved liquid, he did not know it. If strong hands grabbed at him, he did not feel them.

He knew only darkness and descent and, at last, the absence of worry, freedom from disgrace.

One final thought took hold before he slipped into oblivion. The whores had been right: He was truly invincible.

Chapter One

Il conte è morto.

Contessa Caterina Donati whispered the words as her hired carriage rumbled past the scattered huts marking the seaside village of Belmare. She whispered them again in English. No matter how many times she said them, in either language, out loud or to herself, they seemed no more real than they had on that gloomy morning a month earlier when her husband's sodden, lifeless body was delivered unceremoniously to the family palazzo.

But they were real enough to the rest of the world. Her present situation provided bitter proof.

Her shoulders slanted from side to side as the poorly sprung gig jounced through the narrow, twisting streets, the buildings clustered closer now as she entered the heart of the village she had once

7

thought might be her home. The thought had been fleeting. It lasted two nights.

With a sense of foreboding, she looked through the carriage window at the occasional passing villagers. Without exception they stared back with dark, angry eyes, watching from the roadside as she slowly rode by, their numbers increasing as she rode deeper into town.

Her heart grew heavy, the hope she brought with her fluttering weakly. They knew who she was, though no identifying flag flew from the carriage, no family crest adorned the passenger door. Other than a few servants who once worked in the Donati villa and its fields, she had met none of them; during her brief stay in their part of the world, she had kept indoors at Pietro's insistence.

Yet they knew her. More puzzling, what mystic power of communication had told them that she would arrive today? How had they known she would ever return?

Her breathing grew shallow. More than five years had passed since a Donati visited this small, poor village that clung to a narrow stretch of jagged Tuscan coast. Five long years, but the hatred of the people remained. It drifted into the carriage like the hot summer wind coming off the dark sea. She felt it more now than when she had come here as a bride.

Kate understood that hate. The Donatis had

brought ruin to them all. A month ago, incapable of harming anyone else, the last of the noble family had brought ruin to himself.

Il conte è morto.

But the harm he had wreaked lived on. His death had not been enough to ease their hatred. It festered in their eyes.

Like her late husband, she bore the despised name of Donati. She would take it to her grave, along with the title she had never wanted. That had been her father's obsession. Like the conte, he was gone, the two men who had held complete power over her, who had abandoned her to a fate she was powerless to avoid.

A thick twist of yellow hair lay heavily against the back of her neck, sending rivulets of perspiration down her spine, and the black silk mourning gown clung to her sweat-slick skin. Her lips cracked from lack of moisture. How comforting it would be to order the carriage to a halt, to step into the street and ask for a cup of water. She would gladly part with one of the few coins in her purse for such a respite.

More, she would tell the villagers she knew the suffering that had resulted when Pietro closed Donati fields to them, departed the villa, left the servants and farmers with nothing but the meager living they could wrest from the sea. She could go further and tell them that all yet might be well.

9

But such reassurance might prove to be a lie. The eyes of the villagers, roughly clad men and women, and children, too, told her not to dare.

She wanted to grab the bonnet resting on the cracked leather seat beside her and cram it back in place, letting its sides act as blinders against their ill will. Instead, she clutched her hands together in her lap and held her head high.

Without warning, the carriage lurched to a stop, and she was flung forward, one shoulder striking sharply against the hard wall in front of her. She righted herself, gingerly flexed the muscles of her injured shoulder, and pressed gloved fingers to the perspiration on her forehead. What now? She could not venture to guess.

"Contessa Donati?"

She stared at the scowling face in the window. It belonged to a young man, coarse-featured and thick of body, his unruly black hair cut short beneath a narrow cap that marked officialdom. She recognized him right away, not by name but by his station in life. He was what passed for authority in the village.

Over the past few weeks she had learned to recognize authority very well, no matter the form it took.

"*Si*, Constable," she said, forcing herself into the Italian of her late husband's people, the language that now and evermore would be hers. "Is there anything wrong?"

He viewed her with a mixture of arrogance and curiosity, neither of which he would have openly revealed when she was rich.

"In the name of Grand Duke Leopold, I wish only to learn if your journey has been a safe one."

He dared lower his eyes to take in the length of her neck, the sloping shoulders, the black silk sculpted by sweat against the curve of her breasts.

"The road between here and Florence can be a hazardous one for a woman traveling alone," he added, his voice thick with mock concern.

Kate almost laughed. He spoke as if thieves were her worst worry. The hired gig showed no sign its lone occupant would offer much in the way of booty. Not once had she been threatened, even when she traveled in the dark of night.

Talk of the grand duke's concern was even more ludicrous. Early in their marriage she and the conte had visited Leopold in the Pitti Palace, on their final journey from Belmare to Venice, a journey that took them through the Florentine city. He had shown little interest in them, and that had been when they were not yet destitute, when the conte still retained a portion of his inherited wealth and all of hers.

Pietro had not sensed the grand duke's slights. Though she had already experienced the extremes of her husband's cruelty, she had been embarrassed for him.

Leopold, she knew, would not be interested in her now.

In stopping the carriage, the constable had acted on his own, eager to boast over an evening flagon of wine how he had detained the once mighty contessa, had brazenly looked her over, had determined she was a pitiful creature indeed. This much she understood far too well.

Kate's eyes, normally far too large in her too-thin face, narrowed in a rush of anger, but she kept her voice modulated. Anger was an emotion she was too poor to afford.

"*Per favore,* inform the grand duke that the journey went well and that I am grateful to return to the duchy over which he so honorably rules."

She could scarcely keep the sarcasm from her voice. Leopold was no more tyrant than any of the other dukes in this loosely allied collection of states known as Italy. But he was in authority. And he was a man. It was, she knew far too well, an unfortunate combination of traits.

With a glance over his shoulder at his audience, the constable raised his voice.

"The grand duke worries also about the villa you have chosen as your home." Another lie.

"And why is that?" she asked. Did not Leopold know it was the only home left to her, the Venetian palazzo and apartments in Milan having gone to creditors? Of course he knew. And so did everyone staring at her in the shabby hired gig. Anywhere in the world, in Boston as well as in Tuscany, bad news, especially the kind involving an enemy, traveled fast.

The constable was intrepid in his purpose. He wanted much to talk about over the wine.

"La maledetta," he said, putting all the operatic drama he could into the word. "The curse of the falcon."

"I do not believe in curses," she said. She, too, spoke loud enough for all to hear.

A sneer rippled across the constable's coarse features. "I forget you are Americana."

"My birthplace has little to do with my beliefs." But of course it did. Had not the conte reminded her more than once that she came from a land of barbarians?

In the stillness that followed her pronouncement, she looked beyond the young man to the villagers gathered at the edge of the road. Above all else, she wanted to smile, to nod, to let them know she was not a foolish foreigner who chose to ignore their ways. Nor was she a scornful aristocrat who viewed lesser mortals as beneath contempt.

In Belmare she was the lesser mortal. Not one day of her life had been spent in anything close to hard labor, while their days had known little else.

But the smile would not come. She lacked the strength. And from the time she learned to walk and talk she had understood the necessity of keeping her feelings to herself.

Weariness washed over her, and a desire to be done with this interminable journey. She was about to sit back and wait for the gig to resume its lurching progress when she saw him, a tall figure standing behind the other villagers, hatless in the noonday sun, his long black hair catching the ruthless rays like polished obsidian.

He stood unmoving, still as a Michelangelo sculpture, but there was nothing of cold marble in the gilded skin that stretched over prominent cheekbones, high forehead, and strong, square jaw, no coldness in the midnight eyes that studied her like a bird of prey.

Like others around him, he wore a thickly woven shirt the color of Tuscan dust, but in the way he held himself it rested on his broad shoulders more grandly than any silken cloak Pietro had ever owned. He throbbed with life. A peasant, no doubt, a villager. His clothing, his place in the crowd said it was so, though he stood apart from them, unremarked for all his distinctive appearance, like a ghost only she could see.

But he was no ghost, not with such vibrancy rising off him like heat waves from the land itself. He

14

was also the most handsome man she had ever seen.

She shrank into the shadow of the carriage, her own throbbing breath caught in her throat. A whip cracked in the hot, still air and the carriage jerked into motion once again.

Scarcely aware of the jostling, she knew only the burn of shame flushing her cheeks, for in the instant before she retreated, their eyes had met and he had read her interest. He had shown it in a barely perceptible nod, a movement meant only for her.

Her shame was foolish, uncalled for; her interest sprang from nothing more wanton than a curiosity about the people who would be her neighbors. He had stood out, not because of his height or physical power, or even his good looks, but because his had been the only eyes not burning with hate.

One lingering thought would not go away, the idea that she had seen him before, that he came to her on this momentous day from out of her past. The thought was absurd. She had never seen anyone like him in her life. But she knew she would see him again.

Within minutes, the driver of the gig reined away from Belmare onto an even narrower, more rutted road winding up a hillside toward the villa that was all she had left in the world, and she was able to put the stranger out of her mind. She even dared

15

thrust her head outside the window, felt a breeze ruffle her hair, stared up to the top of the hill at her waiting home.

With its central tower and outstretched wings to the right and left, the Villa Falcone resembled the bird for which it had been named, the assassin that had brought about the curse on Donati land.

Waves of heat made the wings appear to move, as if warning her away. Kate blinked and the wings grew still. She had spoken truthfully when she denied a belief in curses. In truth, she believed in little except the small hard knot of pride that pulsed where other women kept a heart.

Her father had almost destroyed that pride, as had her husband. No man would have the chance again. Somehow, on her own, in ways she had only tentatively explored in her mind, she would survive.

Such brave words, little indicating the enormity of what she wanted to do. Over the next days, months and years, it would be her challenge to prove the words true.

Shifting her gaze from the villa, she stared out at the passing fields of yellow broom with their clusters of dying flowers, the valiant oaks clinging to the dry soil, the browning shrubbery, willing her mind not to think. If she thought too much, she might dwell on the past, on the depravity that had been visited upon her at the villa, on the details of that depravity she could never quite forget.

But that was long ago. The conte was dead.

She twisted enough so that she could see behind her the expanse of water over which she had sailed on her first journey to the villa. Out of sight in the distant mist lay the island of Elba, once the prison of a man who had known power of which the rest of the world could scarcely dream.

Was the Villa Falcone to be her prison, the way the island had been for Napoleon? It was a question she could not answer readily. It was a question she did not want to ask, and so she turned her gaze upward to the villa on the hill, the hope in her breast as faint as her heartbeat. But like that pulse, it persisted. She could not let it die.

What would the villagers think if they knew of her doubts, of her dreams? She thought of one villager, the dark, handsome stranger who had given her a knowing nod. She sensed he would understand. But would he, or any of them, approve? It was another question she did not want to ask.

It was another answer she would find out all too soon.

·

Chapter Two

A high stone wall surrounded the villa itself, reminding Kate of a fortress. The massive wrought-iron gate that crossed the road had been left open, its heavy bell silent.

As the gig creaked onto the circular driveway, a sudden gust of hot wind rattled the gate, drawing a lone, mournful clang from the bell, as if on this bright, cloudless day the forces of darkness felt compelled to announce her arrival.

Darkness indeed, she thought, as the carriage moved slowly up the final yards to the front of the house. What had come over her? She must be made of sterner stuff.

Though he moved slowly, her lone servant, Alfiero, awaited her, opening the door and offering a hand to help her alight.

The sight of him gave her heart a lift and quickened its beat. His early arrival must have alerted the villagers to her momentary arrival. She felt foolish for thinking the news had sprung from anything supernatural.

She smiled at the dear man, tall, thin, his back bent too soon with age. His hair was streaked with gray, his deep-set eyes and aquiline nose set in a heavily lined face, reminding her of his long years of servitude for a family that got the most from its hired help.

There was a weariness, too, in his dark eyes, as if he had seen far too much unpleasantness in his long life. He tried to mask the weariness when he was around her—he was doing so now—but she could see it when his guard was down.

Of all the Donati servants, he had been the only one to remain at her side when the creditors at last departed. He had even volunteered to come early to the villa and ready it for her arrival. Her gratitude was boundless, but when she tried to tell him so, he murmured that he knew his duty, and his position in the world, though others seemed to have forgotten theirs.

She had not taken his response as a rebuff. He knew the hardships she would be facing, hardships he would also bear. No matter how formal he remained, it had to be more than duty that kept him at her side.

On legs weary from the long journey south, she walked toward the carved wooden double doors of the Villa Falcone. On her first visit all those years ago, when she and the conte were newlyweds, they had traveled by ship, and she had been far more rested.

She had also been innocent. She was innocent no more.

"Quickly," Alfiero snapped behind her, his words directed to the coachman, "the contessa's belongings. Inside. They bake in the sun."

Despite his sixty years, he spoke with an aristocratic command she could never muster. It wasn't her shaky use of Italian that deterred her. As the late conte had been quick to point out, she lacked the proper attitude.

The coachman moved hastily with a deference he would never have shown to her. She had to hurry to get inside ahead of the two worn valises that he dropped onto the entryway's stone floor. Payment for the journey had already been made, but she fumbled through her purse for a few coins.

"That will be all," Alfiero said with a firmness that wiped the expectant look from the coachman's face, and he was soon on his way, stirring up dust as the gig rumbled away from the villa, through the rigidly silent iron gate, and down the hill.

Alfiero closed the massive doors, their solid thud reminding Kate of the conte's coffin lid as it fell over his remains. For a moment, as if buried alive in the centuries-old villa, Kate could scarcely breathe. She was back. She truly was back, though she had once vowed never to return.

Like the clang of the bell, the walls of the entryway whispered a mournful welcome. She was certain of it, though the exact words were not clear. They brushed across her skin like the passing of warm air, or the movement of spirits made restless by her unexpected presence. A sense of foreboding gripped her, warring with a feeling of anticipation. She did not know which was the stronger, which sensation would eventually prevail.

Oblivious to all that assailed her, Alfiero turned with a bow. "Welcome to the Villa Falcone, Contessa Donati," he said. How normal he sounded, how much his usual self, his voice the lone sound as it echoed against the walls. She was able to take a deep breath. She yearned for the handshake of a friend, even a quick, affectionate embrace, but he would have been horrified at such familiarity.

He was right, of course, to retain such an attitude. At this point in her life, a display of affection, of gentleness, might be her undoing.

He lifted the valises, light burdens even for his stooped figure, though they contained all the personal possessions she could now claim. "I will show you to your room."

She glanced around the wide entryway, to the

high stuccoed walls that were the color of ripe peach flesh, paler in places where once valuable tapestries had hung, to the overhead chandelier with its myriad unlit candle stubs, to the high window over the doors that provided a shaft of natural light.

The air was cool, the old walls sufficiently thick to fend off the summer heat. A chill shivered through her, but not from the change in temperature. Despite her earlier residence, she was a stranger here, an unwanted one from the hatred in the villagers' eyes, taking her residence in this rambling, cursed structure because, like Alfiero, she had no place else to go. It was possible the wind, the bell, the walls had not been welcoming her but rather ordering her to leave.

She shook off the chill, and, too, the sense of foreboding. Where was her Yankee sensibility? Faintness of heart must not be tolerated, nor dispiriting memories. She was alive, she was in good health and she had a plan, vague though it was.

She smiled at Alfiero. "Yes, please show me to my room. The bright one, I hope, with the balcony overlooking the terrace. Though it's been years, I remember it with fondness."

As well she should. It had been the one place in all the villa where she had felt safe.

Walking up the winding staircase, she thought of the first time she had trod this way. In those days, the villa had abounded with servants, and there had been excitement in the air. When the ruling Donati was in residence, visitors came, and parties lasted well into the early morning. A new contessa, still a bride, called for very special entertainment indeed.

It was an excitement she had not been able to share. Two weeks before that first arrival, she and the conte had been married in Venice with much pomp and ceremony in the magnificent baroque church of Santa Maria della Salute, surrounded by paintings of Titian and Tintorello, the onlookers the wealthy and titled of the city and beyond, the presiding priest the archbishop himself.

In the audience had been her father, puffed with pride that she had made such a marriage when back in Boston she attracted primarily grasping men who wanted nothing but her fortune. That he had allowed her to associate with no one she would have considered eligible was not a fact he could ever admit. The Bohemian artist, the writer, the scholar—these were men whose callings were removed from the world of commerce and therefore beneath his contempt, though she would have liked to encourage a deeper acquaintance with them.

Placid though she had been in Boston, she had fought him on the marriage, sensing that this fawning Italian aristocrat who praised her beauty with poetic excess might be no better than the greedy suitors in America. She was not beautiful. But she was rich.

Eager to return to Boston with news of his only child's triumph, her father had not listened. His arguments had worn her down. Always she had been a dutiful daughter, accepting of her fate. Perhaps, she had told herself, the conte would not be so bad. Certainly he was surrounded by friends and admirers. And he displayed a wealth as great as her own.

They had set sail immediately for Tuscany, that time of year in Venice being cold and damp. Her father also departed, but, she was to find out weeks later, his ship had gone down in an Atlantic storm. He never knew the fate to which he had consigned his only child.

The wedding night was to be spent in the conte's luxurious cabin. He had made lewd suggestions about the rhythms of the water aiding the pleasure that awaited them. But those same rhythms had rendered him helplessly sick. When she tried to attend him, he shoved her from the stateroom, using the little strength left to him, and she had spent the first weeks of their marriage walking the deck, observing the beauty of the sea, pushing from her mind what awaited her in Tuscany.

On land, he immediately began his recuperation. Two days in the villa and he ordered her to his bedchamber on the second floor of the central tower. Her room lay another flight up, selected by her for its balcony and the view of the countryside. Pietro Donati had not been so interested in the landscape, and he disliked climbing stairs.

Besides, as she found out soon enough, he delighted in ordering that she come like a supplicant to him in his own darker but far grander bedchamber.

Now, as she passed the hallway leading to that chamber, she found the air musty, close, cloying, the darkness impenetrable. She refused to give the hallway a glance; the air and the gloom held too vividly the smell and color of remembered cruelty. Nothing she could do, nothing she could tell herself, would erase the memory of that first night with the conte, their long-delayed wedding night, the night she learned the hell into which she had been delivered. She would seal off the chamber, seal off the entire floor if she could.

When she entered her own sparsely furnished room, it was exactly as she remembered it, spacious and light, with windows opening out on the hills.

"You've readied it for me," she said to Alfiero.

He nodded, short of breath.

Her conscience struck. "Please, don't come up those stairs again. I forbid it." That brought a lift of his brows. She never forbade anything that remained forbidden long.

This time she was adamant. "Whatever needs to be done up here, I can handle it."

He murmured dissent but soon saw her word was not to be brooked. She suspected that in his heart he was secretly relieved.

After he departed, she looked at the white iron bed with its white bedcovers, at the matching white lace curtains, the ochre walls that, except for a large mirror, were without decoration. Like the mistress of the house, she thought as she stared at her reflection. Pale skin, pale hair, overlarge watery blue eyes, gaunt cheeks, a tall, thin body clad in a loose-fitting, incongruous black gown. The dark-eyed villager must have been laughing to himself when he viewed this latest contessa who had come to claim the Villa Falcone. Like the villa itself, she had nothing of value to show.

But looks could be deceiving, in men and women both. Throwing open the windows, she stared out at the land that was now hers, taking in the sweep of the fields and the far hills in one exhilarating glance. Drawing a deep breath, she told herself that eventually all would be well.

Later, when she had changed from the cloying silk into a lighter gown—still black, of course, so that she might conform to the outward trappings of grief—after she had supped on a thick bean soup and the saltless Tuscan bread the conte had detested and she had come to love, after a useless attempt to rest, she hurried to the outside stone steps that led from her bedroom balcony down two floors to the terrace, then onto another shorter set of stairs leading to the overgrown rolling land at the rear of the Villa Falcone.

It was on this second set of stairs that she met with an accident. A stone in one of the high steps came loose under her weight and she stumbled, tripping down the stairs, landing on her bottom on the hard ground, one sleeve ripping open on the corner of the final step.

With a groan, she looked at the tear. A thin line of blood appeared on her forearm; she blotted it away with the cloth. It was nothing, a minor scratch. Gingerly she pulled herself to her feet. Other than a loss of dignity, she seemed little worse for the fall.

Chagrined by her clumsiness, she managed a smile. *All right, Contessa, you must do better to act your part.*

And so she would, when the need arose, but she would have to be careful. Like Venice and Milan, Tuscany was an alien land to her.

But how beautiful it was, rolling hills lined with rows of tall cypress trees, an endless stretch of sky, a land of ancient peoples, of grand art and music, of riches her native country could not emulate. And at its most dramatic boundary, beneath a high limestone cliff topped by thick shrubbery, lay the deep, dark Mediterranean that flowed beyond Elba to equally exotic climes—France, Spain, the edge of mysterious Africa.

In contrast, America, especially Boston, seemed isolated indeed.

She breathed deeply, taking in the hint of lavender and the sweet, fragrant broom that hung on the cooling air, their scents laced with a hint of the sea. With the setting sun at her back, she found herself drawn past a long-dead flower garden directly behind the terrace, across rolling land to another weed-choked garden, this one formerly a source of food for the Donati table, through the simple iron gate in the back section of the stone wall to the far fields with their mixture of olive trees and grapevines, everything wild, neglected, challenging.

In vain she tried to remember how the fields had appeared all those years ago. But so much had occupied her inside the house, not the least of which was Pietro's order that she stay far from the laborers who toiled in his fields, she had not been concerned with such unimportant matters as the land on which she lived. She had contented herself—if contented could describe her tormented state— with looking at the fields from the windows of her room.

On this bright July day, the marriage was past; land was everything now.

Ignoring the weeds that tugged at her skirt, she followed an uneven path that led to the first of the fields, her steps emboldened by a rush of freedom that left her light-headed. No whispers, no bells assailed her now, only the sky and the sun and the hard earth under her shoes. In truth, though this was an ancient land, she felt like an infant born into a new world.

The feeling came unexpectedly and made her smile. Ah, if only she could be as innocent as an infant, her fertile mind blank but eager to discover the wonders of the world.

But she was not innocent. The conte had seen to that.

A breeze tugged at her hair. Alone, she felt free to unbind it and let the long locks flow freely. She even dared loosen the top buttons of her gown, pulling the snug collar away from her neck and the rise of her breasts. Closing her eyes for a moment, she let the air play with her in intimate ways she had never allowed the conte.

Freedom was the wine from which she would sip, more intoxicating by far than any that the rampant grapes lying before her could yield. No man would understand. Men were born to freedom. Some women, too, she admitted. But not Kate. She had much to experience, much to learn.

29

Once again taking up her desultory pace, she wandered farther from the villa, halting just past a gnarled, leafless elm, its limbs draped thickly with ungoverned vines. The tree's long, late-evening shadow fell across her path. An errant vine hung from one of the limbs, and in the shadow took on the appearance of a noose around her neck, or so the image seemed as it fell across the parched ground before her.

An omen? A reminder of the curse? Foolish thoughts. The shadow was a coincidence, the invention of a weary woman's imagination.

She stirred the dust, but the image remained. And then she saw another image, a shadow looming next to hers, the shadow of a man. Like a ghost, he had moved silently into her path, the hangman come to ply his trade.

With a scream, she bolted forward, stumbled on the uneven terrain and fell, pushed herself around to a sitting position and dared to look at her executioner.

The scream became a gasp. She was caught in the gaze of the man from the village, the tall one with the penetrating eyes, the beautiful one—there was no other way to describe him. The only villager who had not looked at her with hatred.

But the hatred was there now, flashing briefly in his black eyes, so powerful it pinned her to the ground.

Chapter Three

"*Mi scusi*, Contessa Donati," the intruder said with a bow that Kate supposed he intended as humble. "I did not mean to startle you."

He lied. An underlying edge in his voice, rumbling out of a broad chest, told her the truth. Startling her had been his exact goal. He had succeeded far better than she could let him know.

"I did not expect the contessa to be so *timido*," he added, this time including a shrug that strained the shirt across his shoulders.

The movement caught her eye. Then she realized what he had said, and her face stung from the insult. Without thinking, she replied in English.

"Timid! What else did you expect when you crept up on me the way you did? You frightened me out of my wits."

His thick black brows cocked a fraction, another fascinating movement. She forced herself to calmness, grateful that her anger, momentary though it was, had overtaken fear. Returning to Italian, she matched his mock courtesy.

"I did not expect a trespasser on my land, signore."

"Again I apologize."

It was the one thing he definitely was *not* doing. She had to give him credit. He lied with dignity, his Italian different from that of the Venetians and Milanese, accents to which she had grown accustomed. He had to be a Tuscan laborer, as she had first suspected from the coarseness of his clothes, though there was something in his speech, and everything in his bearing, that denied any hint of peasantry.

As she had thought in the village, he wore his shirt very well, though it was perhaps a shade undersized, his upper body being incredibly well formed. How she could have thought he looked familiar would forever remain a mystery.

Still shaken, she forced her gaze from his eyes, past the sun-gilded skin pulled taut over a high-cheeked, unsmiling face, away from the thick, black collar-length hair, down the strong neck, past the open throat of the shirt, ignoring the sample of dusky chest hair in the opening, down one arm with its sleeve rolled back to reveal more

32

brown skin, more fine, black hair, finally stopping at the outstretched hand offering assistance.

Like the rest of him, the hand was strong, brown, unshaking, confident that she would accept his help. He gave her no chance to decline. When his fingers wrapped around hers, she felt a jolt so strong it made her spine tingle. Did he feel the same current? If so, he gave no sign.

Without effort, he pulled her to her feet, and she stepped quickly away, out of his reach, clenching the hand he had touched into a fist and burying it in the folds of her skirt. It was either that or grab his hand again, to test whether the jolt had been a one-time thing.

He noticed everything she did, and his lips came close to a smile. Whoever or whatever he was, he did not act humble very well.

"You've hurt yourself," he said, his attention turned to the tear in her sleeve.

"It's nothing. It happened earlier." She brushed the dust and twigs from her skirt. "You should have made yourself known to me," she added, sounding peckish when she wanted to sound in control.

Resting his strong, blunt fingers against his muscled thigh, he lowered his eyes, but she knew that as he did so he studied all of her, much as she had studied him. And what did he see? A woman too tall, too thin, pale blue eyes set too wide in a pale, gaunt face, her thick yellow hair blowing wantonly in the breeze.

Italians preferred women shorter, darker, more voluptuous, or so the conte had said. Her intruder gave no sign of pleasure or displeasure, not even when he paused at the bared skin below her throat, but what did that prove? Some men cared little for a woman's appearance, as long as she had a woman's parts. In his pursuit of every skirt that swished past him, the conte had taught her that.

Forcing her eyes from him, she looked around at the deserted landscape. Her stomach tightened. She and the stranger were very much alone. If she cried for help, who would come to her rescue? Alfiero, pitting his frail body against this magnificent specimen?

And how dare she think anything about the intruder was magnificent? He truly was a boor for frightening her so. She should have told him in language he could understand.

She wanted to stamp her feet in anger, as much as she wanted to touch his skin, to discover whether he was as hot as she. So much for the newfound freedom from men that had sent joy rushing through her only minutes before. So much for being newly born.

"This is my land," she said, for the first time in five years sounding a little like a contessa. "Who are you? What are you doing here?"

Once again a glimmer of hatred flashed briefly in his eyes. But was it hate? She was no longer sure. Whatever thoughts burned in his mind, the spark they struck came from an emotion so stark she could not put a name to it.

In that moment he truly frightened her, not because of anything dreamed up in her agitated mind but because of the harsh, undefinable forces she saw in him. Whether or not he revealed his true purpose, she sensed that by her presence in this field, figuratively and physically, she was standing in his way.

His lips twitched, full, sensuous lips without being anything less than masculine, and her fear took on an edge of something else she could not identify, something dark and primal, a stirring deep within.

"My name is Roberto Vela, though that should mean nothing to you, Contessa."

He looked beyond her to the rolling landscape with its neglected growth. As he did so, a different spark colored his eyes. Pride, she thought, and was surprised.

"I once worked this land of yours."

"For my husband."

"No. Never. For the conte before him."

Kate had never met Pietro's father. He had died long before her father brought her to Venice on the fateful journey undertaken from Boston to give his daughter a knowledge of the world—or so he had said. What he had wanted for her was a husband.

But she had heard stories about Renaldo Donati, a tall, handsome, domineering man, an aristocrat born to command, very much different from his short, squat son, his only heir, who could not command even himself.

She shook herself. No matter what the future held, or even the present, she must stop living in the past.

"Why are you here now, Signore Vela?" she asked, wishing he would go away, yet unable to stop her questions. "None of the other villagers seem inclined to have anything to do with me. They, too, worked for my husband's family."

"The work was taken from them, Contessa Donati. I left a long time before that sad occurrence." The look in his eyes became shuttered, absent of hate or pride. "It was my choice to leave."

He spoke flatly, as if purposely keeping out all emotion. But he must have felt deeply about the work. Otherwise, why return? And what had driven him away in the first place? Family? An ambition to succeed elsewhere?

Or had his reason been something darker? She suspected this was so, though she did not know why.

She wanted to tell him that the closing of the

villa was not her doing. But she would sound defensive, belligerent, hurt that she could be so misjudged. She was none of those things. Besides, she could not completely dismiss the thought that perhaps she had been a little at fault. She had been so ignorant.

Maybe she could have made Pietro happy in these Tuscan hills, had she not been so repulsed by his notions of lovemaking. As far as she knew, they were not so different from those of other men. Perhaps all wives submitted to such indignities.

Her repulsion had sent him to the village girls who had likewise, after a while, turned on him. Had she been more compliant, perhaps he would not have dragged her to the cities of the north, where he could find the satisfaction he craved.

He claimed it was the curse of the falcon—the poor crops and bad grapes—that drove him away. But Pietro had never been a man who could find satisfaction in anything so simple as a good yield from his land. Even then, so early in their marriage, she had known that about him.

She wondered how much she would ever know about the man standing before her. What little this Roberto Vela said convinced her there was far more he would not say.

"This land could bring profits again," he said.

She looked away before he could read the surprise in her eyes. Had she not been thinking the very same thing? Only not with such certainty. Her considerations had been diluted by doubt, nourished by nothing but hope.

She studied the bent, overgrown olive trees, between them the wild growth of grapevines long ago overtaking whatever stakes had kept them from spreading their fruit on the ground.

"I don't see how," she said, afraid to let him know of her hopes. Anything she had been considering was too new, too fragile, to discuss with anyone as confident as he, though he seemed to be supporting those very possibilities she nurtured so tenderly.

"Of course you don't. And if you did, would you have the strength to do what is necessary? Would you have the will?"

The words stung, as much from their truth as their boldness.

"You dare say such things because you once worked on this land?"

He knelt, scooped up a handful of dirt and stood to his full height, letting the soil drift from between his fingers, purposely letting the breeze catch the fine particles and blow them back on her. She tasted grit, but all she could see was him.

"Tuscan land is like a woman, Contessa Donati." He moved close, until she could detect the small flecks of light in his dark eyes, could breathe his animal scent. "She must be treated right, plowed and then watered, nourished in the growing season to bring out her full ripeness."

His words, provocative, seductive, made her dizzy. She did not know herself. The surface of her skin felt raw, in need of soothing, and her pulse throbbed in her throat. "She must also be loved," she said, wondering if he would touch her, wondering if she would touch him. He could not possibly be as hot as she.

"If conditions are ideal." His voice turned harsh. "As they so rarely are."

It was a rebuff. It brought her to her senses and cooled her body heat. What was she doing? What was she thinking? She jumped away as if he had burned her.

"Please leave, signore," she said. "You have no right to be here."

He took a moment to answer. "No, I have no right." Again he spoke flatly, and again she felt a turmoil inside him he could barely contain.

He bowed but still was not humble. "First I will see that you return to the villa safely."

Wind whispered through the gray-green leaves of the olive trees. She glanced beyond him to the dead elm and the hanging vine that had reminded her of a noose. For a moment she had fancied him her executioner. And so he still could be. Already he had slain her peace of mind.

"The light is sufficient to guide me home. There

are those who await me." Alfiero would forgive her for making him plural. "Good evening, Signore Vela."

She gave him too wide a berth, fighting the urge to break into a run. He must think her a foolish, skittish woman, fearful the urge to grab her would overwhelm him if she came close. He might even think she would be tempted to grab him right back.

She did not care. Think what he would, this laborer with his arrogant air and provocative words, she did not want so much as her skirt to touch any part of him. She could not have told him why.

Caterina.

Her name filled the surrounding air like a sigh. It was a name she scarcely thought of as hers. She was Kate, plain Kate, the Italian translation having little to do with her real identity. Still, the sound of it stopped her. Surely he had not called her name. It was the wind rustling the leaves; her overwrought imagination, already aroused since the moment of her arrival, worked too hard on this strange night. First the noose, and now . . .

She refused to look back at him, but she felt his eyes on her as she hurried along the uneven, upward pathway back to the villa. Was that his laughter urging her on her way? No, it was still the wind, coming off the water to the west, coming from a sky turned bloodred by the setting sun.

Hurriedly she focused on the villa. When she

had first arrived—could it be only an hour or two ago?—the walls themselves had seemed forbidding. After her experience in the field, it had become her sanctuary.

Most of the windows were dark, except for the light in her bedroom window and another on the balustrade that lined the terrace beneath her balcony. Alfiero, dear man, did indeed await her return.

When she was through the back gate and halfway to the terrace, she dared one last glance over her shoulder, but Roberto Vela was not to be seen. Looking up, she saw a broad-winged bird swoop over the grove, its dark shape visible against the evening sky.

"The falcon has returned."

Jumping, she turned to see Alfiero standing close at her side. His eyes lowered, but not before she detected a sharp concern he had not shown to her before.

"Forgive me, Contessa Donati. I startled you."

Unlike Roberto Vela, he sounded truly contrite.

"You didn't, not really. I'm just a little skittish tonight." She hesitated a moment. "There was a man out in the field."

"Is the contessa all right?"

"He didn't harm me. He just surprised me. Roberto Vela was his name. He said he used to work here in the fields. Do you remember him?"

"This is a name I do not know."

"It's no matter. I shouldn't have mentioned meeting him."

She meant what she said. Asking about Vela gave him more importance than he deserved. Already the strange influence he had cast over her waned. She was more exhausted than she had realized.

She glanced back at the peregrine, watching as it swooped and soared, then headed back for its nest in the distant hills. She knew little about the curse, except that the family into which she had married and all who had business with them believed in it with all their hearts.

Being an American and therefore a barbarian, she could not believe.

Wearily, she brushed at her eyes, her gaze falling to the ground. A curious sight awaited. Alfiero's normally well-polished shoes were covered in the same dirt that comprised the distant fields, its color paler than the dark soil within the high stone wall. Had he been following her? Watching her? Standing guard?

Or seeing what his mistress was about, this curious foreigner who had never adjusted to the ways of her new country?

She should ask him, but she did not want to hear another lie.

"It's late," she said. "We both need our rest. We have a long day tomorrow."

When they arrived at the base of the steps leading to the terrace, she pointed out the loose stone that had tripped her earlier, then hurried up to bed. Snuggling under a light cover, she pushed visions of the falcon from her mind.

The visions were replaced by another, more unsettling one, that of a man, a stranger with the face of a god and the voice of a devil. She called herself a fool. Despite his looks, despite his sense of presence, Roberto Vela meant little to her in this new world she occupied. By tomorrow she probably would find it difficult to recall his name.

Chapter Four

Kate awoke late in the morning with the intruder's name on her lips and cursed herself. It must have been a dream that brought Roberto Vela to mind, or a nightmare, one she had already forgotten though her mind was filled with vague images of tangled vines and feral birds.

Like the dream, she would surely forget him.

Shaking off everything but thoughts of what her day might hold, she dressed hurriedly. When she went downstairs, her eyes averted from the hallway that led to the conte's room, her first visitor to the Villa Falcone awaited—not counting Vela, who scarcely mattered, she reminded herself. Why, oh why, did she keep recalling his name?

Stefano Braggio stood in the *soggiorno,* the large, open room off the entryway that had once

44

been the center of life for the Donatis. For the past
two generations, Signore Braggio and his late father before him had been the agents of business for
the family; he was part of her inheritance, it now
seemed. Without her asking him to do so, he had
represented her in those dark days after Pietro's
death, when the creditors had swooped in like the
assassin birds her husband had very much feared.

An even-featured, handsome man not much
taller than she, Braggio bore the coloring of many
Italians from the north—fair hair and deep brown
eyes—and, being a man who worked indoors,
fawn-colored skin that had picked up no additional
darkness from the sun. He wore his hair slicked
back, every strand in place. Indeed, everything
about him was meticulous, from his fine suit and
neatly tied cravat to his polished shoes. How he
managed the latter in such a dusty land, she did
not know.

In keeping with his appearance, his gestures
were smooth, infallibly polite, though his eyes were
watchful. She could have sworn he looked at her
sometimes when he thought she didn't know with
a regard that was far from impersonal, but he never
spoke out of turn, never made her feel uncomfortable.

Sometimes she wished he would look ruffled,
distressed, but she could never tell him so. He
would have taken her well-meant comment as crit-

icism. She owed him too much for that. To her regret, other than a small retainer, too little for him to live upon, gratitude was the only payment she could afford. She owed him much more. Because of his dealings with the conte's creditors, the villa was still hers.

She also knew that if he had his way, it would not remain so for long. It was the one area upon which the two of them disagreed.

He bowed over her extended hand. "Contessa Donati, what a relief it is to find you safely arrived."

"You surprise me, Signore Braggio," she said with a smile that was almost genuine. "I did not expect you so soon."

He waved a hand. "Forgive me. My intention was to be here to greet you, but business detained me in Florence."

He spoke as if he expected her to ask about that business. When she did not, he went on.

"You are aware, Contessa Donati, of the growing community of exiles in that beautiful city. People from your own country and from England, too, have found a veritable paradise in the Tuscan hills, or so they say."

"I believe you have mentioned the colony once or twice."

"Only because of my concern for your well-being. More than ever, I have hopes of finding a

46

buyer for this villa. The proceeds would provide enough income for you to live comfortably in the Florentine community, surrounded by people of your own kind."

And what kind was she? she wanted to ask. A nearly destitute widow? An alien in this tradition-bound country? A commoner with an aristocratic name? Or a little of all three, alien being at the top of the list.

She managed to conceal her irritation. He was only trying to help.

"I've just arrived, Signore Braggio. Give me some time to see if I can settle in."

"Of course. Please accept my apology. You are still weary from your journey."

Surprisingly, she wasn't, but with a nod she let him believe he was right.

"Would the contessa and Signore Braggio be wanting breakfast?" Alfiero asked from behind her.

The agent declined, asking only for coffee, which, at her request, Alfiero served on the terrace. The idea of enclosing herself in the dining room, large as it was, stifled her. Outside her bedchamber, she still felt uncomfortable in her new home. Time, she prayed, would help her adjust.

Though the terrace was bathed in sunlight, the morning air was still cool as they settled on stone benches before the massive marble-topped table that occupied the center of the open space.

The walls of the villa marked the boundary of the terrace on three sides; on the fourth was a balustrade graced at even intervals by four statues of prancing young boys, each statue carved crudely from stone, the lack of finesse adding to their charm. Last evening, in her rush to walk about her land, she had scarcely noticed them.

In the middle of the balustrade was an opening for the steps that led to the gardens, the gate and on to the fields of olive grove and vineyard. Beyond lay the distant cypress-lined hills at the far edge of Donati land.

For a moment she was reminded of her fall on the broken step, then pushed it from her mind. The villa dated to the sixteenth century and had been neglected for more than five years. Accidents were bound to happen. She would have to be careful when she roamed the house and grounds, that was all.

Right now she had Signore Braggio to deal with.

Already the sky was a brilliant blue and the morning was quickly passing. Though he was handsome and polite and in other circumstances his visit might offer a respite from her worries, she wished very much that he had waited at least a day to arrive.

Sipping her coffee, strong and black, she watched as the agent stirred three cubes of sugar into his small cup. He took a small swallow, added another cube and stared past her to the hills.

"You know, of course, Contessa, about the curse."

She could say one thing for Italian men: They certainly knew how to take the joy out of an occasion. The last thing she wanted to be reminded of was the bird of prey that had circled the fields yesterday evening, and, worse, of the implications others might draw from the sighting.

"The conte told me." *You've mentioned it yourself, my dear agent, more than once.* "A Donati some generations past accidently killed a valuable falcon, isn't that the story?"

"Not quite. True, it was a long time ago, that much is correct. Your late husband's ancestor, an impetuous man like the conte himself, attempted to capture a peregrine falcon owned by the Medici family. The falcon fought, slashing him in the face, disfiguring the man, or so the story goes, and in retaliation he slew the bird."

"Not an accident, then," she said, only half listening, thinking instead of what she would do when her visitor was gone.

"No, not an accident. The Medicis, as you no doubt know, were a powerful family. Our great Michelangelo himself called a Medici his patron. As you can well understand, there were those in the family who were angered by the loss, though there is nothing on record that says they acted on that anger." He shook his head sadly. "But records kept by the Donatis themselves do show that from that unfortunate day, things began to go wrong at the villa—poor crops, bad vintage, a storm that carried away the casks of wine the family stored in the grotto."

"A grotto?" Kate asked, stirred to attention. Here was a detail concerning the villa she had never heard.

"It lies beneath your land and opens to the sea. I'm not sure where, exactly, but it is a dangerous place, or so I have been told. You should not concern yourself with its location. I know you are not given to accepting my advice, but in this I beg you to listen."

Kate nodded, though in her mind she tucked away the information for later investigation. At the moment, she had too much to deal with to seek out trouble. She knew without a doubt, trouble would seek her out, though she doubted it would come in the form of a watery cave.

Braggio continued. "It was the villagers, a superstitious lot, who first began the talk of a curse. Whenever ill fortune befell the Donatis, someone— more than one, usually—claimed to have seen a falcon flying over the villa. Such is possible, as they breed in the far hills."

As if in response to his solemn words, a bank of

clouds appeared over those same hills and blotted out the morning sun.

Kate shivered, again remembering the soaring bird of last night. The falcon had nothing to do with her arrival, of that she was sure. She had spoken true in claiming she did not believe in curses. The shiver came not from a premonition but from a sudden chill.

As if he could read her mind, Braggio said, "I am a man of business and, I like to think, of science as well, and I would normally scoff at such a tale. But I also know there are things in this world we cannot understand."

She tried to interrupt, but he hurried on. Men did, she knew, like to be instructive, especially when faced with a helpless woman. And in her experience, all Italian men thought women helpless—useful at times, but helpless where the important matters of life were concerned.

"Ill fortune has, in truth, befallen six generations of Donatis, beginning with the slain bird and continuing to the conte's unfortunate demise. His own mother, the late contessa, died after repeated attempts to give her husband additional heirs. Conte Renaldo Donati became ill while in his prime, before he could take another wife and give his only son a brother."

"Surely these instances were circumstantial. Pietro told me his mother had never been strong."

"And what of the contessas who preceded her, the wives of a half-dozen contes who had never been able to bear more than one son? What of them? I do not say their barrenness resulted from the curse, but it is a fact that cannot be ignored."

Kate held herself very still. "One son for each contessa? This I had not heard."

"The record should be in the village church."

"I don't doubt you." She attempted a smile. "If you're worried that I hope for a large family, please do not. I plan never to marry again. Once was enough."

She tried to keep her voice light, but she could not ignore the agent's frown, brief though it was.

He leveled his dark eyes on her. She had never seen him more serious, not even on that sad day when they stood together and watched creditors rip the valuable artwork from the palazzo walls.

"You would do well to tread cautiously, Contessa. I speak as one who wishes only your well-being. Consider selling the villa."

He almost had her, but at that moment the sun chose to appear from behind the cloud and cast its light onto one of the prancing boys. She could almost hear laughter issue from the stone lips. If dire happenings in the past could be taken as a warning, so could such a happy image.

"I promise caution," she said with a shake of her head, "but I cannot promise more. Not so soon."

She should have gone on and told him of her
hopes, her desires, but the words caught in her
throat. And they would not have put his mind at
ease.

He blinked a half-dozen times before he spoke.

"I understand," he said, but she could see he did
not. "If you change your mind about remaining at
the villa, I will be in the village for the next few
days"—he named a small inn she remembered
passing on her journey, one fronting on Belmare's
main piazza—"and you can reach me there."

Later, after Braggio was gone, Kate sought out Alfiero in the wide, high-ceilinged kitchen with its
bank of ovens that had prepared feasts for a thousand celebrations. What a waste, she thought, as
were the dozen bedrooms and dressing areas, the
soggiorno, the alcoves, the huge dining room with
its long trestle table and massive wrought-iron can-
delabras, empty now of candles because they were
too expensive.

And what would she do with so much light anyway? In the daytime she had the sun; at night she
would be too exhausted to do more than sleep.

If her life went as she wished.

She found Alfiero at a porcelain sink, an apron
tied incongruously over his suit coat, the sleeves of
which were folded back, his hands sunk in soapy
water. The sight of him removed any oppression

she might have felt at being within the villa's walls.

"I'm not entirely impoverished," she told him with a gentle smile. "Can you go to the village today? Please hire someone to do the kitchen work and help with the cleaning. I will do what I can"— she raised a hand to still his protest—"but this place is too much for just the two of us. We'll close off most of the rooms. I can eat in here, or, when the weather permits, on the terrace."

Alfiero's high brow wrinkled. "A hundred Donatis will be turning in their graves, Contessa."

"I'll bet you could find one or two who would understand."

He frowned, clearly believing otherwise.

"The alternative," she said, "is to do as Signore Braggio proposes and sell the villa. I can't believe that putting the Villa Falcone in the hands of someone other than a Donati, even one through marriage, would make any of my husband's ancestors rest easier."

This land could bring profits again.

Roberto Vela's words came back to her, once again echoing her own thoughts. What if she had repeated them to the agent? He would have done much more than frown as Alfiero was doing.

Do you have the strength to do what is necessary? the intruder had also said. *Do you have the will?*

The questions had been arrogant, highly inappropriate. In the conte's day such effrontery would have earned Vela a beating, or worse.

An image of his hard, brown back—she assumed it was hard and brown—under the whip brought a shudder. She could more easily imagine one of his hard, brown hands taking the whip from his persecutor, snapping it in two and tossing the pieces aside as he would scraps from a half-eaten meal.

And if by then he had not received an answer to his questions, he would ask them again, as he would if he appeared a second time in the villa's woebegone fields.

Over the next days and weeks she would find out how to respond. The questions themselves she would keep to herself, as she would the bolder words he had used to goad her, words so crude, about plowing and water, that she could scarcely recall them without feeling her cheeks burn.

The man was a jumble of inconsistencies, taunting her as if he sought far too personal favors she could never give, then drawing back into himself, his own desires never to be revealed.

What could he want with a scrawny, pallid recluse like her anyway?

She shook herself. What was she thinking, going on in such a way while Alfiero stood at a sink of tepid water watching whatever expressions played on her face? Enough of memory. Enough of useless embarrassment and equally useless speculation. Those were exactly the reactions he had wished, though she could not imagine why.

What she had to do was get on with business. That she had never before directed her own life paled into insignificance.

She smiled at Alfiero. "See if you can find someone in the village who can advise me on how to go about reviving the fields."

Someone short, bald, spindly but strong, if possible.

The servant's frown spread to his eyes and his tightly drawn mouth, and he held himself very still.

"Contessa—"

"I'm hardly that and we both know it," she said softly, insistently, speaking from her heart. "If we're to live here, we must make the Villa Falcone pay for itself."

But Alfiero was not so easily won over.

"Forgive me, but even the late conte could not accomplish what the contessa suggests."

"I intend to try harder. I must find the strength." She felt a swell of confidence. After Braggio's visit, through all her musings, she had come up with the answer to one of Roberto Vela's questions. "Already, my dear friend, I have the will."

To herself, in English, she whispered, "And let the curse be damned."

If she were a vindictive woman, she might very

well have wished the same fate for a cynical, too-handsome laborer with an aristocratic air the late conte had never been able to achieve.

That he might have goaded her into the very strength of purpose she had been questioning was a notion she refused to consider. This battle for an independent life was hers and hers alone.

A fingernail snapped. Kate bit it off and spat the fragment into the freshly turned dirt. This was the third nail she'd lost in the past hour. If she had any left by the time she got back to the villa, she would trim them off to the quick.

Three nails and a nose burned by the sun, despite the floppy straw hat she'd found in the storage shed beneath the terrace and tugged over the knot of hair she'd twisted at the top of her head. And her hands. Already the palms were beginning to blister. And what had she accomplished? Scarcely one square meter of ground turned at the base of one olive tree, one meter out of a thousand, one tree out of hundreds, and that didn't count the grapevines.

There was also the nagging thought that, sitting like this under a tree, her legs folded in front of her, she did not know what she was doing.

Under such circumstances, a woman could become discouraged.

Kate refused. She wanted to get a feel for the

land. The only way to do that was to dig. Besides, Alfiero might return from the village with a dozen laborers willing not only to work for a woman they had for years considered their enemy but also to work alongside her.

And with little pay, of course; certainly not enough to feed themselves and their families. She had come on the newly opened train from Venice to Florence, then by hired gig to Belmare, with few coins in her purse, but, unknown to anyone, in the hem of her heavy black dress she had sewn the golden *lire* secretly stashed away during the years of her marriage. She couldn't live on such a slim reservoir, not for the rest of her life, but she could put it to work and let it grow.

If only she had the dozen men.

A dozen? She would settle for one. In truth, it was her prayer.

She might as well wish for a flock of falcons to descend upon the grove and peck the land into submission. Staring down the row of trees and vines in front of her, knowing dozens of such rows lay to the right and left, understanding this was not the only field she must work, she felt a curious kind of contentment.

Sunlight and shadows, rich soil, Tuscan tradition, all could be her friends. If she held still and the breeze died, she could hear the sea crashing against a cliff only a few hundred yards away. Its saltiness hung on the late-morning air. She allowed herself a moment to ponder exactly where the grotto might be.

How much more pleasant this was, blistered hands and all, than secluding herself in a heavily draped Venetian parlor burying her heart and soul in Italian books she discovered in the seldom-used library of the Venetian palazzo.

But she wasn't here for pleasure. She was wasting time. Sweat beaded on her brow beneath the ineffectual hat. Tossing it aside, she shook out her hair, too long, too thick as it fell against her shoulders and back. Tomorrow she would put it in a braid.

Taking up the pick, after gingerly stroking her blisters, she attacked the dirt once again.

"What are you doing?"

The voice that came from behind her was deep, thick and, of course, cynical. She recognized it right away. Her heart pounded. She did not bother to look around.

Instead of her dreamed-of dozen workers, she had gotten one critic.

Roberto Vela had returned.

Chapter Five

Kate could feel his eyes fixed on her, could sense their dark probing, could see the critical curve of his lips. Unable to breathe, she held still, but only for a moment. Ignoring Roberto Vela would not make him go away.

"Ah, Signore Vela, I should have expected you," she said matter-of-factly. "I'm planting money, of course. I was hoping it would grow, since the grapes have been doing so poorly."

For emphasis, Kate pounded the pick into the hard ground. Her wince brought him around to face her. He knelt, his eyes close to a level with hers. He moved so quickly, with a natural grace that belied his size, she almost yelped. When he settled in front of her, he was very, very close. He blotted out the sun.

In an instant she took in his dark brows, the thickness of his lashes, the sharp line of bone that gave shape to his face. She wanted to touch him to see if he were truly flesh and blood or just some apparition come to bedevil her.

But touching him was out of the question. Why did the notion keep occurring to her? She knew all too well that he was real. Nothing ghostly could make her heart pound the way it did. *Vibrant* was the way she had first thought of him. She had not changed her mind.

Quickly she looked down, determined to hide any emotion stronger than irritation. His was not a visage she could look at impassively for long.

Without warning, he took the pick from her, tossed it aside and turned her hands.

"Most women would protect themselves with gloves," he said as he studied her reddened palms.

Kate fought to keep her hands from trembling beneath his warmth. She fought, too, to keep the trembling from her voice. Concentrating on his lips—not a calming choice but better than his eyes—she tugged free of his grasp.

"I am not like most women, signore. There are those who might enjoy your company. I am not among them. Though I appreciate your concern for my welfare"—a polite lie to show him how politeness was done—"I must ask you to please leave."

His lips flattened. "No."

In one word he mastered matter-of-factness far better than she. She looked into his eyes in astonishment. "What did you say?"

"The contessa heard me all too well."

His tone was strangely deferential, in contrast to all else: the slant of his kneeling figure so close to her, the tension and determination she sensed within him, the words themselves.

She had to concentrate on the words. He called her a contessa, and that she would have to be.

Scrambling to her feet, she backed away, realizing the difficulty of playing an aristocrat while sitting in the dirt. Just as quickly he stood, reminding her once again of his size and the presence that overpowered everything around him without any sign of effort on his part.

Almost everything. The road of her life, to onlookers seemingly paved with gold, had provided in reality too rough a ride for her to give up the reins now. She knew too well what she looked like—a pale, frail woman, pampered, playing at handling a laborer's work, her efforts sprung from whim rather than desperation.

Let Vela believe what he would, as long as he did so from a distance.

She brushed an errant strand of hair from her eyes. "If you won't leave, as any decent person would, I'll have you thrown off."

"By your servant?"

Even in her anger, she saw the absurdity in that.

A terrible thought struck. "Did Alfiero ask you here, on my behalf?"

"No one asked me here. Did you ask him to?"

"Don't be absurd. It was . . . well, never mind. You are here uninvited. If you continue to trespass on Donati land, I will be forced to summon the constable."

He smiled, a small, quick movement of his lips that had little humor in it.

"You speak of the less-than-formidable constable in the village? I was there in Belmare yesterday. But of course this you already know."

He must be remembering how their eyes had met and then, to her embarrassment, how she had shrunk into the shadowy corner of the gig.

As he talked, she took a deep breath, and with it drew in a sense of pride that she needed very, very much.

Roberto Vela was purposely trying to humiliate her. Did he take joy in reminding her of the constable's scorn? He went too far. She could not, she would not let him unnerve her. He must not win this war of words.

She drew herself to her full height. When at last she could speak calmly, she spoke from her heart.

"Signore Vela, if that is truly your name, you are wrong to come onto my property and talk to me any way you wish. Did the villagers ask that you do so? Did they ask you to harass me in such a way? Of course they did. I should have thought of that earlier."

She gave him a chance to deny the accusation. When he did not, when he continued to stand close and watch her lips as she spoke, she determined to go on. Let him look where he wanted. His watchful eyes would have no effect on her.

"Please inform them that whatever happened in the past at the Villa Falcone was none of my doing. You can also tell them that whatever I do here, I carry their interests in my heart as well as my own."

As with Stefano Braggio, she could not tell him all that was in her heart, details about her hopes and dreams. Her agent would have argued; this man would scoff.

With more fervor than caution, she hurried on.

"I am a lone woman, and in the eyes of all Tuscany, no doubt, helpless, but the knowledge that justice lies on my side gives me strength."

He continued to stare at her in silence. For the first time since they'd met, she had truly stopped him. Conflicting urges warred within him; she could sense them although she could not have begun to put a name to them. That he was capable of violence was something she did not doubt. But what could drive him to such a state? That was something else she did not know. Without any reason for doing so, she sensed that the *something* might easily involve her.

She eyed the pick. It lay on the ground a scant few inches from the edge of her gown.

As if he could read her mind, he reached for it and placed it in her hands. After a pause, he also picked up the hat she had so carelessly discarded and settled it on her head, his fingers lightly brushing the loose hair from her cheeks.

"You should wear this, Contessa. Already your face is burned by the sun, and this is but your first day working in the fields."

She could read in his voice the unspoken belief that this day would also be her last. Getting the better of the man was like trying to hold back the heat with her hands. Strangely, the more audacious he became, the more determined she was to respond.

"You mock me, and I do not know why."

"I mock myself. You are correct in saying you are not responsible for the past. You are wrong if you believe I wish to harm you. I am a simple man and I speak the truth. As a boy, I did work these fields. Like many others, I ran away to sea. After many years, I have returned. The villagers have not sent me. I no longer know anyone in Belmare."

"Yesterday you stood in their midst."

"I stood as a stranger. I am here today with one purpose: to offer what you so obviously need."

Without explaining what he meant, he bowed curtly and walked away, disappearing over the top of the hillside grove, leaving her to look after him, her pride unable to overcome the trembling in her knees.

The field suddenly became quiet, no crickets chirping, no birds to sing, not even the rustle of wind in the leaves. It was as if in leaving he had taken all the life from around her.

I am a simple man.

Kate almost laughed. If Roberto Vela was simple, she was Lucrezia Borgia.

She did not begin to speculate about what he thought she needed. Could he really be speaking as a man to a woman, wanting manly things only a woman could give? If he was so foolish, he would soon find out she was hardened to such enticements, even coming from one who looked the way he did.

Having lost her mother when she was born, she spent her childhood wanting loving tenderness from her father, but love was an emotion he could not feel. Pride, yes, and certainly ambition, but never love. Later, as she moved through adolescence to womanhood, she had wanted a different kind of love. She had wanted passion, had yearned for a man's arousing touch. Scandalous such yearnings had been, though they sprang naturally and unbidden from someplace deep inside her, and she had kept them to herself. She no longer felt even their lingering traces. They had died on her wedding night.

Five long years later, what she needed more than anything else was peace. She needed a chance to prove herself, to mend what the men in her life had broken.

These were needs Roberto Vela could never understand.

•

"I could find no workers for you, Contessa."

Kate stood on the terrace as Alfiero gave his report. As she'd requested, while she began her assault on the grove, he had taken the donkey cart into the village, his dignified figure at odds with the crude conveyance. He had returned not an hour earlier.

At this cool time of day the setting sun cast purple shadows across the rolling fields stretching out from the terrace, obscuring the weeds, the hard-packed ground, the dying grapes. But she knew too well that they were out there, waiting to be dealt with. She could not accept her servant's words.

"Surely someone needs employment. I can't pay well, but something is better than nothing."

"They say the fields are too far gone. That the falcon will bring trouble for them."

"Are they afraid of work or of the curse?"

Alfiero avoided her eye.

"Their lives are hard," he said. "It is not work they fear."

"And it can't be the curse. Some of them, perhaps most, found employment with the Donati family before the conte sent them away." She sighed. "I am the cause of their refusal. How sad, when I want only what will benefit us all."

Though the air was cool, it bore an oppressive weight that settled hard on her and made breathing difficult. She understood that weight. Memories of the conte hung all around her, like a bad smell from an open grave, polluting ground, air, water—everything she touched, everything she needed. Maybe the only solution was a wild storm to rush through her life and wash out all those memories.

But the turbulence would also have to cleanse the minds of the villagers. Like her dozen fantasy laborers, the ones she had imagined returning with Alfiero, she knew no such storm existed. As she had always known, she must depend on herself.

The trouble was, she didn't feel very strong at the moment. She could have cried, but that would have been a waste. Even Alfiero, loyal though he was, would have taken the tears as weakness. Such was the common judgment of men.

She drew her gaze from the purple fields to the statues prancing atop the balustrade, to the stooped figure of her dear and faithful servant.

"I doubt help was available for you either," she said.

His lined face softened. "At first this was so. But when I was on the road leading up to the villa, a woman appeared in front of me. She had heard of my request and said she was in need of employment."

"She defied the will of the other villagers?"

"The signorina comes from Pisa, far away from Belmare. But she has heard of the ill will of the people here. She asks that her employment not be revealed. She would give her name only as Maria."

"You found her satisfactory?"

"This is something I do not yet know. She asks for little in wages, only food and shelter."

"And that her employment be kept secret."

Alfiero nodded. Remembering the scorn in the eyes of the villagers as she rode through Belmare, she understood the woman's request. If she could have asked for help as Kate Cartwright, the name she had borne most of her life, she would have. But she was condemned to being Contessa Caterina Donati, a far worse curse than any that the powerful Medicis could have visited on her, dead falcon or no.

"When does she start?"

"She is here now, Contessa, preparing the evening meal. She says that if you do not approve of what she cooks, she will leave."

"Fair enough. I hope you told her I am not a particular eater."

"Forgive me, but I told her you ate very little at all. She replied that perhaps her food will help your appetite."

"I'd like to dine out on the terrace again, if that's all right. The sky is clear and the moon will provide enough light."

"So I have already instructed."

Warmth rushed through Kate and she was again moved to tears, not from self-pity but from gratitude.

She touched Alfiero's arm. "Thank you, dear friend."

He flushed, but he did not pull away. She wanted to give him an affectionate hug, but that would have sent him scrambling back to the kitchen. She contented herself with another pat, then hurried up the outdoor stairway that led from the terrace to the third-floor balcony of the villa's central tower. Tossing aside the garment she had worn in the field, along with the floppy straw hat, she hurriedly bathed and put on a clean gown—black, of course—brushed and bound her hair into a tight knot, then walked back down the terrace stairs in time to see Alfiero standing in the doorway to the corridor, his back to her, and beyond him the indistinct figure of a woman bearing a tray.

The two huddled together for a moment over the

tray, intent on a conversation she could not understand. Moving to the edge of the terrace, she touched the stone balustrade, still warm from the sun despite the coolness of the air, and watched a lizard scurry over the carved foot of one of the prancing boys.

Remembering her fall, she moved to the steps that led from the terrace to the garden behind the house and saw that the broken step had been repaired. By Alfiero, of course.

"Contessa."

She turned to see Alfiero set the tray on the marble table and pull back the stone bench for her to sit. Looking past him, she saw the woman he had hired, the only one who dared work for a cursed Donati.

The woman known only as Maria was short and dark, with a rounded middle covered by a plain brown apron. Her hair was pulled back from her face, much as Kate wore her own. She had the strong features of the Tuscans, the straight back, the steady stance. Hers was a timeless face, lined without sagging, no heavy jowls or pockets under the eyes. Kate put her age at somewhere between forty and sixty; a wide span, but she could not be more specific.

Only two things distinguished Maria: the wide, white streak that marked the left side of her otherwise black hair and, even more arresting, the open, watchful look in her surprisingly amber eyes.

Kate could not look away. It was as if the woman was trying to tell her something, or perhaps trying to read something in the countenance of her new mistress. The eyes reminded her of another pair. With a start, she remembered their owner: Roberto Vela. More than once he had looked at her in the same way.

The comparison was absurd. Other than a manner of staring, the two were nothing alike. Absurd or not, the idea of a similarity buried itself in her mind and would not go away.

Shaken, Kate took the seat offered by Alfiero and watched as he took the plate from the tray, along with a crystal glass and a bottle of deep red wine. He poured a small portion of the wine for her. She sipped and felt its warmth race through her, nodding that she wanted more.

"It is from the Donati vineyard from ten years past," Alfiero offered. "Maria found it in the small room off the kitchen where she has chosen to stay."

Kate smiled at the woman, who continued to stand close to the open door. "Thank you, Maria. It is very good."

The housekeeper nodded but remained silent.

Kate tasted the pasta, covered in sliced wild mushrooms, and the side dish of fried cheese, served with the saltless Tuscan bread, along with slices of tomatoes as red as the wine. Served in the open air, a hint of lingering spring flowers and lavender hanging on the breeze, the dinner was the best she had ever eaten, an observation she passed on to the cook.

Maria nodded, as if she had expected nothing less in the reaction of her mistress, then turned and left without having uttered a word. Kate did not leave the terrace until she had consumed every bite and drunk half the bottle of wine. It was with contentment that she went up the stairs, changed the black dress for a white nightgown and brushed her hair until it crackled with electricity.

Perhaps she would sleep through the night, the first time since she had left Boston. Maybe she would have done just that if, the moment she pulled the light cover up to her chin, her mind hadn't begun its nightly chore of remembering and analyzing. Tomorrow the fields awaited with their crops she knew nothing about. Until this moment she had not realized how much she depended upon Alfiero finding her help.

Worse, she realized what had passed between her old servant and her new, in that moment when they'd paused in the corridor doorway. There had been more than conversation. Alfiero had been tasting her food.

Did he think the freshly prepared meal had already spoiled? No, not at all. He was making sure that everything was safe for her to eat. As if someone might try to poison her.

What could possibly have given him such an idea? Had something happened in the village that he had not told her about? If she put the question to him, he would say she'd misunderstood his purpose. He wanted only to determine that the meal was to a contessa's standards.

It would be an obvious lie. He knew she was rarely aware of what she ate.

Perhaps she was mistaken about the tasting. Perhaps she was imagining more problems than she already faced. She assured herself that such was the case.

And so she put her thoughts to more practical pursuits. She was hated, she who had never purposely harmed anyone in her life, hated by an entire village of people whom she had never met.

This latter fact was the only one she could change. A long time later, after she had determined an immediate plan of action, she dropped into a brief and troubled sleep.

Chapter Six

By the time Kate eased down from the donkey cart, the central piazza of Belmare was bathed in the warm golden glow of the mid-morning sun. The stuccoed buildings rose on three sides, their walls the same peach-flesh color as those at the Villa Falcone, only without the pale rectangles where valuable tapestries had once hung.

In the center of the stone clearing was a blue mosaic fountain with an arched dolphin leaping from the middle of geometrically patterned tile. The fountain was dry and looked as if it had not been used in years.

The buildings to the right and left were fronted by stalls with tables of goods for sale, on one side items of clothing, on the other produce from the farms surrounding the village. An overhang from the tile roofs kept the stalls shaded from the July sun.

Few customers shopped at the stalls. The only villagers in the piazza were seated at wooden tables directly opposite her, beyond the dry fountain, in front of the inn where her agent Stefano Braggio had said he would be staying. All of the villagers at the tables were men, their rough brown hands cradling small cups of coffee or resting near small glasses of a clear liquid she took to be grappa.

The conte once told her grappa could turn a sober man into a drunk after only two swallows. These men with their watchful eyes looked sober enough, and solemn as they stared at her, as if expecting the news that somebody close to them had died.

The only two women in sight stood by the tables of clothing. Like the men, they did not in any way acknowledge her arrival, except, of course, for the way they stared.

They should have at least smiled. She must make quite an amusing picture, the once powerful contessa alighting awkwardly from a donkey cart, helped down by a lone servant who should have retired years ago.

Alfiero sidled close, his voice low. "If the contessa wishes, we will return to the villa. The produce can wait."

"No. I'll be all right."

She spoke with more confidence than she was feeling. Belmare was to be her home. She wondered if the greeting of today would be the one she would face whenever she left her high hill and came to town.

She was about to step toward the inn when a child's laughter broke the stillness and a girl of no more than five broke into the piazza at a run, her dark braids flying behind her, small brown feet pounding upon the stone-covered ground.

"Stella," a woman's voice rang out from somewhere behind her, "do not run from me. You have forgotten your sandals again."

Unmindful of where she was going, the child named Stella ran straight into Kate. She righted herself and her brown eyes darted upward. The eyes widened and the laughter died.

The little girl was so small, so filled with life, Kate thought, her young warmth infused with the sweet smell of a child's sweat. Stella had been playing hard. Kate's heart melted. She smiled and knelt.

"Don't be afraid," she said softly.

Stella stared at her, speechless.

"Are you hurt?" Kate asked. Her hand ached to touch her. A child. Pleasure blossomed inside her. A precious, innocent child.

Slowly the child shook her head.

"Good. Then there's no harm done." She dared

to brush Stella's smooth cheek. "Your face is smudged. Have you been playing in the dirt?"

She was rewarded with a serious nod. Half the child's face was taken up with round brown eyes.

"Playing in the dirt is fun." Or so she supposed. It was something she had never been allowed to do. She discounted yesterday in the field. The occupation of yesterday had not been play.

The child's lips parted, as if she would speak, but her mother's shrill cry stopped her.

"Stella, get away from her!"

Kate watched the light in the little girl's eyes die. The blossoming, once warm and tender inside her, died as well. She felt as if a little bit of heaven had unexpectedly been offered to her and just as quickly been snatched away.

She was not surprised. No matter how successful her mission today or her plans for the coming years, a child was the one thing she could never have. She had said as much to Stefano Braggio. She knew the truth now more than ever. What she had not added was the rest of it: She would have given the Villa Falcone itself to hold her own infant in her arms.

And to be able to care properly for him or her. That went along with the holding and the loving. The pain of her loss—such was the only way to put it—was almost too much to bear.

"It's all right," she said soothingly to the child. "Do as your mother says."

She stood and looked over the top of the child's head to the woman striding toward her from the far side of the piazza. The mother kept her eyes lowered, even when she reached her daughter and took her by the arm, her grip unnecessarily firm when wrapped around such slenderness.

"She meant no harm," Kate said, and then, with embarrassment as she realized the true cause of the woman's anger, added, "I meant no harm."

The woman dared one quick glance at Kate, then bent so that she might hold her child close and hurried past Belmare's dreadful Contessa Donati, disappearing around the side of the building where clothing was being sold.

Kate could feel the eyes of the villagers boring in on her, but they no longer mattered. In the aftermath of the encounter, she thought about the look on the woman's face. She had been angry, true, but she had also been afraid. Anger she could understand—the contessa bore the weight of many past sins—but not fear. The child had been in no danger.

Despite the warmth of the sun flooding the piazza, Kate felt a chill.

She shook it off. The one thing she had known about her mission today was that it would not be easy. Holding herself with as much dignity as possible, she walked around the unused fountain, her destination the open front door of the inn. She got no closer than the first of the outside tables before Stefano Braggio came hurrying out, working furiously at buttoning his short dark coat and straightening his off-center tie.

Halting in front of her, he ran a hasty hand through his normally slicked-back hair. Today it was badly in need of a comb. She had never seen him so disheveled. He also looked more handsome than ever, and very much concerned. If she had any sense . . .

But of course she did not.

"Signore Braggio, I fear my arrival is at an awkward time."

"No, no," he said, catching his breath. "Work kept me awake until early morning. I fear I slept far beyond my usual hour." He gestured to one of the empty tables. "Please, have a seat. I will order us coffee."

It seemed very important that she allow him to do so, as an apology for his appearance. She nodded and took a chair, wondering as she did what work had occupied him most of the night. Surely nothing that involved the once-grand Donati fortune, or her own, both fortunes having been disposed of long ago.

After he had gone inside the inn, she rested her hands in her lap and did the only thing she could do: She let the villagers look at her. After a dawn awakening, she had spent a long time selecting the proper gown for the journey, one simple without showing any signs of wear, although to most she was sure each black frock was very much like the next.

Equal care had gone into pinning up her hair and adding the least frivolous bonnet in her wardrobe. This took less time. Except for one feathered monstrosity ordered for her by the conte, all her bonnets were plain.

She was striving to look like a woman intent on serious business, with no hint of the frivolous nature the long-time residents of Belmare must attribute to her. How well she succeeded in her goal was impossible to tell.

From out of nowhere came an image of Alfiero standing between her and last evening's tray of food. He had feared someone wished her harm. Was that someone—or maybe more than one—watching her now?

With great purpose, she pushed the image aside and studied the front of the inn. A six-foot-high trellis flanked each side of the double door, each one entwined with thick grapevines that looked as old as the Villa Falcone, the vines wandering from their anchoring trellis onto the tile roof. Green grapes hung in clusters from the thick stalks, the entire scene painted in Tuscan sunlight. She had never seen anything more beautiful, or more typical of her new homeland.

Did the beauty hide the threat of a viper? She refused to believe it was so.

The agent returned, followed by a waiter bearing a laden tray. Neither of them spoke until the waiter had gone and Braggio had sweetened his coffee. They both sipped the hot brew. Then Kate got to the point.

"I have a favor to ask. I would like to talk to as many villagers as you can gather as soon as possible."

Braggio lifted his eyebrows, then smiled regretfully, as if he was dealing with someone simpleminded.

"Contessa Donati, forgive my intrusion, but what would be the purpose? In time they will learn to forgive what they view as the transgressions of the family into which you married. But they will not do so today, or tomorrow, or even into the next year."

As always, Braggio took many words to get his message across. She had to listen carefully, to translate in her mind, if she was to understand him.

"I don't want their forgiveness. I want their help."

He looked at her with even more pitying eyes. "You cannot have one without the other. Please tell me what it is you require of the people of Belmare

82

and perhaps I can provide this help you say you need. They have little money, of course. . . ."

His voice trailed off, but she understood his implication: He suggested she wanted their charity.

He did not understand her; but then, he was a man.

She raised her voice so that the onlookers, the number of whom had grown, could more easily hear what she had to say.

"Please, Signore Braggio, I want only to speak to them." She struggled to find the exact words. "I do not seek any of their *lire,* nor anything of value from them except their time."

That was true of this morning. She did not add that over the coming weeks and months she wanted more, much more.

She dared look at the men at the tables and the ones standing around the edges of the piazza, and the women who had gathered close to the stalls.

"Since when has the mistress of the Villa Falcone come and asked such a thing?" she asked. "Never, I think. I want them to listen to me, and after I have said what I came to say, I will listen to them."

The skepticism was stark on the faces of the people. But there was confusion as well. Good. Confusion as to her motives was not exactly goodwill, but eventually that was where it might lead.

She fell silent, sat back in her chair and let them stare at her. Outwardly she was calm, but her stomach was in a knot and her heart pulsed strongly with the rhythm of a funeral bell. She glanced covetously at a glass of grappa on the nearest table. She should have asked for that instead of coffee. Perhaps it would give her a jolt of necessary courage.

No, she must remain clearheaded. She had often seen the conte after drinking too much wine. Sober he was merely foolish; drunk, he became absurd.

Reluctantly, Braggio stood and began to circulate among the villagers. What he said to them she did not know, but gradually their numbers began to swell, men and women with a scattering of children among them. She did not see Stella or her distraught mother. She was not surprised.

Only one person did she recognize, the village constable, standing in the midst of the others, looking as officious as ever. If she could be grateful for anything, it was his silence. Later, when she was gone, he could—and would—say whatever he wished.

After a quarter hour of watching and being watched, she stood and walked to the edge of the fountain, a path clearing before her. She thought about standing up on the side of the fountain, but she was taller than most of the Italians and thought they could see her without any trouble.

Besides, as anxious as she was, she would probably fall and impale herself on some part of the sculpted dolphin. It would be just her luck.

In her mind she had gone over a hundred ways to begin, declaring herself a friend of the villagers, admitting and apologizing for the Donati sins, appealing to their sense of fairness. Most important of all, she did not want them to pity her. Like a falcon, they would fall on her as their prey.

None of the ways she thought of worked. So she told the truth, without sugaring it the way Stefano Braggio did his coffee.

"I want to open the vineyards once again, and the olive groves. I cannot do it alone."

No response. Her palms grew damp.

"There is good land up there, land that can bring sustenance for us all."

Silence. It screamed in her ears.

She walked around the perimeter of the fountain, searching for a single look of interest, succeeding only in finding that the ill will so apparent three days ago when she first arrived had not abated.

They were a handsome people, lean from the work of their days, their olive skin clear, their dark eyes deep and unblinking. And they held themselves with pride. Every one of them.

She appealed to that pride.

"We need to help ourselves, you and I, if we are to get along. We can do that together. After expenses have been paid, I will personally take nothing more from the land than you do."

It was her strongest point. It did not change the silent response.

At last someone, a man from within the crowd, spoke up.

"How much do you pay?"

She felt the sweat trickle down her back.

"I must be honest with you: I can offer little other than your fair portion of the crops, but it will be more than the percentage you received before."

"There are no crops," another said. "The land lies fallow."

She tried in vain to pick out the speakers, but what difference did it make? They spoke for everyone.

"The land lies waiting," she said, hearing the edge of desperation in her voice and hating it. "It was fertile before. That has not changed."

This time a woman. "You ask us to sacrifice." She said it as an accusation.

"I will work beside you. We all work and we all gain."

She could feel the animosity in the piazza grow stronger. It rose like a wall between her and the people of the town. She had told herself to expect it, but still it hurt. This meeting that she had so desperately wanted could not be going worse.

Then she saw a tall dark figure in the background, standing at the corner of the inn. Roberto Vela had come to witness her failure. Heat burned her cheeks, a deeper kind than any delivered by the sun.

Damn him. She damned herself, too, for letting him affect her so strongly.

"Go to your work, go to your homes," she said, "and consider what I ask. Signore Braggio will be at the inn for a while should you wish to send word to me that you will help make the oil and the wine that has been so much a part of your village."

She spoke without conviction. They would not come to the inn as she asked. They knew it and so did she. She held her place by the fountain and watched the people leave. Even the men at the tables departed. Within minutes she was left with Alfiero and the donkey cart on the road that wound past the piazza, one woman at each of the stalls, and Stefano Braggio, who had taken a place in the shadows by the inn's front doors.

And, of course, Roberto Vela, who had not moved.

She tilted her chin in his direction, daring him with her eyes to smile, or even to nod. He met her stare. After an eternity he turned and was gone.

With a heavy heart she watched her agent striding toward her. She smiled brightly, an effort that made her face hurt.

"Please let me know if you hear from any of the villagers."

"Contessa Donati—"

She waved him off before he could begin a lecture or, worse, offer an expression of sympathy. "Of course I don't imagine that you will, but one never knows. If you will excuse me, I have some shopping to take care of. Please come to dinner some evening before you leave. I have a new cook and housekeeper to help Alfiero. She is quite good."

Without waiting for a reply, she gestured Alfiero toward the produce stalls while she went to the tables of clothing. Within the half hour she was once again bouncing beside her servant on the hard seat of the donkey cart, fresh fruit and vegetables in the back, along with a pair of men's work shoes that almost fit her narrow feet, two nondescript skirts and blouses, a broad-brimmed hat and a pair of leather work gloves.

The woman who sold her the clothes had observed her selections without comment, had put a ridiculously high price on them and smirked when Kate did not protest, but she had not been able to hide completely her surprise when Kate said she was making the purchases for herself.

Contessas did not work in the fields. The words were in the woman's eyes.

Kate stared right back. This contessa did.

When she arrived at the villa, she ate a small plate of cheese and bread, followed by a slice of the watermelon Alfiero had selected in town. He did the serving. Maria was nowhere in sight.

Upstairs she changed into the new clothes, which were not new at all but worn by another woman at some time in the past, before being put out for sale.

Kate couldn't begin to guess why the still serviceable clothing was no longer worn by the original owner. Death? Illness? Family tragedy? Or perhaps it was simply that the woman had needed money. It was a motivation Kate understood.

Besides, everything she had purchased was clean and sturdy. The coarseness of the cloth felt good against her skin after the slickness of the garments purchased by the conte.

As she hurried down the steps leading from the terrace, she glanced back at the watching Alfiero.

"Thank you for repairing the step so quickly. You did a good job."

His brow furrowed.

"I did not repair the step, Contessa. Forgive me, but I forgot."

"Then who? It couldn't have been Maria. The repair was made before she arrived."

"Again, forgive me, Contessa. Perhaps the step was not broken."

"But it was. I saw the loose stone myself, the first evening we arrived."

But had she? The light had been dim, she had been tired but intent on getting to the vineyard. Hadn't she imagined a vine to be a noose? Perhaps clumsiness had caused her to fall.

One thing she knew for sure was that if Alfiero said he had not repaired the step, then he had not. He did not lie. Why should he? What could he possibly gain?

She smiled at him. "I'm sure you're right. Put it out of your mind."

Carrying her gloves and newly purchased hat, her hair braided into a thick plait that hung against her back, she walked away from the terrace through the once-beautiful rose garden and the weed-choked furrows that had once grown the family's produce, hurried down a small incline, through the gate, then up to the first of the hillside fields where so much work needed to be done.

The work had already started. Halfway down one of the central rows, his back to her, Roberto Vela was wielding a pick over one of the hundred pitiful grapevines that had fallen from their stakes and crawled across the ground.

Three olive trees behind him had already been cleared of the wild growth that was choking them. He must have been at work for close to an hour. How had he gotten here so quickly? As slow as the hardworking donkey was, the cart moved fast enough even along the upward portion of the road. Vela had been nowhere in sight.

She pushed the consideration from her mind. It mattered not the path he chose. It got him here, where he did not belong.

She quickened her step. This was too much. People she wanted in the fields stayed away; the one she did not want was hard at work.

He turned as she approached, and she got a good look at him. His form-fitting brown trousers were tucked into a pair of sturdy work boots. His brown shirt, open to the waist, was tucked beneath a wide black leather belt, all that he wore accenting the long legs and the broad shoulders that tapered to a flat stomach and narrow hips.

His black hair was blacker than ever with sweat, and his olive skin was covered with a fine, damp sheen on the taut skin of his face and neck, the hair-dusted chest too clearly visible in the unbuttoned shirt.

She noticed everything, including the knife bound inside a band of leather attached to the belt. Like his skin, the curved blade bore a wicked sheen.

He set down the pick and pulled off his work gloves, tossed them on the ground and returned her stare.

That she was staring there could be no doubt.

Whatever admonitions she had intended to throw at him caught in her throat. The most she managed was to draw her gaze from his body to his hands. They looked strong and hard, and she wondered what they would feel like against her warm skin. Would they be gentle? Would they be rough?

Her stomach knotted and her blood pumped hard. Uncontrollably and totally absurdly, she wanted to unbutton her gown and open it like his shirt, to feel the sun and the sweat and the occasional gentle breeze that danced across the landscape.

Would he look at her as she was looking at him?

Something was passing between them, but she knew not what. She had no experience with the tingles that were racing through her. The closest had been her adolescent dreams, which she had always thought scandalous. Compared to what she was feeling now, those undefined yearnings paled into childishness.

But she was too cowardly, or too cautious, to explore the feeling. Forcing her eyes from him, more fearful of appearing foolish than of the man himself or his knife, she looked into the sky. A falcon circled in the distance, swooping and soaring, an assassin bird searching for its prey. The sight, both beautiful and frightening, even from a distance, snapped the spell into which she had fallen.

She was able to look at her intruder coolly and to speak.

"What are you—"

He did not let her get far. "I know. What am I doing here? Contessa Donati, you have a curious way of ignoring the obvious. You need me now more than ever. You need what I can do for you."

He took a step closer to her and another. She could smell his sweat and the dirt in which he had been working, and the greenness of the newly cut weeds and vines.

"Let us move to the shade," he said. "The sun must not rob us of the strength we will need to do what we both know must be done."

Chapter Seven

Kate stared at him in disbelief. She and her intruder, for that was how she tried to think of him, had been together for an hour, and he had talked for the entire time. About what she needed? What he needed? What they could do for each other?

Most definitely. But only as it pertained to the Villa Falcone.

Not that he talked without passion. When he wasn't sitting so close his shoulder brushed against hers, he was pacing in front of her, gesturing right and left, eyeing her when he presented a new idea and sometimes when he didn't.

What had she learned about him that she hadn't known? He wasn't interested in her physically, despite all the provocative things he had said to her on earlier occasions. She was glad. And relieved. Most definitely relieved.

If her thoughts kept straying to the way he moved his hands or held his head or the way the hair lay against the back of his neck, she knew it was because she had never been so close to such a man before. She was curious about how he was put together. Her conclusion? He was put together very well.

Even more important—definitely more important—he was a man of the soil, though she had already decided that about him the night his shadow appeared by hers and she had thought him her executioner. She still wasn't sure whether the latter had been a total misconception. There were ways a man could kill a woman without leaving a bruise.

Though she learned little about his personal life, she did hear details about the olive trees and the grapevines, about soil and weather and markets, all of them details that were more valuable to her than gold. His passion for everything he said pulsed through him into her. He made her feel the possibilities, and gradually her vague dreams began to take form and shape. If he was manipulating her to a way of thinking that benefited him, she was alert enough to see it benefited her, too. He held her in thrall, in every way that he could.

He had begun by explaining the seemingly careless mixture of crops in the same field. Trees and vines and vegetables had been planted close together so that when the worker took home his share of the produce he could have a little of everything that he needed.

Her response?

What's wrong with that? It seems fair.

It leeches the land without giving it a chance to yield all that it could.

So what way is better?

Terrace one hillside in olive trees, another as a vineyard, melons and squash and corn set off by themselves.

Doesn't that mean that whoever works the vineyard gets only grapes?

If that's the way he's to be paid.

How else?

Coin.

I don't have enough for the workers I need. And that's providing I get any workers at all.

He had let that one go, changing instead to the kinds of grapes best suited to Donati soil. There was nothing wrong with the variety the family had always grown, but they had been picked before full maturity and the wine served young.

So I'll pick them later and age the wine.

Even if she was able to do that, to miraculously get the vineyard going and the process of wine-making begun, she would still have an inferior product.

You said there was nothing wrong with the grapes.

They need to be mixed with Sangiovese grapes to produce a good Chianti. Perhaps a great one.

And how do I get these Sangiovese grapes?

She would have to buy them, or go into partnership with another vineyard.

The more he talked, the less she knew; at least that was how she felt. When he got on the subject of the olive trees, about the steps necessary to get the best oil, about the terracing, and keeping the trees trimmed so that birds might fly through their branches without touching the leaves, she could do nothing but stare toward the sea and wonder if maybe she shouldn't try fishing instead.

"Why are you telling me all this?" she asked at the end of the hour lecture. "I've already told you I don't have enough money to give a living wage to anyone right away. Not if he has a family to support."

"I have no family."

Sitting once again beside her, he spoke flatly, the way he had before, when she suspected he was fighting a deep turmoil. When she looked at him, he was staring toward the sea as she had done, but she saw in his eyes the same anger or hate or despair she had seen before, the deep emotion she could not name but could feel coming from within him like heat from a smouldering fire.

As before, the emotion, the turmoil, was gone as quickly as it had come. Why she wanted to console him, she did not know. Whatever he wanted from her, it wasn't consolation.

He looked at her, his face close, his breath warm on her cheek. "I have given you much to think about."

More than he knew.

She stood and walked up the hill to another weed-choked furrow, stopping beside the dead elm tree with the noose-shaped hanging vine. She felt him move close behind her. She directed her question to the row of cypress trees that lined the ridge of the distant hills.

"What do you really want? Please don't put me off again, Signore Vela. There's a reason behind all you've told me. You want something." She dared glance back at him. "It's time to tell me."

He stood rigid for a moment, his eyes locked with hers, and she felt the force of his will; it robbed her lungs of air. "I want many things." He hesitated, and she thought for a moment he was going to touch her. But he didn't, and she was able to breathe once more.

"First, I want to work the land again. This land. The Villa Falcone."

"Why would you want to do that?" she asked,

startled, and yet, on a deeper level, not startled at all.

"It was a happy time of my life, when I had hope."

He lied. She did not know how she knew whenever he did so, but she did. Perhaps in those long-ago days he had been filled with the hope he claimed, hope that came with being young. But he had also been filled with despair.

She turned to stare at him. Because she was standing uphill, their eyes were on a level. She suspected that was why he had stopped where he had, to give her a sense of being equal in whatever was being discussed. Was he really so calculating? She knew the answer was yes, and her heart turned heavy within her breast. Her disappointment was as foolish as it was real.

Everyone wanted something from her. The problem was to figure out what that something was.

"You wish to work here. Without pay. Forgive me for correcting you, Signore Vela, but I do not believe your time spent in the fields of the villa was as happy as you say."

He shrugged. He put a great deal of muscle into the simple movement. His eyes did not leave hers.

Kate's heart lurched.

"Not all times are happy for anyone," he said. "The past is done. We must consider only what is happening in the present and what will come."

"You surprise me." It was an understatement. "Clearly you have worked this soil. And yet you are far more"—she searched for the Italian word—*"filosófico,* philosophical, than I would have expected."

"Do not make me more than I am, Contessa."

Or less.

She looked away. "I understand forgetting the past," she said, though she did not, at least not in his case. "But I do not understand your working without pay."

"I'll want food."

"And shelter."

"No, shelter is my concern."

Studying the field around them, she saw the hours, the months, the years of backbreaking labor required to accomplish all that he said was needed. Annual crops such as vegetables could bring in a small income, but it was in the olive grove and the vineyard that more than a simple living could be made.

"My Italian is not so good, signore. I must be misunderstanding you."

"There is more."

She read a thousand meanings in his words, and at the same time none at all. She had expected something like this, but still his comment came like a slap.

Of course there was more. A man who looked

the way he did could have any woman of his choice. It would be a triumph to get the Contessa Donati to lie beneath him and spread her legs. After all, there were many women in the village, but there was only one contessa, scrawny and pale though she was.

Kate got a sudden vivid picture of exactly that happening, right here in the dirt, her coarse skirt bunched at her waist, undergarments slung aside as he—

She swallowed a cry. A flush stole over her face. What was happening? What had she allowed herself to feel? A woman of peace, she felt the urge to hit him, but that would be denying the deep heat and the indecent images tearing at her, all of them coming from her own desperate imagination, inspired by nothing more than the presence of an obscenely virile man. She ought to clasp her hands over her ears and run from him, but she wanted even more to touch his bare skin and ask him to go on.

If he read even half of what raced through her mind, he ought to be laughing, or leaving, or throwing her in the dirt to take what he could. Instead, he stood watching her, without expression. Strange how he could keep his own thoughts secret at the same time she felt a tremendous tension in him, a tamped-down pressure that was about to explode.

But the explosion did not come. Instead, he spoke as he had been speaking, firmly, an iron will underlying every word, watching her reaction, making sure she understood what he said.

"I will work for you and make you wealthy once again. But make no mistake: I want equal wealth. We share all that we earn."

It was no more than she had offered the people in the village. Kate wanted the ground to open and swallow her. He did not want her body. He wanted her purse.

She grabbed the noose-shaped vine and hung on for support.

"You ask much," she managed.

"I will give you much."

Everything he said had a double meaning. Or was it her love-starved mind that made it so?

It wasn't love she had been considering. Love had nothing to do with lust.

What he offered would give him power over her. It was a condition she could not tolerate. He was far too evidently a man, a kind of man with whom she had never before dealt. She ought to tell him to leave and take his offer to other vineyards, other fields.

A small voice whispered that that would be a foolish thing to do. She needed him—not as a lover, certainly never that—but as a worker who knew what had to be done to bring about the future she had envisioned for the villa. She truly hated to put such power in his hands; perhaps later they could renegotiate. For the moment, she had no other choice.

Even as she made the decision, she felt a bitterness in her heart. He was using her because of her weak situation. She would have to use him, too.

It was possible that when he saw she truly meant they would share nothing but business, nothing but work, when the toiling became hot and hard, with little but his daily sustenance as a reward, a man of strength and purpose such as he would not stay around.

And once again she would be alone, taking care of herself as she had wanted from the beginning of her widowhood. Her task was to see that she benefited from his knowledge, from his strength and purpose, taking as much of it for herself as she could.

First, before all this could play out, she wanted one thing made clear.

"This is a business arrangement."

"Of course. What else?"

"I am a woman alone. But I am not without power."

His eyes narrowed. "No woman is without power."

She wanted very much to believe that was so, and to believe that he believed it. In an intimate relationship, how much power would any woman have over him? Very little. It was another reason for keeping distance between them.

Besides, no man she had ever known truly believed in the strength of a woman, or her ability to think for herself.

"The land is mine," she said.

"You were married to the late conte. You must have earned it a thousand times over."

"You speak too bluntly."

"It is a failing of mine."

"And your other failings? Should I know them before I agree to your proposal?"

He took a long time answering. "For you, Contessa Donati, and for our purpose, I will keep them under control."

So many double meanings. He made her mind whirl, and just when she had to think clearly.

She held out a hand. "Half of what we make, and nothing but food in payment until then, no matter how hard we have to work or how long it takes to find success."

He stared at her hand, then let his gaze trail up her arm to her throat, to her lips, to her eyes.

"The labor will be more difficult than you can imagine."

"I am not faint of heart."

"It is not your heart that is my concern. I think of your body. You are not strong."

Her temper flared. "Do not misjudge me. I am stronger than you know."

She read the skepticism in his eyes. "I will be careful, as you say, not to misjudge you. I ask the same of you. Will you be guided by me? Will you take my advice on all that needs to be done in the fields?"

"You ask much."

"I am not the only one, Contessa. I could work for a year, for longer, and then be removed from the villa on some excuse that occurs to you."

"You insult me. I am a woman of my word. I will have my agent draw up an agreement that says unless you harm me or betray our pact in a way that threatens the possibility of our success, our partnership will remain."

At last he took her hand. His warmth burned through her skin and her blood pulsed fast. The premonition struck that she was agreeing to far more than had been verbally expressed.

"No signed agreement is necessary," he said. "You will find I am a man of my word. I will not harm you. I will do nothing to threaten our success."

She watched as he strode back to the furrow where he had been working. Pulling the knife from its holder, he stood with legs apart and slashed at a vine that had entwined itself in one of the olive trees. She could see the muscles working beneath his shirt, could imagine the clenching of his buttocks and thighs as he applied force to each swinging motion.

She looked away, unable to trust her thoughts when he was in sight. Everything had happened so quickly, from despair in the piazza to a glimmer of hope up here on the hill. How coincidental his appearance and his offer, following so soon after she had been publicly rebuffed in the village. He must have known such a thing would happen. Alfiero had been there before her and met with a similar response. It was inevitable she would fare no better.

And so he had waited to put his proposition to her when she was most likely to agree. Yes, he was a calculating man. Around him, she must always be on her guard.

Most disturbing was the flash of light in his eyes just before he turned from her to resume his work. It was the light of triumph.

As she stared at him, unable to look away, one question burned in her mind: What had she done?

Chapter Eight

Over the next week Kate found out exactly what her alliance with Roberto Vela meant. It meant work.

Not her feeble first efforts with the pick, when she had moaned over snapped nails and a couple of blisters, but the backbreaking, bone-grinding kind that every evening left her scarcely able to walk from the field, up the terrace stairs and to her bed, unmindful of the grime and sweat she carried with her.

It was the kind of labor he had warned her about, the labor she had proudly, and brashly, claimed she could tolerate. She had spoken in ignorance.

Alfiero always stood on the terrace to watch her exit in the early morning shortly after dawn after a hastily downed breakfast, every muscle in her body urging her to return to bed. He was there, too, for her return when the evening sun was resting close to the edge of the sea and her muscles were too weak to urge anything except immediate unconsciousness.

"The contessa should remain indoors and rest today," Alfiero said each morning as he handed her a basket of food for herself and her lone helper.

"A tray waits in your room," he said in the evening as she handed him the empty basket and trudged toward the stairs.

On each occasion she thanked him and went about what she was driven to do. Sometimes she ate from the evening tray; sometimes she found herself too weary to lift a fork, able only to pull her filthy clothes from her body and set them outside her door, where she always found waiting the clothes she had set out the previous night, freshly laundered.

Sometimes she woke in the middle of the night, bathed herself in the water that was always waiting, then fell back into bed naked, too weary to pull on a gown.

The mysterious housekeeper Maria must be providing the food, the water and the clean clothes, but Kate never saw her. It was as if she had a ghost attending to her needs.

A very thorough ghost who thought of everything. Kate decided she had been wrong about Alfiero tasting her food. Maria could not possibly wish her harm, not with the care she was providing.

And what was the work that tested every muscle in her body? She hacked at vines and weeds, learned to choose the tender shoots that would make new olive trees and grapevines, to surround them with loose dirt dampened with water from the well that had been dug a century ago between the two fields, to set the shoots aside until a suitable spot could be prepared for their planting.

Outside her work, two things drew her attention: the falcon that had begun circling overhead every day, a curiosity that even Alfiero commented on during his brief communications, and, of course, Roberto Vela.

The falcon put on the showier display, soaring and diving over the land, dark wings spread wide, then swooping over the thick growth at the cliff top to the west and skimming the surface of the sea for a wayward fish that dared swim toward the sky.

The falcon signified nothing, she assured herself, despite the warning expression on her servant's face, and despite, too, the shiver that went down her spine when she first saw her soaring visitor each day. She told herself this slice of Tuscany had been the predator's home far longer than it had been hers.

In his quieter way, Roberto proved of far more significance, and not just because of the knowledge he imparted. He was in the field when she arrived; he stayed after she trudged wearily back toward the villa. Though he never admitted it, she knew that as the sun was setting he kept his eyes on her until she was inside the iron gate, close to the terrace and the waiting Alfiero.

Was he watching to make sure she arrived safely? Or was he waiting for her to collapse and cry that she could not go on? She did not know and did not even care. Speculation took too much energy.

They seldom talked. But she watched him as she toiled. From the corner of her eye, from beneath the broad brim of her hat, she observed everything he did, his powerful stroke with the ax, the delicate touch of his strong hands as he held the tender shoots, the long stride as he moved from row to row, muscles working in harmony up and down the length of his backside. From the smoothness of that stride, they did not look like muscles that ached.

The most curious thing about him was the dignity with which he did the most menial tasks. He might have been a conte himself, turning his hand to the care of his own land. The notion stuck in her mind and would not go away. He truly did work as if the trees, the vines, the weeds themselves were his own. She was the intruder in these fields, not he.

After the first few days, in the afternoon he removed his shirt, wrapped a strip of cloth around his head to hold the sweat from his eyes and slapped oil on his bare skin before taking up the pick or the ax or the knife and turning his attention to the task at hand.

The first time he undressed, she protested without thinking.

"You go too far, Signore Vela. We're out here all alone."

"Roberto. Call me Roberto."

The use of his name seemed more intimate than viewing his half-naked state. She took another look at his glistening chest, and her hands got their familiar itch. All right, not quite so intimate. But close.

"Perhaps the contessa would like to take off her own shirt. In that way we will not be different. As you have said, we are out here alone."

She tried to summon a portion of the dignity that came so easily to him.

"I am a lady, signore."

"You are a woman. And you are right to be offended. We are different. Removing your clothes would prove it all the more."

Cheeks burning, she looked down at the stained blouse clinging damply to her body, thought about her smudged face and the unkempt condition of her equally damp hair, and she held her protest. If she had ever truly been a lady, in the strict Boston sense of the word, she was one no more.

But she was definitely a woman. She had never felt her sex more than now.

"Do what you want," she said, then added, "Roberto," letting him know such familiarity meant nothing to her. "We must get back to work."

On shaky legs she walked around him, purposely letting her hips sway from side to side as she strode to the well and splashed water over her face. She let it run in cooling rivulets down her throat, beneath her blouse, trickling between her breasts. He watched. She felt like a silver fish in the water, the coveted object of a bird of prey.

"Enjoy the view," she said in her native English, throwing the words out as if he could understand them. "You will not catch me with your beak."

When she turned to face him, he was working diligently at hacking off an olive tree limb.

Over the ensuing days she had to make several trips to the well to cool herself off. On these journeys he seemed to direct his attention elsewhere. More than once she was tempted to do as he had suggested, to remove her blouse and splash the water liberally over her breasts. But she did not. She had been too carefully Boston bred.

Not that she was always ignored. Their goal, as he explained it to her on a morning when he was still clothed, was to clear this first field of grapevines, to prune the neglected olive trees, to turn the soil and plant the cuttings so that more trees would grow, making sure to define more clearly the terracing of the rows. The distant field would be a vineyard, likewise terraced. They could use parts of the ripped-out trees as stakes for the vines.

He spoke with politeness, with deference, keeping a respectful distance, and he did not talk down to her as if she were a child. His attitude puzzled and intrigued her as much as the workings of the muscles across his back. If she had not known the idea to be absurd, she would have thought he was drawing her into some kind of trap.

Everything he said seemed so logical, so right. The fact that at their current rate of progress they would be well into the new century forty years distant before they saw any income from their labor was something she refused to consider. She placed its unimportance right alongside her questions about why he was even there.

At the end of the first week, while she was digging at a particularly tough root, trying to forget he was working close by half naked, wondering whether she wasn't about to wear out her new-bought gloves, a shadow fell across her. Her attention shot to the dirt-covered boots resting close to her dirt-stained skirt. She set down her knife and drew a deep breath.

Pushing back her hat, she allowed her eyes to trail up the long line of his trousers, moving quickly past the juncture of his thighs and abdomen, easing more slowly up the expanse of muscle and oiled golden skin that was his chest, forcing herself to look into his eyes.

The power she saw there was as hot as the sun. He blinded her. "Good gracious," she said in English, then hurriedly looked down at the ground. "Am I doing something wrong?"

He kneeled beside her. As he bent, his joints did not crackle the way hers did when she assumed the same position. He was in splendid condition both inside and out.

When he tossed her hat aside, she yelped in protest.

"Take off your gloves," he said.

She stared at him. The cloth he had wrapped around his head made him look like an Indian warrior from the American West, a feared chieftain whose picture she had seen in a Boston periodical a long time ago, chiseled face, thick black hair and all. With his patina of civilization, and his proximity, Roberto Vela appeared far more dangerous than the painted savage.

She dared defy him. "No. I have hours left—"

The defiance did not last any longer than it took for him to remove the gloves, then hold out a small pottery jar she hadn't seen at first. Trying hard to ignore the tingle where his skin touched hers, she asked, "What's in there?"

"An oil rendered from sheep's wool."

He might as well have said moondust. She stared at him uncomprehendingly.

"Do you want me to put it on for you?" he asked.

"Put it on?"

It wasn't the most intelligent thing she had ever asked. No longer did she consider simply touching him with her hands. She also thought of using her tongue. Already she could taste his salt.

Her free hand extended toward his bare chest, shining in the sunlight, as much from sweat as from the oil. Her fingers hovered close enough for her to feel his heat.

"It's what you rub on yourself," she said.

"Not for vanity's sake, if that's what you're thinking. The Tuscan sun is cruel, Contessa. Look at your arms."

On this particularly warm day she had rolled her sleeves almost to her shoulders, wanting to feel even the slightest breeze against her sweaty flesh. Already the skin was beginning to burn.

Taking one of her arms, he gave her no chance to care for herself. His long brown fingers dipped into the jar and he began to rub the warm oil from the back of her hand all the way to her shoulder, gliding over the tender flesh in an incredibly sensuous massage, then turning the arm to move back down the paler inside. The arm was close to her body, so he came tauntingly close to her breast, taking his time, giving special attention to the crook in her elbow, then easing on down until he was massaging her fingers, one by one, pulling at them with far more attention than they deserved.

Not knowing where to look, unable to protest, she watched his hands, swallowed when he moved to the other arm, thinking that he was finding sensitive spots on mundane parts of her body, like the inside of her upper arm, her elbow, the palm of each work-sore hand.

And he was affecting parts he did not touch—the pit of her stomach, the tips of her suddenly sensitive breasts, her heart with its peculiarly erratic beat.

"Close your eyes," he said.

Of course she did not, instead looking up at him through her lashes, feeling languorous and aroused at the same time. "Why?" she asked in little more than a whisper.

"They are beautiful. I want to protect them."

For just a moment she believed him. Then reality set in, and she snapped out of her spell, the languor evaporating into the hot air. She knew all too well

116

her physical shortcomings. They had been pointed out with regularity by her father and the conte.

"Please, don't say such things. They're insulting. There is nothing beautiful about me."

He shook his head. "If you have been made to believe this, the conte truly was a fool."

His words made her light-headed. No one had ever talked to her this way, bluntly and yet caressingly. Confused, she had no reply, no sharp retort, not even a whisper. All she could do was stare at him in wonder. Once again she slipped into the spell of believing. He made her feel lovely. She almost smiled.

She caught herself in time, before she made a complete fool of herself. Her pale skin had taken on a hideous tint of red, her crude clothes were filthy, her hair damp, tangled, beyond repair. Worst of all, since he was kneeling downwind of her, he had surely discovered the scent rising from her did not exactly perfume the air with sweetness.

Lovely? The man was insane. Or else he was cunningly able to ferret out the words that would make her the most vulnerable.

He wasn't cunning enough. He ought to stay with the truth.

Taking the jar from his hand, she took a dollop of the oil on the tips of her fingers and smoothed it over her nose and cheeks with far greater efficiency than he had employed.

117

"Did you know Pietro?" she asked, satisfied she could sound so casual.

"I worked for his father."

"So you said. But I wondered if you ever met my late husband. You speak as if you had."

She could feel him withdrawing inside himself, though he held very still.

"Everyone knew Pietro Donati. Men and women both."

Of course they had. The women especially. Pietro had not kept his assignations a secret.

"They knew him," she said, "but they did not like him. That seems to be what you mean."

"Such is not for me to say."

"Then speak for yourself. How did you feel?"

"His father provided me with work."

It was not an answer and both of them knew it. The man was a master of many things, not the least of them evasions about his past.

She smoothed the oil down her neck and onto the skin exposed by the opening of her blouse. His eyes followed the movement of her hand. They flickered once, but they did not stray. Once again her heart took up its erratic beat. She bit at her lower lip.

"I don't understand you," she said.

His laugh was short, sharp. "There are times I do not understand myself."

She set down the jar and rested her hands in her

lap. "For the first time I believe you are speaking the truth."

"I have told you many truths. One of them is that you have beautiful eyes."

He leaned close; with no more than his gaze he drew her to him.

"When I returned to Tuscany," he added, "I knew you would be at the Villa Falcone."

She looked at him in surprise.

"It was no secret," he said. "Everyone did. But you are not what I expected."

"How am I different?" she asked, afraid he might tell her, equally afraid he might not.

"A thousand ways. I have not discovered all of them yet."

Evasion.

"I am what I am," she said flatly, "a widow who was once rich but is rich no more."

"These matters are unimportant. Do you not know that?"

"But it is the hope for riches that brought you here."

He stared at her throat as if he could see her racing pulse. "I am no longer sure."

Neither spoke for a moment. She stared at his lips. He was far too smooth, far too appealing, far, far too mysterious for her to contend with, much less understand. In defense of her sanity she looked beyond him and saw the falcon circling in the sky.

As if he looked for a victim to snare in his deadly talons. She could almost call Roberto *Il Falcone*. The Falcon. A raptor bent on capturing a woman's heart.

Whatever had been passing between them was gone. Hastily she picked up her gloves and shoved her hands inside. Slick from the coating of oil, they slipped easily into place, though the leather was growing stiff with dirt and sweat.

"You're wrong," she said. "Poverty is very important. We're wasting time."

He stood, accepting her change of mood. Again she heard no crackle of the knees.

"You should roll down your sleeves, Contessa. So much exposed skin can do you harm."

She almost told him that his exposed skin was far more dangerous to her than her own. Instead, she picked up the knife. He leaned down to take it from her.

"I need to work, Roberto," she said with genuine irritation.

"Not with this."

His tone was different, not baiting, not provocative and certainly not polite.

She stood and stared at the knife resting in his hand. With little effort, he pulled it into two pieces, the sharp, curved blade separating easily from the wooden handle.

"I didn't realize I was hitting so hard at the root," she said.

"You weren't. Observe."

She stared at where he was pointing. The slot in the handle into which the flat end of the blade should have fitted was splintered, made wider than it should have been.

"I did that?"

"Someone did. I doubt if you damaged your own tool."

"I found this knife in the back of the storage shed. It must have been there forever. I suppose years of use wore down the handle."

"This damage is fresh. Look at the color of the wood beneath the splinters."

"It's a different color. It's paler."

He nodded. She tried to work through what he was saying.

"Someone played with this?" she asked, refusing to believe what seemed apparent to him.

"I doubt it was play. If you had continued to pound at the ground as you were doing, the blade would have separated as it is now. You could have sliced off a finger."

Her hands tensed.

"You can't mean someone wants to harm me. I know the villagers bear ill will toward the Donatis, but this seems beyond what any of them would do."

121

"Where did you leave it last night?"

"I should have put it away. I was careless. I left it on the ground just inside the gate. But I had no idea—"

She shuddered.

He slipped both blade and handle into the sheath at his waist. "Work is done for the day."

"What do you suggest I do? Go back to my room and worry?"

"Sleep would be more beneficial."

"And impossible. Though I'm not accepting your claim someone really wanted to harm me. No, Roberto, I prefer to keep busy. I'm already greased like a pig for the spit—"

His lips twitched.

"—so I might as well bake a little longer out here."

She braced herself for more argument; instead, he nodded brusquely and retrieved a small digging tool from where he had been working.

"Remove more dirt from around the root," he said as he placed it in her hands. "Let me know when you are done. It will take an ax to remove it completely."

A gentle warmth settled in her heart. He was treating her with respect, with consideration for what she had to do. For Kate, it was a new experience and, like everything else about him, far too pleasing. If he truly was setting some kind of trap for her, he did it very well.

With renewed vigor she threw herself into her work, concentrating mightily on the root and the dirt, refusing to consider what might have happened to the knife, refusing also to think about her chaotic feelings concerning Roberto Vela, feelings that grew more complicated as each day passed.

On this evening, when she could no longer see well enough to dig, he escorted her all the way to the terrace. Alfiero stood at the top of the steps, watching. As far as she knew, this was the first time he had got a close view of her business associate, for that was how she wanted to regard him. The servant's face was rigid, not disapproving outright but certainly not accepting, either.

At least, Kate thought with a sigh, Roberto had put on his shirt before walking her from the field. She introduced the two men. They each nodded in silence. She sensed something passing between them—questions, warnings—but she had no idea what it could be. It was probably nothing. She couldn't be right in wondering if they had known each other before this day. Clear thinking was beyond her. She was still skittish from the incident with the knife.

Then Roberto did a curious thing: He knelt to inspect the once-broken step.

"You repaired it," Kate said.

"You had fallen," was all he said.

She remembered that first day when she had hurried out to view her property, remembered the torn sleeve, the thin, bloodied scratch on her arm. She had told him it was nothing, but he had seen through her lie. He had investigated and corrected a problem she had not discussed.

He must stop being so kind. She did not know how to react.

Or maybe it wasn't kindness. He had an interest in keeping her safe. She needed to keep that in mind.

Three days later her life took another turn. One of the villagers showed up in the field and Roberto put him to work. The man, short, barrel-chested and muscular, refused to so much as look at her.

"He's tired of traveling to faraway fields to find work," Roberto said. "Pay him a few *lire* and provide food during the day. He will work from dawn to dusk."

"He seems too good to be true. I need to introduce myself."

"No. He does not wish to speak to the contessa. And do not give him orders. They must come from me."

She tried not to be hurt.

Roberto was not done. "He asks that you not reveal to anyone in town that he is here."

"Can I know his name? All right, don't tell me. I already know the answer to that."

Two days later, just as she was getting used to her mystery worker, another villager appeared, this one also short but lean instead of round, his arms and legs tight like a wire. His working conditions were the same.

She took Roberto aside.

"What's going on?" she asked.

"Believe what they say."

She looked beyond him to the two, who were already wielding pick and shovel. "I can't."

"Would you feel better if I told them to leave?"

"Don't you dare."

He grinned. It wasn't a big grin and it didn't last long, but compared to his usual sobriety, it was like a boisterous laugh. Her heart twisted. Embarrassed, she looked down at the ground.

"I guess instead of forty years," she said, "we'll have the villa profitable in twenty."

"What I want for the villa should come much sooner."

Kate brushed at a strand of hair caught on her cheek, forgetting she had on a dirty leather glove.

He wiped away the smudge. It was a familiar gesture, gentle, almost affectionate. But it was strong enough to send shivers down her spine. Inside her work boots her toes curled.

Confused, she stepped away. "Don't do that."

He bowed, all sign of affection gone. "I apologize, Contessa Donati."

"There's no need. It's just that—"

She had no idea how to go on. Confused, she turned from him and threw herself into her work. In English she muttered the truth. She did not want him to ever stop.

Something was happening to her, something she had not expected. She would have described herself as happy, but since she had no idea how that particular emotion felt, she could easily be wrong.

Certainly she wasn't solemn the way she had been. At times, while working, she heard herself humming. In all her life she could not remember doing such a thing. And she did not truly fear the feelings of pleasure she got from looking at Roberto. They were natural, if disconcerting. And they would pass. Or would they?

One thing she knew for sure: She was getting stronger physically. Her muscles no longer ached every time she took a breath. She was certain she had not gained weight, but her body felt sturdier, healthier, stronger. And she did not feel so awkward walking across the uneven fields. At times she even ran, uphill and down, an impossible feat when she first walked out on her land.

As good as she felt, she did not look at herself in the mirror. She did not want to see herself as others saw her. She corrected herself: as Roberto saw her.

What difference did her appearance make to him? None, she was sure. The trouble was, though she had never been vain, she needed her pride. That the two could be mixed together was something she had never before considered.

She cursed this way of thinking. She was going through too many changes, too fast. No matter how much help she got, she was still a woman alone, a woman who must ultimately depend on herself.

With that said, she still felt an elation that would not go away. She knew all was going too well—experience told her it would not last—but she could not avoid the smiles that stole across her lips, or the soft humming she tried very hard to keep to herself.

Halfway through the third week, with the sun's early rays lighting her path, she went out to the field with her usual basket of food, now packed for four, her gloves and hat tucked inside. Roberto awaited her alone, in the shade of an ancient olive tree.

Without thinking, she smoothed her hair from her face, toward the thick braid that fell down her back. And she straightened, putting her all-too-thin figure at its best advantage.

She looked around for the workers, the round

one she had named Michelangelo—she pictured him putting his muscles to work on the seventeen-foot slab of marble that had become the sculptor's incredible David—and the wiry man she called Leonardo. The latter's delicate touch with the grape-vine shoots, in an artistic genius, could have produced the Mona Lisa.

She kept the names to herself, of course, since neither man wished her to address him. But they gave the pair an identity, made them more than anonymous laborers who came and went with the sun.

Neither artist of the soil was in view today. She looked questioningly at Roberto as she came close.

"We've had trouble," he said. His face was stone, his voice harsh.

She closed her eyes for a moment and felt the joy go out of the day.

Here was the bad news she had been expecting. She stared at him as she set the basket aside.

"Tell me, Roberto. Don't keep anything back."

Chapter Nine

Roberto did not equivocate or pause.

"Last night one of the workers stayed late. The one who first came to the villa."

Michelangelo.

Kate's stomach knotted.

"While he was out in the field preparing to leave, someone attacked him."

"What do you mean, attacked him?"

"He was struck across the back of the head."

She swallowed a cry. "Is he all right?"

"A bruise, a slight loss of blood, nothing permanent. He'll have a lump on his head for a while, and a formidable ache, but that is all."

"Thank God. Where is he now?"

"I took him to the village. He's being cared for."

The full import of what Roberto said hit her. "I

don't understand. Who could have done such a thing? Did he see who it was? Did you?"

"Unfortunately, the answer to both is no. He says he heard nothing, saw nothing until he returned to consciousness. I was not here when the blow was struck. He was to leave shortly after I did. There was still light, and he wanted to finish taking down one of the trees in the far field. Ironically a branch from that tree was the weapon used to strike him. After I had been gone a while, I sensed that all was not well. The feeling would not go away, and I returned at midnight and found him."

Kate listened in growing horror, picturing the scene; the furrowed ground, the air chilled by the nightly breeze from the sea, leaves rustling, everything ghostlike in the light of the full moon.

And lying in the middle of the distant field, the unconscious worker.

"Poor man. But for you, he could have lain outside for hours longer."

"I should not have left him."

"Don't blame yourself. Who would think such a thing could happen?" She rubbed her arms. "Who could have done it? I keep coming back to that. Who? Did he have money on him? Does he have enemies?"

"He lives in a hut in the hills, isolated from Belmare. He is a simple farmer and has been all his life. He has no family and little money." Roberto hesitated. "Perhaps his enemies, if he has them, are not involved. I have not told you everything. There is more."

She should have known there would be.

"The new plants you put into the cleared ground are gone."

She rubbed at her temples, feeling stupid, slow to understand. "What do you mean, gone?"

"Just that. They have been ripped out of the dirt. This morning I found a few of them close to the cliff. The rest had obviously been thrown into the sea and washed away by the waves."

Slowly, stunned by his layers of bad news, she looked toward the wind-whipped trees and the wild shrubbery and the pile of boulders, some larger than the donkey cart, that marked the seaside edge of her property. She had been meaning to make her way there, to stand close to the sharp limestone drop-off and study the churning sea at its base. She had never found the time. Her days were far too busy.

But someone had gone there. Someone intent on destruction. An enemy. And not Michelangelo's.

"I don't believe the attack was planned," Roberto said. "Whoever came here thought he would be without witnesses when he did what he did."

"But the destruction was planned." She lifted her hands in a helpless gesture. "Could the villagers hate me so much they would harm an innocent man?"

He gave her a long stare before he spoke. "I do not know. I had not thought so. But I do not know."

Something in his voice, in his stance, in the stark darkness of his eyes told her that he was as shaken as she. The work had been his, too, and the worker, a simple farmer, had been hired by him. Perhaps they had been friends. No, that couldn't be. Roberto had said he had been gone so long he was a stranger in these hills.

"And the other man." Leonardo. "He is all right?"

"He was here earlier, but he knew nothing of what had happened. I sent him away for the day, to consider whether he wanted to return."

Kate let out a tremulous sigh. One worker assaulted, both of them gone, the delicate fruits of their labor destroyed. And just when everything was going so well.

She had known scorn before, and isolation. But this hatred, and the form of violence it had taken, was too new, too raw for her heart to accept.

The enormity of it all overcame her. The ground unexpectedly dropped from beneath her, and her knees gave way. In an instant she was in his arms. The tears came, though she had not cried in years. Tears of frustration and anger and helplessness.

She did not try to stop them. She doubted if she could.

He held her tight as she buried her face in his shirt. She let him hold her for a long time. She let him comfort her. If it was a weakness, she would worry about it later. At the moment she needed him more than she had ever needed anyone.

Neither spoke. Gradually she became aware of what she was truly doing. She was burying herself in a man's arms, eager to absorb his strength, his warmth, the consolation offered by his solid presence slowly turning into something far different from simple sympathy.

For a woman stunned by misfortune, she was far too aware of his physicality, the breadth and firmness of his chest, the scent of manliness, the power of his arms. She looked up at him, at his lips and then into his eyes. She forgot to breathe.

He bent his head. His lips moved closer. A tremor went through him, moved from his body into hers, connecting them in a way that was purely sexual. Her mouth opened but no sound came out. She heard nothing but the buzzing in her ears.

Again the unexpected happened. He was supposed to cover her mouth with his, to connect the two of them with a searing kiss, as if he would pull her into him and keep her there with that kiss. It was what she wanted, and he wanted it, too. Or so she thought.

Instead, he pressed his lips to her forehead and eased her away, holding on to her arms for a moment until she could stand on her own. He need not have bothered. Once the shock subsided—and it took only a few seconds—her knees were no longer weak.

"You have received bad news," he said, as if that explained anything, as if he told her something she did not already know, expressing in simple words the reason he had pushed her away. "I do not wish to take advantage," he added softly, and then more softly, almost to himself, "though you are more tempting than you realize."

Added to the burden of everything he had already told her, she now felt foolish, all her secret wounds exposed. Her lone consolation came from his voice, which was not so strong, not so sure as she had grown used to.

She stepped away. "Nothing was going to happen."

But of course it was, and he knew it. More, he would remember how easily she had offered herself to him, pressing her body against his, her breasts, her thighs. The choice not to kiss her—to really kiss her—had been his, not hers.

In the bath of summer sunlight flooding the hillside, she felt cold. It cleared her head.

"It all seemed too much," she said airily, "that's why I reacted as I did." She could not tell whether he believed her, but he should. She almost believed herself. "I had allowed myself to feel good about the work we were accomplishing. Things did not seem so bleak, not with the additional help, and I allowed myself to hope that we could accomplish what we set out to do. I will not allow myself such a luxury again."

The more she talked, the more she heard the truth in her own words. Like wine, hope was an intoxicant that blurred the edges of reality. She would indeed be careful how much of that hope she allowed herself.

He studied her as if he would see beyond those words. This watchfulness was not, for her, his most endearing trait. He made her feel vulnerable at the moment she most needed to feel strong.

"You have said this is too much, and so it is. Go back to your bed, Contessa."

"I can't do that. After what happened, we have more work to do than ever."

She tried to get around him, but he blocked her path. She might as well have been arguing with the sun.

"Rest is needed. You have worked hard, and you are exhausted, even now at the beginning of the day. When you looked in the mirror, did you not see the bruising around your eyes?"

"I don't look in mirrors."

"You should."

"To see how tired I appear?"

"To see other things as well."

"More reason not to look," she said, thinking of the gaunt face, blistered by the sun, the straggly hair that refused to stay in its bun, and yes, the bruised eyes that would be in her reflection.

He did not try to argue with her. "We would not accomplish much today," he said. "Tomorrow is soon enough to see what must be done to repair the damage."

He made good sense, again not an endearing trait.

Worse, his words brought a rush of chagrin. How could she have forgotten, even temporarily, the darkest part of this turn of events? The injured man, the destroyed sprigs of grape and olive plants—these were of importance, not any temporary, womanly aberration on her part.

So he hadn't kissed her. Except for a moment's weakness, she hadn't wanted him to. If she told herself that often enough, she might eventually believe it was so.

"And will you also rest?" she asked.

"As to that, I cannot say. But I will not be in the fields. It is best that you not be here alone."

"Surely no one in broad daylight would—"

She knew the answer without finishing the question.

She looked around her, at the openness, the sky,

the far hills. And, of course, the peregrine falcon, which had returned to swoop and search for its daily prey. Had he been witness to the attack? Did he fly at night? Or did he, like her, tuck himself away with the fall of the sun and not come out again until the early rays once again warmed the earth?

"So much space, so much land, yet if I walk away this morning I'll feel like a prisoner in my own home."

Eyes hooded, he watched her. "We are all prisoners of one kind or another."

"Don't try to tell me that you are any such thing. I don't believe it."

"Believe what you must. Our needs and our wants keep us from doing everything we wish."

Like really kissing me? If she asked him, he would probably say yes. He would probably lie.

You are more tempting than you realize. Another lie.

She must, she truly must, stop coming back to what had almost happened between them.

"Claim what you will," she said, "there is no way I can look upon you as a prisoner of any kind."

Her words, meant as an end to the discussion, seemed only to goad him.

"You think I have no wants?" He spoke in anger. She realized with a start that for all his measured rationality and calm, he had been holding in a great emotion. Then, even harsher, as if the words were torn from him, he threw at her, "You think I have no needs?"

Before she could respond, he swept her into his arms, and this time his mouth covered hers, his tongue parting her lips as he gave her a far more explosive kiss than she had expected before. Stunned, she could not push him away, and then she did not want to. He covered her in fire. Shock turned to heat and burned away the world. She clutched at his sleeves and thrust her body hard against him, her blood racing, her body pulsing with an ache she had never known she could feel, not outside her imagination, not outside her dreams.

His strong, hard hands moved with wondrous gentleness across her shoulders, down her sides, brushing against her trembling breasts, gripping her waist and holding her hips more firmly against him.

Through her worn skirt she could feel the contours of his body, and she knew he felt the same ache as she. She wanted him shirtless, as she had seen him so many times. She wanted to press her bare breasts against his slick, hard chest, she wanted . . .

He thrust her from him, as suddenly as he had pulled her into his arms, leaving her once again to straighten herself, to still her heart, to focus her senses on anything other than him. This time the straightening, the focusing came much more slowly. Aware of the turning of the earth, wondering if she might spin off into space, she felt she might never think clearly again.

She pressed her fingers to her lips, yearning to capture the feel of his mouth covering hers, needing just as passionately to wipe the feel of him away.

She looked away from him. Standing so close, his chest heaving with ragged breaths, he was far too much to contemplate with any degree of calmness. She stared toward the dark sea, trying to think of what to say, what to do.

Something had happened here on this hillside, though she did not know what it was. Something beyond a kiss. Something that would change them both.

She felt him watching her, heard the ragged breathing he could not control, and knew he was as shaken as she. It was small consolation, but it enabled her to speak.

"That was not supposed to happen."

"Not that way." He seemed to speak without thinking.

"What are you talking about?"

Even as she asked the question, she could feel him getting control of himself, distancing himself. Among his many talents, he had the ability to pull away without taking the smallest of steps.

"You are Contessa Donati. I am a laborer, a peasant."

Kate knew it was the only explanation she would get. If only he knew how little she felt like an aristocrat, he would laugh. Or perhaps take her here on the ground. She could not let the thought linger in her mind.

She backed away from him. Perhaps he did not need physical distance between them to hold himself separate, but she did.

"You're right about one thing," she said, turning the conversation away from her inappropriate thoughts. "I need to rest. If you should want to talk to me, send word to Alfiero. Otherwise I will see you here tomorrow morning. And we will both forget what happened this morning."

To her own ears her voice sounded pinched, but his reaction was all she could have wished.

"Of course, Contessa," he said, as formal as she.

"And please let me know if there's anything I can do for Mi—"—she caught herself—"for the worker. I hope that both of the men return, but I won't blame them if they do not."

As she walked away from him, fighting the impulse to run, exhaustion dogged her every step and she could not hold her back straight, though she knew he watched. Roberto was right: She was as weary as if she had put in a day of hard labor. And she was more than ever heartsick about Michelangelo and about the plants.

But if she thought these were her most serious worries, as she certainly should if she were a decent kind of woman, she was wrong. With one kiss, Roberto had turned her world upside down. All her admonitions could not change that frightening fact.

Had she so soon forgotten how much a man could hurt a woman? Apparently the answer was yes.

What she was to do about her lapse, she did not know. What if another such situation arose, a time when in distress she forgot herself? What if they were not in such an open place? What if they were in private, where no one else could see? He might not be so quick to thrust her away. And she might not so readily let him.

She could little control what he said or did, but she would have to do something about herself before she made the worst mistake of her life.

Chapter Ten

Kate made an attempt at rest, but she could not so much as close her eyes, much less sleep. Closed eyes would bring images to her mind. Sleep would bring dreams.

She dressed in one of the black mourning gowns she had brought with her from Venice, binding her hair loosely at the back of her neck, as always avoiding looking at herself in the mirror, refusing to view the havoc sun and wind and hard labor had wreaked on her person.

She went down the inside steps of the villa in search of Alfiero, hurrying past the middle floor and the closed chamber that had been the conte's. She found her servant in the kitchen with Maria. She had not seen him when she returned from the field only an hour after taking the food basket and departing, and she did not know if he knew what had occurred.

She was thinking only of the assaults on the worker and the land. If he ever found out about anything else—he or anyone else—she would never be able to look him in the eye again.

Neither did she want to tell him about poor Michelangelo. He still disapproved of what she was doing, although after his initial reaction three weeks earlier, he had not been so rude as to show his disapproval with more than a lift of his brows. Unlike his mistress, he maintained the proprieties.

But he—and Maria, too—deserved to know someone had been assaulted not very far away. Someone who worked for her.

She saw right away, from the look in their eyes, that they already knew.

"Maria told me," Alfiero explained before she could even speak.

She looked at the woman, who appeared much as she had the first day she came to work: wearing a simple blouse and skirt and a clean apron covering her round figure, dark hair pulled tightly back, making the white streak down the left side appear more startling than ever.

And of course there were the deep, piercing brown eyes, out of place in the plain, flat features of her ageless face.

"How did you find out?" Kate asked.

The woman gave her a smile as bland as a cat's. "I know things."

Kate shook her head. Already her mind could scarcely stop its racing. Now here was something else to contemplate.

"I don't understand," she said, but she had the uncomfortable feeling that perhaps she did.

"I have the gift."

"You have the gift of knowing things you have not been told?"

Maria nodded.

Kate glanced toward Alfiero.

"There are those who say it is so," he said. From his expression, he might as well have been telling her what would be on her dinner tray.

"Who are the ones who say this? I thought Maria was not known in the village."

"Her name is known, as well as her reputation."

She rubbed at her temple, a growing habit on this strange day. "And what is that?"

Maria spoke up. "I am known as *la maga*, a sorceress, though it is a term I would not myself use."

Kate wanted to laugh. A sorceress was the last person she needed preparing her food. No wonder Alfiero had tasted the first meal the woman had prepared.

But the revelation really wasn't humorous. She thought of the witches of Salem and the fear they had aroused. Those women—most of them—had proclaimed their innocence. Not so Maria. But then, the Salem women had not lived in Tuscany, a land where civilization dated far back before Roman centurions walked these hills.

"Isn't a sorceress evil?" she asked.

"I am not evil, Contessa Donati. My powers are limited to my gift."

"Which is knowing things without being told." She shot Alfiero a sharp look. "You might have told me this before."

"Maria is a hard worker. She is a good cook."

He seemed satisfied with his explanation. She wondered what it would take to shake him out of his stoic mien. Letting the issue go, she shifted her attention to the food basket resting on a worktable at the side of the room.

"When I went out this morning, I set it down and forgot all about it. How did it get here?"

"The signora suggested it should be brought inside," Alfiero said.

Kate looked at Maria. "You knew I had left it."

"I knew."

Kate did not try to hide her skepticism. All of Tuscany might believe in the powers of her new housekeeper, but that did not make the powers real, any more than the women of Salem had really been witches. Maria could have followed her mistress as she left for the day. As stunned as Kate had been at Roberto's news, she would not have noticed a horde of gladiators at her heels.

"What else do you know? Who injured the worker? Who destroyed much of what we had accomplished?"

"This I cannot say, Contessa Donati. I have the gift, but it is not without its limits."

She sounded apologetic, and most of all sincere. Perhaps she had not followed. But she must have been outside, or looking through a window, when Kate returned. She could have hurried to the field and asked Roberto what had taken place. Of course; that was it. The Villa Falcone already had the curse of the falcon to contend with; a mystic in the kitchen might just be too much.

But she couldn't resist questioning Maria further.

"And Signore Vela, the man who is helping me revive the grove and vineyard—where is he now?"

The woman's demeanor changed, though Kate could not have said exactly how.

"Signore Vela? Is that what he calls himself?" she asked.

Kate tensed. "You know something about him?"

"I know nothing. I have told you, my gift is limited."

"Yet you question his name."

"I question the truthfulness of all men."

"Including that of Roberto Vela. Or whoever he is."

"The signore is very much a man, as the contessa knows."

Kate took a long, slow breath to steady her heart. What if Maria truly had a gift? What if she had seen everything that had taken place in the field? Worse, what if she told everything she knew? This conversation was rapidly going down a truly treacherous path.

Kate changed its direction. "Please help me understand, Maria. You did not learn about the assault from Signore Vela this morning. You just sensed it, right? But you can't sense where he is at this moment or what he is doing."

"The contessa misunderstands. He searches in the village for the villain who brought trouble to your home."

What she said sounded completely logical. It was something Roberto would very likely do. As little as Kate knew about him, she knew that.

"Does his search put him in danger?"

She tried to put the question casually, as if she cared for him as an associate and nothing more, as if she had not only an hour and a half ago done things with him she had never done with any man. The shrewd look in Maria's eyes told her that she failed.

"Roberto Vela is a man who takes care of himself. If he comes to harm, it will not be at the hands of a coward who strikes an unarmed man in the dark."

Kate gave up looking unconcerned. "Who will harm him?"

"A woman."

Maria's eyes trapped her, and she asked the question she did not want to ask. "What woman?"

"This I cannot say."

"How will he be harmed?"

"In the ways a woman can hurt a man."

"I don't know of these ways."

"Not yet, perhaps. When the time comes, if you are that woman, you will know."

The suggestion that she could actually hurt Roberto was ludicrous, as if she might use some mysterious womanly wiles. But Maria almost made her believe in the possibility.

For a moment no one spoke. The three seemed caught in a tableau, one certainly not of Kate's making, and not of Alfiero's. The silence seemed interminable.

She attempted a laugh. "I don't know what we're talking about. Thank you, Maria, for fetching the basket. It was careless of me to leave it in the field." She turned to Alfiero. "Since I'm not outdoors today, I find myself with time on my hands. Is there anything I can help with?"

"Do not concern yourself with matters of the

villa. Unless you have found something unsatisfactory."

"Not in the least."

She hadn't, not until the past few minutes with the talk of Maria's gift. For a moment she had been taken in, as much by the woman's stare as by her insistent voice. But Kate was far too entrenched in Yankee sensibility to believe such a thing as second sight could really exist.

Excusing herself, she did what she had been putting off since she arrived. How long ago had it been? Three weeks ago today. Not once had bells clanged mysteriously, or walls whispered their dubious welcome.

She needed to inspect her home.

At the north of the villa was the *ferro battuto,* the ornate wrought-iron gate through which she had ridden in the hired gig. The terrace lay to the west, surrounded on three sides by rooms—the kitchen, the dining room, various quarters for servants Kate no longer had and, of course, by the tower. On the east was another wing, this one with a courtyard enclosed on all four sides by accommodations for additional family members and guests. This part of the villa she had never truly explored, not in the past weeks, not five years earlier during her only other period of residence.

It was in this direction that she began her tour. Like the entryway and the *soggiorno* through which she had to pass, the narrow, high-ceilinged corridor leading around the east wing was silent. Without windows to provide natural light, the way was dim, and she walked slowly along the stone floors, worn smooth by a thousand residents over the past centuries, the only whisper the rustle of her skirts. The walls were thick, the air cool, redolent of perfumes and powders from those who had passed this way.

The odors were subtle at first, though not particularly pleasant. Kate was a woman who preferred the verdant scents of the land, of sun and wind coming off the sea. A half-dozen steps farther along the corridor and the air became cloying, sickly sweet, attacking her the way the whispers had her first day at the villa.

Her throat constricted and she hurried along, rattling the stubborn knobs of the chamber doors that taunted her at intervals. Her head grew light. With the little breath left to her, she flung herself against one of the doors and stumbled inside, scarcely able to right herself, avoiding a bruising fall on the hard, bare floor.

Light streamed through the uncurtained windows, dust motes dancing in the beams. It brought her no cheer, except that here she could breathe, short, shallow gasps that did not still her racing heart.

"Stop being ridiculous."

Her admonition echoed from wall to wall in the empty room, but it served to calm her. As she looked around her, she could not keep from wondering what had taken place here over the past centuries.

Her moment of calm contemplation did not last. With growing horror she saw in an unlit corner shadows moving about, dancers in satin gowns and brocade coats, in another shifting shapes that metamorphosed into a naked man and woman grappling at buttocks and thighs with rapacious hands. Everything soundless, everything in pantomime, vague and transparent, as if made out of mist.

"Who are you?"

Her voice sounded harsh and loud in the midst of such unreality. The figures paid her no mind.

Unable to return to the corridor, she saw her only escape, a second door leading to the courtyard, and to the clean, warm comfort of Tuscan air. She forced herself to cross the half dozen yards that separated her from relief. Something cold brushed across her cheek. Not air. The windows were closed and locked. With a scream she threw herself through the door into the enclosed courtyard. Her shrill cry echoed from wall to wall, broken only by the slam of the chamber door behind her.

She turned coward and squeezed her eyes closed, drawing in deep gulps of air. Hand over her pounding heart, she willed it to slow, and at last her heart obeyed. Slowly she opened her eyes to bright day. Her gaze darted from right to left, to the rows of windows and doors, the tiled roof, on one side the tall facade of the central tower behind which lay her own room. If only she could levitate to the highest window and crawl inside, she would grope her way to her bed and pull the covers over her head.

A bird sang, its sweet trill hovering in the air. It was a very ordinary sound on this far from ordinary day, but it served a purpose. As quickly as her terror had come, it was gone, leaving her dizzy and confused and, as the confusion cleared, embarrassed because she had behaved so crazily. Her head cleared. There was nothing out here to frighten her, and there had been nothing in the room, except an overtired woman with an overactive imagination. Dancers and naked lovers, indeed. What was happening to her?

Oh, yes, she was truly a coward. How Roberto would sneer. Alfiero would nod, as if he had seen such an attack coming, and Maria . . . she might already know how foolishly her mistress had behaved.

If there had been spirits inside that bedchamber—and of course there had not been—they told her this was where they belonged. Not she. What had they actually done except spread their sickly perfumes and, of course, frighten her out of her wits?

She had come on this tour expecting such a demonstration, though she had not consciously realized it was so. What had started her imagination working? A gust of wind when she first crossed through the front gate weeks ago. Today's troubles in the field had put her on edge. She could explain everything. If she could not yet sigh with relief, it was only because the memory of her panic was still too fresh.

Hand at her throat, she forced her attention to the courtyard, which was breathtakingly commonplace as such courtyards went. Weeds had poked their way through the stone foundation, and she counted three lizards scurrying about as she walked around. She had never observed such beautiful creatures in all her life.

In the center was a fountain that resembled the one in the piazza in front of the Belmare inn, from its blue tile to the leaping dolphin to the dryness that must have existed for years. The same artisan must have fashioned them both. She could not escape one sobering thought: Here in this courtyard, around this fountain, Pietro had held his drunken parties. After their first night together, he had never complained when she said a headache kept her away.

More interesting even than the fountain were the

frescoes painted on all four walls, a series of pictures that seemed to illustrate scenes from Italy's past, though they were so covered with grime from exposure to the elements she could not be sure. Such paintings were not unusual in this part of the world, but these were special because they were hers. Someday, if she had the means, she vowed to see that they were restored.

Would Roberto help here as he was helping in the fields? Probably not. Early in their association he had refused an invitation to come to the villa for an evening meal. He had said he did not belong. The closest he had ever come was this morning, when he brought her to the back steps of the terrace.

A more important question occurred: Why was she thinking of him now? And who was he, really, this man who called himself a peasant but who carried himself like a duke? Maria had questioned his name, and now so did she. More important, he had a life entirely separate from hers. He was here for purely economic reasons and, he had hinted, the return to a life he had known as a boy. A passionate kiss with his aristocratic confederate would be an added bonus.

Even the conte had suggested she could take a lover if she chose, as long as she was discreet, as long as she allowed the man of her choice, peasant

or otherwise, to teach her how she should behave
in bed.

Anything sexual that passed between her and
Roberto would be nothing but a temporary search
for pleasure, certainly for him. If she couldn't look
at their encounters in quite such a way, she would
have a problem, one for which she would get no
sympathy; not from him, not from herself.

There was no way on earth she could ever harm
him. But there were a thousand ways he could
harm her. Imagined spirits were as nothing when
compared to him. She needed to protect herself.
And now she knew what she had to do.

After venturing one quick look inside the chamber, making sure the ghosts had gone and her courage was making a return, she entered the main
entryway of the villa by way of a door into the
tower and hurried up the stairs. Instead of passing
the middle level, she stopped in the hallway and
stared at the door leading to the bedchamber that
had belonged to her husband. It was here she had
first learned how cruel a man could be.

She needed a reminder. Perhaps Roberto Vela
would never behave in such a way—she blushed
to think the occasion for him to do so might ever
arise—but perhaps he might. It was a possibility
she could not risk.

What she contemplated would be difficult, more
so after her experience of the past half hour. But

she had put it off too long. Hiding from worry never solved anything. She should have learned that long ago.

It was time she laid all her ghosts to rest. Wiping her palms on her skirt, she turned the ornate knob and opened what she would always regard as Pietro's door. Stiffening her back, she went inside.

Chapter Eleven

Shutting the door behind her, Kate leaned back and closed her eyes, letting the scents assail her first. Other than wine and tobacco smoke, the only odor she had ever associated with Pietro was the sour scent of frustration and failure.

She could find no trace of him now, not even the wine, which even in those early days he had consumed in copious amounts. Certainly there were no traces of perfume or powder, as there had been in the eastern wing. She had not expected otherwise. Out of a twisted sense of propriety, Pietro had never brought other women to this room, his late mother's chamber lying across the hall and his father's down the way, directly under the airy room that became Kate's.

Her husband held no such compunction about

vino. At first he made excuses for his drunkenness, claiming the illness at sea had left him dehydrated, but he didn't keep up that excuse for long. He simply drank. Rarely had she come to his bed when he was sober. She used to wonder how he would behave in such a condition. And then she did not care.

On their delayed wedding night the room had been in darkness, as it was now so many years later, on this day the draperies drawn against the summer sun. Somehow creditors had overlooked the furnishings of this room. Especially the high, wide bed, visible in silhouette, as it had been all those years ago.

Instead of a black mourning gown, on that night she had worn white, a thin cotton nightgown she had purchased for its high neck and long sleeves and for its opacity. She should not have bothered. He tore it off her almost immediately.

Vieni qui, moglia.

"Come here, wife."

She could hear his slurred words drifting from the direction of the bed as if he spoke them on this day, in the wheedling way he had used with her that first night, for a short while.

The words drew her into the past.

"Gattina," he had whispered. "Kitten, I will feel your claws." He chuckled. "And you will feel my whip."

She'd thought he was teasing, using a euphemism to describe what he carried between his legs. Eventually she had discovered he was not a man for metaphor. He said what he meant, and he did whatever he chose.

"Of course, Pietro," she had answered in her halting Italian.

She had walked toward him, grateful for the dark. This was her duty, she told herself. He was her husband. Some things must pass between them, and then she could retire to her room on the upper floor.

The lamp beside the bed suddenly flared, killing the welcome darkness as he raised the wick, illuminating the bed, the carpet, his naked, supine body. He lay atop the covers, and she knew for certain what she had suspected from the moment they became betrothed: He would not be a subtle lover, bringing her slowly to an understanding of the duties she owed him as his wife.

He would not be concerned with her pleasure, any more than he would her sensibilities.

She stared at the carpet, trying to forget the quick glimpse she had got of him, the hairy arms and legs, the pale paunch that was his middle, the stubby fingers adorned with rings, stroking the appendage between his legs. Not yet forty, he was already losing the hair on his head, but it grew profusely everywhere else.

The stroking quickened, as though he willed her to watch. No, he would not be subtle.

"Vieni," he ordered more sharply. "I would look upon my contessa."

A cold dread robbed her of breath. She must respond with meekness and ready submission, let him take his pleasure, then leave when he was done. Instinct told her this was the only way to survive.

She eased more fully into the light.

He cursed. "What is that damnable thing you are wearing?"

"A nightgown—"

"Simpleton. I know what it is."

She had never been talked to in such a way. Most often, she had been ignored. Her temper flared, and for a moment she forgot her plan of submission.

"Pietro, I am your wife. You should treat me with respect."

"Respect? Come here and I will show you respect."

Still bold with indignation, she dared a small rebellion and took a step backward. With a roar, he came out of the bed. She would not have thought he could move so fast. His rings scraped the underside of her chin as he gripped the gown at the neck and tore downward. He was stronger than his paunchiness made him appear. The sound of the fabric ripping was as frightening as anything she had yet seen or heard. She could not take another step away.

The sound seemed to subdue him as well, for he dropped his hands and looked at the pale, slender body he had exposed . . . the small, high breasts with their pink nipples shriveled as if from cold, the narrow waist and slight flare of hips, the long legs that were, like the rest of her, far too thin.

The darkest, most visible thing about her was the triangle of black hair beneath her stomach and abdomen. It was this that drew his attention.

"At least you've got all your parts," he growled.

It was not the soothing compliment a bride hoped to hear from her husband on their wedding night.

His fat lips twisted. "Or do you?"

He grabbed one of the sleeves that still hung limp around her wrists and jerked her toward him. She stumbled and fell against him. He felt clammy and warm, like a worm disturbed from its resting place beneath a rock. Holding her wrist in a cruel vise, he thrust his free hand between her legs and explored with his fingers.

She struggled to get away, pounding his chest with her fist. He twisted her arm to her back and tugged upward. She winced with pain, but she did not cease her struggles until he wrenched her arm higher and she grew faint. His fingers pinched and probed, violating her most private area, as if she were a pig he was planning to buy. Or a whore.

He chuckled. "A virgin, if I am any judge. You are just as your fool of a father promised."

Dropping her arm, he turned toward the bed, as if nothing had passed between them, as if he had not violated her with his hand. Rubbing her arm, she could not help viewing his backside, as white and round and soft as the front.

"*Vieni.* Come," he said, in what she had quickly learned was his standard command. He was not a man who varied his speech any more than he varied his behavior. "Satisfy me."

He waved toward a painting that hung over the bed. "Do not shame me before the Conte. Do not shame yourself."

She looked at the painting, a portrait of her late father-in-law, Conte Renaldo Donati. The cruel twist of his mouth made her shudder and kept her from giving the painting more than a quick glance. She had never looked at it again.

Pietro offered all the cruelty she could stand. She thought about running to the door and down the stairs and into the night, taking her chances with whatever dangers awaited in the dark. But he would send his servants looking for her. Loyal to the Donati family, they would drag her back, all the way to this room, and there was little knowing what cruelties he would inflict upon her then.

All her life she had been lectured about the importance of appearances. What would her father advise her now?

Submit. You are his wife.

Shivering, Kate felt lost, lonely, abandoned to a fate she could not escape. She would try submission again, out of a lifetime habit of obedience.

She closed her eyes, but no prayers came. Somehow she must get through the next minutes or hours or however long it took for him to find this satisfaction she was to provide. She must not arouse him to anger again.

He threw the covers to the foot of the bed. The mattress groaned as he lay down. "And take off that ridiculous shroud you call a nightgown. You look pathetic."

She eased her arms from the sleeves, and the ruined gown fell to the floor. Removing her slippers, she circled the bed.

"What are you doing?" he snapped.

"I'm going to lie down beside you."

He growled his impatience. Grabbing a bottle of wine from the bedside table, he took a long drink, his throat working hard, drawing the last drops between his pink, wet lips before he tossed the bottle onto the floor beside him. She thought he paid her no mind, but she was wrong. She had no sooner put her head on the pillow than he was on top of her, hands gripping her wrists and pinning them on the pillow over her head.

The first time happened fast, knees wedging between her legs, separating them with his body, his paunch rubbing against her belly as he thrust inside her; a lucky aim, she later learned. He was never so quick again. She cried out from the pain, but it seemed only to encourage him as he pounded more fiercely against her savaged flesh. With an explosive grunt he fell on top of her and lay still.

An eternity of seconds passed before he began to snore. She tried to slip out from beneath him, but he snorted and buried her deeper into the soft mattress as he breathed sourly into her face. She could feel his flaccid appendage between her legs, and also the stickiness, the semen and blood that had trailed down the insides of her thighs.

She had never felt filthier in her life.

There was no escape. Her only recourse was to hold still and let him sleep, praying he would slip deeper into his drunken stupor and allow her to get away.

It was not a night for getting what she wanted. When she could stand the weight and smell of him no longer, she pulled free, jerking her wrists from his limp hands, still extended over her head. She almost made it out of the bed. With a roar, he grabbed her around the waist and dragged her back against him. He wound his fingers in her hair and jerked hard. Tears came to her eyes and she lashed out at him with her fists, the blows landing weakly against his chest. Desperate, she rammed one knee between his legs and caught him where he was most vulnerable.

He roared in pain and fell to his side away from her, clutching at his genitals. She sprang to her feet and made a dash around the bed.

"Cagna!" he roared. Bitch!

He came after her, catching her at the door and throwing her to the floor, rubbing at himself and, incredibly, grinning.

"The pain was momentary. You did not catch me full on, *moglia*. It was a mistake."

He turned the key in the lock and threw it across the room. She heard it land sharply against the marble hearth, close to where the logs burned into ash. Instead of going for her, he moved to the massive wardrobe crammed with his many clothes, threw open the door, then turned to her with a triumphant light in his eyes.

His hand gripped tightly the handle of a long and snaking leather whip. He snapped it in the air. The crack was deafening.

"The first time is easy," he hissed. "Already you have made the second easy as well. I like a woman who begs for punishment, but I did not think you would so oblige me as you have. Pain can be an aphrodisiac. For us both."

165

She saw in an instant that even if her quickly abandoned submission had been longer-lived, it would have done her little good. On hands and knees, moving sideways, she edged from him toward the bed. More than five years later she could still feel the raw terror that gripped her, the need to lash out at him before he could lash out at her. Desperately her hands felt about the carpet. Her fingers found the empty wine bottle. She could not think, could not plan. The whip was raised. Gripping the bottle by the neck, she launched herself off the floor and like a wild woman ran at him, crashing the hard, solid end of the glass against his face, without aim, knowing only the satisfactory thud as it landed against his flesh.

He cried out, then whimpered and like a wounded animal backed away, staring at her in incomprehension, the whip dropping from his hand as he reached for the corner of his lip where the bottle had struck. A thin line of blood ran from the cut and onto his fingers. He stared at the blood.

And then he settled his small, hard eyes on her. She could do nothing but return the stare, the two of them injured, naked, a husband and wife on what was supposed to be their first night together, the night that would bind them in wedlock for eternity.

On that night they became enemies.

"I will kill you," he said.

"No," she answered, though she did not know how she would keep him from it.

Something flickered across his face—fear, indecision, confusion, she did not know which—and then she remembered he was still drunk. It made her stronger than he.

And she discovered something else. He was a coward, even as he sneered at her, even as he spoke.

"You will never strike me again," he said, "or I will have you punished." The words came out weak, though she doubted he realized it.

"You will never raise the whip to me."

"You are my wife." As if that gave him power to do what he wished. "I have made you so tonight."

And so he had. Despite his cowardice, the victory had been his. Somehow he had marked her, in a way that killed all passions within her. She had known that no man would ever want her again. And she would want no man.

For more than five years she had been right. Until Roberto Vela came into her life.

On that long-ago night she had gathered her torn gown and her slippers, holding them against her in a foolish attempt at modesty, had scrambled around on the hearth until she found the key, then let herself out of the hellish chamber. She sensed people watching, servants, for there were no visitors in the villa. They scurried away like insects so that they would not view her shame.

In her room she had found the same water in which she had bathed before she presented herself to the conte. She bathed again, scrubbing ruthlessly until her skin turned as raw as her pride. Her movements slow and methodical, she put on one of the simple gowns she had brought with her from Boston and lay down, ready to leave if she should have to, though she had no place to go. Closing her eyes, she wondered if sleep would come.

The next thing she knew she was opening her eyes to the sun streaming in through an open window. The air was chill. She had eased her aching body from the bed, smoothed her wrinkled gown, combed her hair and gone down to find out what kind of life she would lead.

Pietro had not arisen and sent word he would remain in his room for the day. Only his manservant was allowed to see him. What the servant reported to the others, she never heard. She ate breakfast alone in the dining room, sitting at the foot of a table that could hold two dozen more diners, the pair of massive candelabra ablaze with light until she asked that the tapers be extinguished. The servants tiptoed around her, bringing more and more food, although she took only a few bites. Though she could have been wrong, she thought they looked at her with new respect.

She could have told them that she viewed herself with shame.

Alfiero remained closest to her, directing the others, and she somehow understood that he, and through him the others, were trying to make up for what she had endured.

Two weeks later she received word that her father's ship had gone down in an Atlantic storm off the coast of Liverpool. He had never reached Boston, had never been able to boast to the wealthy of that city how his daughter, at twenty-two close to a spinster in her own land, had conquered Europe and become a contessa.

Neither she nor the conte ever mentioned that first night again, though for the rest of his life he bore the small scar she had inflicted at the corner of his mouth. He did not send for her until a week had passed, and when he did, she came to him, wearing a gown similar to the first, slipping out of it when she came into the room, letting him take his pleasure.

He called her names, some she recognized, some she did not, but she knew that none were flattering. On their first night as husband and wife, she had gone from kitten to bitch, a permanent transition. It was a small price to pay for what she had gained. He was never gentle with her, but he never hurt her on purpose again, though she knew that all the time she was with him, every time, he trembled with an urge for cruelty.

Sometimes the trembling rendered him impotent. Those were the times she feared him most, for they lasted the longest. If he was drunk, he wept and clasped her against his sweaty body, so tightly she could scarcely breathe; if, on more rare occasions, he was sober, he used harsh words, terrible words, that bit into her like the whip.

As for herself, she played her part well, a meek and dutiful wife who did not object when her husband sought his pleasures elsewhere, when he squandered his money and then hers. To his friends, to the other aristocrats, she was an American and therefore ignorant and simple, unworthy of consideration. She did not disabuse them of their belief.

As the years passed and he sank further into depravity, the conte sent for her less and less often. Those years ate at her conscience, years in which he ranted against the memory of a harsh father and moaned over the loss of a mother who had deserted him too soon. He saw himself as a victim. And so he was.

Perhaps if she had worked harder to make theirs a real marriage, things might have turned out differently. She tried to talk to him once, when they were staying in the Donati apartments in Milan, away from the sensual temptations of Venice. She wanted to see if they could make peace, but he told her that as long as he had her money, he had no use for her.

And here she was, returned after all these years to the room where their strange marriage had truly begun. The mustiness, the dark, disturbed her. She threw open the draperies and tried to open the window, but it was wedged shut with the dirt and grime of the years.

In the light filtering through the smudged glass, she spied beside the wardrobe the trunk she had brought with her from Boston. In it she found a half-dozen dresses, some from Boston, two that had been purchased for her in Venice. Choosing one from each of her two countries, she set them on the bed and opened the wardrobe. It was empty. When they had left the villa after that one unfortunate stay, he had taken with him all his personal belongings.

A long, narrow box on the top shelf caught her eye. She took it down and opened it to find her husband's pistol and a small packet of ammunition. He had bragged to her that the Conte had given it to him when he was twelve, on the eve of his becoming a man.

But the bragging had not been filled with true pride. The pistol was small, not the heavy, long-barreled weapon that should have celebrated his approaching status. Somehow the little weapon had been left behind.

She glanced toward the wall over the bed, expecting to see the painting of Conte Renaldo Donati. The wall was bare. She was surprised. Surely the creditors had not taken it. Even Pietro had told her the painting was a poor one, worth little, kept by him only because of sentiment. Kate suspected another truth. He kept the portrait not out of respect but out of fear, thinking that if he removed it, the late Conte would come for him out of his grave.

Wrapping the dresses around the box, she took her collection with her to the hallway, closing the door firmly behind her, moving rapidly up the stairs.

In the privacy of her room she shook out the Boston dress, a simple yellow gown, and put it on, brushed her hair, letting it fall long and loose against her shoulders, then dared to look into the mirror. A pair of startlingly blue eyes stared back. Like her arms and hands, her face had lost its pallor, her complexion having taken on an almost golden glow, bringing out the color of her eyes, while her hair had been bleached to a shimmery, buttery shade from exposure to the sun.

She scarcely recognized herself. Roberto had called her eyes beautiful. Maybe he had not been completely wrong.

Too, she filled out the dress differently. It was looser in the waist, more fitted in the hips and bosom. Why hard labor should make her breasts fuller, she had no idea, but it must, for the evidence was unmistakable in her reflection. She was sturdier, hardier, but she was also more voluptuous. At least she felt so. She felt sensuous.

Suddenly she realized she was ravenous, a surprising reaction to what she had just gone through. Hurrying down the inside stairs, she made her way to the kitchen. Maria was there alone. Turning from the stove, she stared at Kate in surprise and then, in an instant, with a knowing nod.

Kate did not ask what she was thinking. She did not want to know.

"Neither you nor Alfiero should bother with a tray this evening. I'll take my meal in the dining room. If your gift can tell you where another bottle of Donati wine is hidden, I would be most grateful."

She had reason to celebrate. Had she not faced the ghosts of the Villa Falcone and emerged shaken but unhurt? More important, in entering Pietro's room she had faced a demon from her past and had come out stronger. But was she strong enough?

For years she had thought her body defiled, that it bore a visible shame for how it had been used. She no longer felt that way. The conte had hurt her body, true, but he had not touched her heart.

The real hurt had come later. Until she'd heard the details of the curse, she had thought that hurt was done. As in so many other areas of her life, she had been wrong. How foolish it had been to think in her sensible Yankee way that the curse could not touch her. But it did, in ways she could never reveal.

That did not mean she could welcome the touch of a man. She only hoped that her determination to stay out of Roberto's arms had been strengthened to the same degree as her spirit. The test would come tomorrow when she saw him again.

Her thoughts were troubled throughout dinner, and even the wine did little to calm her. She seemed to feel Roberto in the room, surrounding her, occupying the air she breathed, the shadows cast by the candlelight, his spirit brushing against her as she lifted her trembling glass, as if he belonged there far more than she, he the Donati and she the interloper.

Spirit was too weak a word for his unseen presence. She felt his eyes watching, waiting for her to do something, but she did not know what that something could be.

Her sense of him became unbearable and she ran from the room. She was halfway up the inside stairs when she heard her name.

"Contessa Donati."

She looked down to see Maria staring up at her from the entryway. Swaying, she gripped the banister.

"Beware of Roberto Vela."

Kate's heart pounded.

"What are you talking about?" Her voice was faint.

"He is not for you."

She tried to laugh at the woman's absurdity, but the sound caught in her throat.

"In what way?"

"In the way a woman is for a man, and a man is for a woman."

She felt Roberto's lips brush against hers. Quickly she covered her mouth with her fingers, to still a cry and wipe away remembered warmth. His ghost seemed beside her on the stairs, as much as in the dining room. She needed all her strength to remain standing.

"Earlier you said that he would come to harm at the hands of a woman. You even hinted that I might be that woman."

"When we spoke, you inquired about danger to him. You did not ask about yourself."

She spoke with such solemnity, such conviction, that Kate was tempted to believe her. In this centuries-old villa, the scene of countless births and deaths, of love and betrayal, anything seemed possible.

"Who are you, Maria? What do you know?"

"I have told you what I can. Heed what I say. If you do not, you put yourself in peril."

"But—"

The servant was gone before she could finish her question, leaving the warning to hover in the air and to chill her heart.

Kate closed her eyes. This was impossible. She could not believe in seers, any more than in the existence of spirits. Whoever Maria was, whatever her background, she was bent on mischief, using her new mistress's fears to agitate an already troubled household. If Kate was to take seriously the admonition she had just heard, she might as well admit to the power of the falcon's curse.

Dismissing the woman was tempting, but that would return the burden of running the household to the bent back of Alfiero. And with the villagers feeling as they did, there would be no one to replace her.

The lone solution, as least for the present, was to ignore Maria's superstitious belief in her own power. After all, what had she actually said? That Roberto was not for her? That he was a danger? As if she did not already know that.

Lifting her skirt, she quickly climbed the stairs and went up to the sanctuary of her room.

*   *   *

Later, after going over the expense accounts she was keeping in case her agent Stefano Braggio asked if she kept such books, Kate stood at the window of her bedchamber and looked out on the sun setting over the sea. From this vantage, she could see no more than a patch of water, but it was enough to enjoy the orange light dancing on the waves.

Here she felt no one's presence other than her own. Gradually she began to return to the woman who had first arrived at the Villa Falcone, the one who needed more than anything else the fortitude that came with independence, a fortitude that would see her through these difficult times. She needed Roberto Vela; but then, he needed her, too, else he would be cast off the land he claimed to want as his new home.

They would use each other in ways that were mutually beneficial, but no emotion, no passion could be involved.

Directly below her, the terrace was in shadows. A movement caught her eye. At first she thought it was one of the statues on the balustrade, but that was absurd. Statues did not move. Even the few sips of wine at dinner must have been too much.

Besides, the moving figure was cloaked too heavily for such a warm night. To Kate's surprise, an arm was lifted, gesturing for her to come down.

She sighed heavily. What sort of charade was

being played out for her now? Was the entire world trying to frighten her?

The wine, curiosity, the strange day—everything combined to send her out of the room and down to the terrace, a lamp in one hand, the conte's small loaded pistol hidden in the pocket of her gown.

She would speak to whoever beckoned, whether man or woman she could not be sure. Reaching the last of the outside stairs, she raised the lamp in time to see the figure hurrying across the ground that had once been the rose garden, not far from the back of the terrace.

Patting the gun, not thinking further, Kate hurried after.

Chapter Twelve

The figure moved swiftly on a winding trail through the gathering dark, barely visible in the mist that had, without warning, rolled inland from the sea and across the fields.

"Stop," she shouted, to no effect.

She glanced over her shoulder, wondering if anyone was watching from an open window. Perhaps Maria knew what was happening. For a change Kate wished that she did.

It was the last thought she gave to the sanctuary of the villa. The chase pumped her blood and took her breath, prickly weeds tore at her gown, but on she ran through the dusk, as if a chain bound her to the runner, through the back gate and beyond.

As she ran, a strange sense of freedom began to burn through her, strengthening with each step, breaking a barrier she had not known existed. Her spirit no longer ruled by caution, she became the pursuer, the beckoning figure the pursued, the only chain binding them her determination to see the chase through to the end.

The lamp in her hand grew cumbersome, but she held it tight, not so lost to rationality that she would plunge herself into the dark. The pocketed gun bounced against her thigh.

The figure darted, twisted, then turned toward the thick shrubbery and the cluster of boulders that marked the cliff-side end of Donati property.

Work had made Kate tough; she put that toughness to use as she darted across the uneven land. Still, she felt herself losing ground, the distance between herself and the swirling cape increasing. Suddenly she lost sight of it. One moment the cape was there close to the shrubbery, and then it was gone. She slowed her step, came to a halt and listened. Wind whistled through the leaves. Even the mist took on a keening sound as it brushed coldly against her cheek.

And, too, she heard the sea as it threw itself against the base of the cliff twenty yards to the west and another twenty yards straight down.

Beads of moisture caught in her tangled hair and along the surface of her too-thin gown. Chilled, she rubbed her arm, conceding the wisdom of the cape as protection against the damp night air.

She lifted the lantern high but saw only shadows.

"This way," a voice whispered. It came from behind the row of brush. Kate jumped at its proximity. Man or woman, she still could not tell.

"Who are you?" she called out.

"A friend."

The speaker sounded close enough to touch. It must be a trick of the night. Kate had never felt so alone.

She drew out the pistol. "I'm armed," she said.

"I mean you no harm. Come this way." And when she did not move, "There is something you must know."

The words, if not the voice, sounded very much like something Maria might say.

A shiver ran down Kate's spine. Holding the lantern aloft in one hand, the gun gripped in the other, she followed the summons of the whisper, pushing her way carefully through the dense growth. Her ankle turned on a pebble and she almost fell. Heart pounding, she straightened and moved on more slowly, rocking the light from side to side to spread its beams into the dark.

A step, then another. One more and she felt her feet give way to emptiness, pulling her down into a narrow fissure, as if the earth opened up just wide enough to swallow her. She had no chance to think, to reason, to protect herself. The earth became a carnivore, its teeth sharp as jagged rocks as she fell deeper, deeper into its maw, light and gun forgotten, the teeth slashing at her, cutting, bruising, the darkness complete as the jaws closed over her.

Once or twice her shoes caught on a projection that slowed her descent. She thought she would fall forever, straight into hell. But something caught at her, someone, hands grabbing, arms enfolding, someone dark, unyielding, omnipotent, the devil himself.

She fought against the restricting arms, lashed out with fists and nails at the relentless hold. This devil was no ghost. His grip was far too fierce, too real. So was his growled command for her to stop fighting him.

Terrified, trapped, she slipped into the welcome void of unconsciousness.

In the distance, she heard a voice calling her name.

"Caterina." And then, "Kate. Can you hear me?"

Her eyes fluttered, letting in a slash of light. She closed them tight against the pain.

She heard a weak moan and realized the pitiful sound came from her own throat. After squeezing her eyes closed for a moment, she forced them open. The light did not hurt so much as it had before. She tried to focus, and looked into the dark eyes of Roberto Vela. She was lying prone in his arms, cradled against his chest. The sound of the sea was close, loud enough for her to touch the water if she chose.

The realization of all this came in an instant. Nothing made sense, not his presence or even the way he spoke. She knew him and yet she didn't. Worst of all, she could not remember what had put her in his arms.

He brushed damp strands of hair from her face. "Say my name," he ordered. "Tell me who I am."

"Robert."

She could scarcely get the name out, and when she did it sounded wrong. His hold was tight, both supporting and imprisoning her, his visage harsh, his eyes burning with a primal fire. She had not descended into hell; she had plummeted into his lair and there was no escape.

She struggled to clear her thoughts.

"Where am I? What's going on?"

"You are where you do not belong. What the hell are you doing here?"

She heard anguish in his voice, as well as anger. Frightened, she put her hand against his chest and felt bare flesh in the opening of his unbuttoned shirt. For just a moment his heart pounded against her fingertips.

She jerked back as if burned and tried to look around her. She lay on a thick black cape atop what appeared to be a cushioning bed of moss, its fecund smell rivaling the salty potency of the sea. A gray rock wall glistening with moisture rose at Roberto's back. Flickering light from a lantern danced along the solid, dank surface, painting shadows in the ragged crevices, sparing enough illumination to play on the hard lines of his face, the tightly drawn mouth, the piercing stare beneath a line of fierce black brows.

Her heart caught. He did not look so handsome as he had in sunlight. In the dimness of his lair, he looked nothing less than dangerous.

His hand touched her face, her hair, probed her throat and around to the back of her neck, feeling its way across her shoulders, the same hand she had seen rip thick roots of olive trees from the subterranean soil, savaging vines that had grown on the hillside for countless years.

On her the hand moved with equal skill, but there was no tearing of the flesh or bruising. He soothed wherever he touched at first; then came a prickling of the skin and a deeper surge of tremors she could not control. Dark emotions churned with a burgeoning insistence both new to her and as natural as each indrawn breath of air.

He was touching her as she had imagined he might, measuring her with his fingers, for what purpose she did not know or care.

Surely he could see her reaction, surely he could

see what he did to her. Embarrassed, far too belatedly, she tried to pull away.

"What are you doing?" she asked, too weakly.

"Checking for any injuries. Hold still. I'm not
done."

Resting her head on the cape, bunched to pillow
her weight, he kneeled beside her and put both
hands to work, moving from her shoulders, down
her arms, bending first one and then the other,
working her fingers until he seemed satisfied and
moved on to her torso, the slippery fabric of her
Boston gown whispering encouragement under the
power of his probing. He stroked down her sides,
passing close to her breasts, to her waist, then past
her hips, lifting each leg and bending it as he had
her arms.

With each touch, each stroke, her breathing
grew more shallow, the tremors coming fast one
on the other, in rhythm with the lapping of the
unseen water, their tempo equal to the beating of
her heart.

In self-defense she cried out, "Robert."

He stood and helped her to her feet, slowly removing his support, letting her stand on her own.

"You fell a long way," he said. "I barely caught
you before you landed."

"I was frightened," she whispered, for a moment
drawn in her mind from him back to her nightmare
fall. "The ground opened up. And now . . ."

She could not go on. A frantic urge drove her to look around herself. The hard, wet walls rose on both sides of them, disappearing into a dark overhead arch. At one end of the enclosure she saw nothing but darkness, at the other the dim outline of the surging sea, its landlocked edge lapping close by at the rock floor beneath her feet. This must be the grotto someone had told her about, though she could not remember who that someone was. Somewhere in the background water dripped steadily, the ping growing louder as she brought her gaze full circle, back to a pair of dark, watchful eyes.

Heat flared in their depths. Every nerve in her body became a receptor of that heat, each pulse of her blood a burn, their isolation a relentless spark. With only his eyes on her, she felt sinful, dirty, without shame, the most humiliating part of all the rush of pleasure the mixture gave her. She was alone with him, where no one else could see. Whatever they did, no one else need ever know.

But caution was not completely rendered into ash, nor was rational thought. She would know what they did, and she would never forget. She must get away from him, now, before it was too late. When she started around him, he gripped her arm.

"Where are you going?" he asked.

She could not meet his eye. "Out. If I can find the way."

"You are too late."

"For what?"

"Escape."

The single word, and the truth of it, drew her gaze to his face. His raw hunger made her sway, and her heart pounded in her throat. He eased his hand from her arm and brushed his thumb across her lips, a tenuous connection as binding as iron chains. A dark yearning pulsed within her. She ought to turn her head but hadn't the power to do so. Yet she felt no weakness. For the first time in her life she knew the domination of desire.

His thumb found her teeth. She bit him, and the heat blazed hotter in his eyes. Sucking at his thumb, she plunged into a sensual insanity. When he caressed her cheek, she knew what she must do.

Whatever soreness she experienced from the fall would come tomorrow. At the moment, with her shadowy granite world throbbing around her and the feel of his hands still hot on her flesh, tomorrow seemed an eternity away.

And the warning that he would be a danger to her was as unimportant as her vow to stay out of his arms. Something was different about him, something different about her, but she was too far gone to guess at what that difference was.

Images flashed through her mind . . . weeks of watching him work shirtless in the sun, trickles of sweat running down his face, his chest, his spine . . . the sideways looks he cast her when he thought she wasn't looking . . . the coldness of her wedding-night memories . . . the heat of his hands searching her body for injury.

Oh, yes, she thought with a strange kind of joy, let the devil himself take the warnings of danger, and take, too, her own vows for a solitary life. She had fallen in more ways than one, but she felt no regret.

She let her gaze trail down him, to his unfastened shirt, his tight trousers, his long legs with their powerful thighs. She had to force her eyes back to his face.

"If I am frightened, only you can make it go away," she said; then again, in a fervent whisper, "Make the fear go away."

She wrapped her hands in the fullness of his shirt and held on tight as he touched her lips with his tongue.

"There is no turning back," he whispered against her opening mouth.

In answer, she took his hand and pressed it against her swelling breast. He rubbed his palm against the hardened tip. She gasped. Five years of dutiful submission in the marriage bed had not prepared her for the wildness coursing through her from that simple motion. Passion, the driving need for more of that same wildness, became her everything.

His tongue danced against her teeth, then slipped deeper inside her. Thrusting her hands into his thick black hair, she held his head close. A thousand sensations stunned her, from the taste and feel of his rough tongue to the gentle massage of her breast, to pulsing sensations that skittered through her, settling low in her abdomen. The muscles of her thighs and buttocks tensed, and she held herself tight against him, instinct driving her. She had no previous desires to equal the smallest portion of what she was feeling now.

Tremors shot from her to him and back again. Urgency growled in his throat. She did to him what he was doing to her, primal desire shared with equal fervor. She felt powerful and yielding at the same time, offering herself to him and demanding all that he could bring to her.

He broke the kiss and, with his hands on her shoulders, eased her to her knees on the cape, his lips pressed against her eyes, her cheeks, her throat, his tongue licking aside the mist-matted hair to free her ear for exploration. He gave her a new sensation, as intimate as the exploration of her mouth.

"Kate," he said, "sweet Kate."

Her body throbbed. "I don't feel sweet."

"You feel ready."

"And you? Are you the same?"

He backed away and looked into her eyes. "You cannot imagine how I feel."

"Then show me."

His gaze burned lower, to the stiff peaks that strained against her bodice. She shifted her trembling fingers from his shoulders to the buttons of her gown, working inexorably downward to the fastening at her waist, and downward more, slower now, hesitant. He stilled her hand, and with the fabric pulled aside, stared at her breasts. His lips parted. She had no need to ask if he liked what he saw.

He brushed a gentle finger against the blue veins visible through the paleness of her skin. Here the sun's rays had not toughened her, nor had a man's tender touch taught her what yearning could really be. Until this moment.

Here, in her breasts, she felt virginal, though the rest of her had been violated far too often. Enough of the past, her mind cried. Tonight she would be made love to for the first time. Because she welcomed what was happening. Because of the man she held in her arms.

"I hadn't pictured you this way," he said.

"How did you picture me?"

"Cold, like marble."

"I didn't know you pictured me at all."

"I have seen you in my mind every day since I first learned of your existence."

"The day I first came to Belmare. The day I first saw you."

He lowered his gaze, thick lashes masking his eyes.

"You tremble," he said. "The air is cold. I am remiss."

"No, never that."

He laid her on the cape. Arching her back, she welcomed the caress of his tongue against her skin. With catlike thoroughness he licked the darkening peaks of each breast. She purred with pleasure.

The laving became more insistent and, too, his hands as he cupped her fullness. Impatience blended with desire.

"I want—"

She could not express what she wanted. Such feelings could not be put into words.

"You want me to undress you."

He did so with expert ease and speed, careful, she suspected, lest he find some injury that had not already shown itself.

"I won't break," she said.

"Good. I have use of you."

"And I of you."

Her boldness stunned her, and at the same time made her more bold. She made no attempt to cover herself. It would have been false modesty.

He shed his clothes more quickly, giving her only a quick glimpse of his magnificence before he put his hands upon her and she forgot all else. His was a direct assault. His fingers found their way between her legs while his lips and tongue played havoc with the rest of her. The rock walls of the grotto became a comforting cocoon, his ragged breathing joined with hers against the orchestral background of the pounding sea.

The rhythms of the earth pulsed through her, beginning and ending with the intimate places he explored. She grasped for him, wanting to hold his power beneath her hands. His skin was slick and damp, his body hard, his muscles tensing everywhere she touched.

Awkwardly she reached for his thighs, wanting to know him as intimately as he was discovering her. He guided her hand, and at last she held his erection in her fingers. It was as slick and hard as any place on his body, the essence of desire. His intake of breath was harsh and satisfying. Caressing him, stroking, she felt her awkwardness slip away.

As much as she wanted to concentrate on him, his erotic assault overwhelmed her. The rhythms quickened, she gasped his name and opened herself to him as naturally as if she had done so a thousand times. When he settled his body between her parted thighs, she kissed his eyes, his lips, as her arms wrapped around him.

"The fates have decided for us," he whispered against her open mouth.

"Be quick," she answered with an urgent sigh, "before they change their minds."

"Too late. Far, far too late."

Cupping her face between his strong brown hands, he eased inside her, slowly stretching her long unused body, and in no more than a half-dozen thrusts he taught her ecstasy.

When she opened her eyes, she had no idea how much time had passed. A minute? An hour? A lifetime? However long, her body retained the remnants of primal pleasure. She held herself very still lest they go away. They were too sweet, these last faint tremblings, too welcome, not to last.

Her mind drugged by satisfaction, she could think of nothing beyond the moment. In joining his body with hers, Roberto had brought her to another world that was at once both shared and private, a world not confined to the deep, narrow cave in which the two of them lay. It was a world of the spirit and the heart. She experienced a contentment more profound than any she had known, a world she had only dreamed existed. Let her mind remain fuzzy. She was happier this way.

She lay on her back, he beside her, one arm resting on her middle. A breeze off the water rippled across her, a cold reminder of her naked state and, more chilling, of her vulnerability. With one shiver, her mind cleared and contentment fled. Only a second ago she had been certain the feelings he had brought her would last.

Could such certainty be an illusion? Of course it could. She had also been certain she would never know any man again, and if she did, that man would not be Roberto Vela.

What had she done? And what was she supposed to do now? Her thoughts ricocheted as wildly as her emotions, like a bullet fired into the confines of the grotto.

She dared glance at him. As always, he was watching her, reminding her once again what a perfectly beautiful creature he was. She turned to him, as desperate to cover herself with his body as to feel the comfort of his warmth. In all her life she had known true uninhibited happiness only this once. Perhaps she could capture it again. If it was an illusion, she did not care.

"Kate," he whispered into her hair.

She met with failure. Happiness refused to return. Too clearly she remembered who she was and who he was and how she had vowed nothing like this could ever happen. With remembrance came another lesson bitterly learned, that when passion was spent, the universe it created eventually dissolved, bringing a harsh return to reality.

"I don't want to talk," she said, her words muffled against his chest.

"All right," he said, stroking her spine, stopping a hand span below her waist. "We won't talk."

How sweet it would be never to speak again, to communicate with touches and kisses and sighs. The prospect beckoned as a perfect world.

Impossible, too. Perfection in any form was not to be hers, not for long. Robert had been perfect and he had made her feel the same, but the time had come to deal with what they had done.

At such a moment, in the aftermath of a lovemaking that was both incredible and incomprehensible, reality not only returned, it returned with barbs.

She pushed away from him. It was the most difficult thing she had ever done.

"We can't . . . we shouldn't, not again."

"But we will."

The possibility that he was right existed far too strongly. She could not let him know.

"This was not in our agreement."

The mention of the agreement stopped him for a moment. She sensed a tension in him that had not been present a moment before.

"Let's see, what was it exactly that we said?" he asked. "Or rather, what you demanded. I was not to hurt you. Did I, Contessa? Tell me honestly."

"Don't call me that."

"Then Kate it will be."

"Don't call me anything." It was an order they both knew made no sense. "As to the agreement, perhaps you did not understand my Ita—"

A new horror took hold.

"We're speaking English."

"And have been since you arrived. When you didn't comment on it, I should have realized your state of mind and not touched you. Even when you begged me to." He spoke harshly.

"I did not," she threw back, but of course she had. At the time he had been holding her close and she had not been thinking clearly. Which was exactly what he was saying.

Her head throbbed. She scrambled to her feet. He rose to stand beside her, close enough to block out the walls of the grotto, the rocky floor, the sea itself. Only he existed. She did not know where to look.

Nervously she stroked her hair. "Please, put on your clothes. I have to think."

He bowed and reached for a shirt. It covered him to his thighs, leaving a pair of long, muscled legs to distract her. Too, she thought of the parts hidden beneath the shirttail, parts she had struggled to hold.

In a cowardly gesture she covered her eyes and was rewarded with the scent of him on her hands.

Heaven help her, she wanted to lick each finger, to sense him in every way she could.

"Please be quick," she said, her voice pitifully weak, then listened without looking while he finished dressing, picturing all the places he covered with his clothes.

"I'm done," he said.

She looked at him. And he looked at her.

"Oh," she said with a cry. "I forgot myself."

His dark eyes glittered in the dim light. "I should have reminded you, but I am not so strong."

Bending, he picked up her gown and undergarments, then placed them on their makeshift bed before turning his back to her. She put them on as quickly as fumbling fingers would allow. Was he picturing what she covered the way she had pictured him? She did not know. Women did not think the same as men.

Before speaking, she stole a minute to stare at him, his height, his strength, the easy way he dominated everything around him. All this she had held in her arms; all this had been hers for a while.

Or had possession existed solely on his part? What kind of a devil was he?

She tried to comb her hair with her fingers, then gave up the task as hopeless. Whatever dignity she presented would have to come from within. Somehow she had to find the woman she knew herself to be.

It was either that or run screaming around him and throw herself into the sea.

"All right, Roberto . . . Robert. Tell me who you really are."

"Of course, Contessa," he said in mock servitude. "After you tell me how you found your way to me tonight."

Chapter Thirteen

Kate stared at him in disbelief. "Surely you don't believe I was looking for you."

He glanced at the stained and wrinkled cape at their feet, lying in a tumble atop the dark green moss. She could almost make out the imprint of their bodies in the folds of cloth.

"You gave me cause," he said.

He spoke as if she had come to him seeking sex, risking her life, her pride, her everything for the chance to throw herself into his arms. She would rather he had hit her than hurl such an accusation. Except that he was not a man to hurl anything. Innuendo was more his style.

He left her speechless, more hurt than he could ever know.

He spoke in her stead. "You think I'm a bastard."

"You gave me cause," she said.

He stared at her for a moment. A mask slipped over his face, a mask of indifference, coming far too quickly in the aftermath of what they had shared. She had been feeling many things about the two of them and what they had done—embarrassment, confusion, shame, as well as other, deeper emotions not yet sorted out—but a sense of indifference had not been among them.

She felt a desolation that was far worse than anger or insult, as if after possessing something precious, she had lost it.

"I'm sorry," she said with all her heart. "I'm saying things I don't really mean." She brushed a hand across her eyes. "It's just that—"

What could she tell him? That with this one brief encounter he had changed her life?

"I am the one who should apologize. I thought you wanted honesty."

"Does honesty always hurt?"

"I have found it so. I am being honest with you when I say that what we did brought me more pleasure than I ever could have imagined. And I honestly hope it did the same for you. Whether you wished it or not."

Was he trying to compensate for the harshness

that kept flaring between them? She did not know. But she heard in his voice a slipping of his indifference, and from that derived a satisfaction that was as sweet as it was insane.

She caught herself. What was she thinking? A flush stole up her throat and cheeks. "I don't wish it again."

"Then I must have disappointed you. How different we are. Right now I want more than anything in the world to rip your clothes off you and—"

She shook her head vehemently. "Please, no."

Her lungs constricted and she could barely breathe. He must not discover they shared the same desire. It had exploded in her with no more than his words.

Turning from him, she began to pace along the side wall of the grotto, her arms crossed over her breasts to hide the hardening of their tips.

"Tell me the truth of who you are," she said. "English, Italian, I don't know anymore."

You taunt equally well in either language.

"I have not lied to you, Contessa Donati. Caterina. Kate."

She ignored his mock attempt at servitude. While he did a number of things with expertise, playing humble was not one of them. He did it no better than she played the part of aristocrat.

"Neither have you told me the entire truth," she said.

Touch me when you tell me, hold me. Speak gently. I need your tenderness.

"I was born here. Is that what you wish to know? And I did work Donati land, from as early as I can remember until I was twelve."

He paused, as if remembering details he could not reveal, his focus on the blackness at the back of the cave.

"What about your parents?"

"My mother was dead."

"And your father?"

"He had long been lost to me."

"I don't understand what that means."

Another pause.

"It means he, too, was dead. There seemed little to keep me here, so, as I told you, I went to sea. My wanderings led me to England, where I lived for many years. But always Tuscany beckoned. I returned to Belmare the day before you arrived. It was long enough to hear the talk of the villagers, to know you would not be welcome."

"But you didn't feel that way."

"No. I held no animosity toward you."

Instinct told her he was being truthful, yet still held something back. Perhaps she was wrong. Instinct had failed her before. She had honestly believed, in the brief two weeks between the wedding ceremony and the marital bed, that if she tried hard enough and was a good wife, she could make her marriage bearable.

The problem was, she had not understood what her husband meant by good.

No, men did not think the same as women, anymore than they looked the same. In that moment, she knew above all else that she needed to protect herself, no matter what Roberto told her, no matter what he did. She must put distance between them on every level that she could. Beginning now.

When he wasn't seducing her with his hands, he was doing so with words. She must try to alienate him the same way.

Her attention fell to the cape.

"And you, having known many women from many lands, decided to make up for the coldness of the villagers." Slowly she raised her eyes to his. "While I, being a member of the aristocracy, albeit one by marriage, decided to find out what it would be like to sleep with the help."

He continued to hold himself very still, but she could see the veins tighten in his neck. The sight was a small victory, but it brought her little joy. To her own ears her words were harsh, unreal, belying everything that was in her heart.

"I ask you outright, did I disappoint?" he asked. "I have confessed my pleasure. Did you like what I did to you? Did you enjoy what you did to me?

Show me the honesty you asked of me. Even if it hurts."

Her lips turned dry. Despite her noblest efforts, she could not resist licking them. Roberto Vela was not an easy man to defeat.

"I liked it all. I wouldn't know how to pretend such things." A hollow little laugh. She felt as if she were falling down the fissure in the earth all over again. She avoided his eye. "Why didn't you tell me you spoke English?"

The question was more than idle. It was a shift to safer topics, and he knew it. She remembered too well, and so must he, the times when in his presence she had used her native tongue to mutter her thoughts, her feelings, confident he could not comprehend.

How civilized she was being right now, with such casual talk, when she wanted to scream.

She let out a long, low breath of air that emptied her lungs. "I should have been told."

"You wish to be a part of this land. I respected that wish."

She laughed sharply. "You lied out of respect? All right, you didn't outright lie, but you let me believe something that was not so. It seems to me everything between us has been a sham."

"Do not belittle our work."

She stared at him. Pride slipped through his mask.

"No," she assured him, "I will not do that."

She listened to the drip of water and wondered how she could go on toiling beside him in the fields.

She rubbed at her arms. "I don't like this place. It must be the grotto Stefano Braggio told me about. I had forgotten it existed."

"So why are you here? You have convinced me it was not to lie in my arms."

At the moment, in light of what had taken place over the last hour, lying with him was a far more compelling reason than the truth. But he had a right to know the details, and so she spoke of the beckoning figure, of the chase, of its sudden end.

"I should have turned back, of course. But I couldn't, not right away, not until I was more convinced danger awaited. I was armed. I know how to use a gun. It was one of the few useful things my father taught me." She gave a bitter laugh. "Much good it did me."

"There are stairs leading down here from the top of the cliff," he said, "but a grating is kept over the opening for safety. Did you not see it?"

"It wasn't in place. Otherwise I wouldn't have—"

She looked at him in dawning alarm. "It must have been moved. Whoever was out there purposely led me into danger."

He did not respond. He let the possibility sink in.

"I can't believe this. I mean no one harm."

"You are a Donati. For some that may be enough."

"For whom? Who could hold such hatred for someone he's never met?"

Light flickered across his face. He looked harsh, unmovable. The same tension, the fury she had seen in his eyes on earlier occasions flashed briefly. The look chilled her soul.

She closed her eyes and remembered the first occasion on which she had spoken to him, her first time in the field behind the villa, when in the gathering dusk she had thought him her executioner. What if he was the caped figure of this bizarre night? What if he had drawn her from her room, to the fissure, to his lair? He could have disappeared in the brush, removed the grate and scrambled down to the grotto, awaiting her, catching her at the last second, pretending to be her rescuer.

And then he became her lover, everything part of a plan. The evidence was lying at her feet, in the form of a wadded cape. It lay, too, in the stains between her thighs, the residue of passion that marked his invasion.

It hid most strongly in her heart. No matter how she must protest to the contrary, he had made her his. Her prayer was that the possession was for only a little while.

"Much has been made of my presence here. What of yours?" She was proud of the strength in her voice. He must not know she was close to collapse.

"I come to the grotto sometimes," he said, answering too quickly, without thought, as if he had been waiting for her question. "It is a place of refuge. But it is also a place of danger. You must not visit it again."

"And why is that?" She almost added, *Because of you?*

He took a long time to answer, and when he did he spoke as if the words had been held in his memory, to spill out in the event a stranger wandered into the grotto. A stranger such as she.

"Once, years ago, the Donatis stored their crates of wine in here, letting the vintage age. A storm sent the water raging inside. Two workers drowned. If such a storm happened once, it could happen again."

"You knew these men?"

"I knew them." His voice took on a sharper edge. "There was a woman, too, in another storm. But that was long before the workers."

Kate felt the tension in him. "Did you know her as well?"

"No. We never met."

207

He spoke with finality. The woman was one of his secrets. She did not ask him more. Instead, she brushed at her tired eyes, for a change thinking beyond Roberto and herself.

"The curse goes on, in so many ways, doesn't it?"

"Crops have failed. Oil from the olives has turned rancid. And of course there are the storms."

"The return of which I'm supposed to fear, though in the past weeks we've known nothing but cloudless days and nights."

"Life here is unpredictable. Have you not yet discovered that?"

"And what about the members of the family? Has the curse descended on them, too, in ways other than economic?"

She knew the answer even as she asked the question. Contessas were given one chance at childbirth before turning barren. It was the worst curse of them all, the one that foolishly twisted her heart.

Robert made no allusion to such. "It made them leave."

Not all of them. She could not speak for her husband's predecessors, but his unsatisfied lechery was as much a cause of their departure as any flight of a falcon. It was not, however, an issue she cared to discuss.

"You are tired, Contessa."

Again, he spoke with finality. This time it put an end to the night.

"I did not tell you," he went on, "but there are places on your body that will bear bruises tomorrow. And there are small abrasions, shallow, barely breaking the skin. You should see to them when you return to your room."

Here was another shame. He knew her body better than she.

"You should have told me."

"Forgive me. They did not seem to pain you." He paused. "And I had other things on my mind."

A few of these other things came back to her, and she blushed. She took consolation in the fact that she could still do so.

She swallowed and looked around at the encroaching rock walls. "How do I get out of here? Is the tunnel the only way?" A sense of falling made her shudder. "I don't think I can use it. Not now. Not so soon."

"I have a horse stabled not far away. You can be in your bed within the hour."

She nodded her assent. Picking up the cape, he shook it out and rested it on her shoulders, taking care not to touch her. He left her for a moment, then returned from the back of the grotto with her gun and lamp, its flame long since dead.

"These are yours, I believe. Take them."

Ah, here was the Roberto she knew. But she

could not think of him as Roberto. He spoke English far too well, his accent more like someone who had lived in London all his life. He was Robert, though who Robert really was she still did not know.

He scooped her up in his arms and made straight for the open water, his boots falling on a narrow ridge that led to the entrance of the grotto. Outside, on a wider, rocky beach strewn with massive boulders and smaller rocks, she looked up at the full moon, and at the canopy of stars. No storm tonight. Except inside her. With her arms around his neck, her body jostling against his, she raged inside.

He could easily dash her on these rocks, if destruction was his intent. Perhaps he chose a different method. He would shatter her heart and mind.

He did not put her down until they had reached a wooded area at the edge of the village. Here in a small barnlike shed off a seldom-used trail, he showed her the horse he had promised. The animal whinnied and nuzzled against Robert's chest.

He slung the saddle into place with the same expert ease he gave to every task—every task, including making love. Mounting, he reached down to lift her off the ground and set her across his thighs, her legs dangling to one side. He was solid beneath her, and his breath was hot on her cheek.

Through the layers of clothes and cape, she felt his muscles tense.

"You give pleasure, Kate, in unusual ways."

"You should not say such a thing."

"I made no promises the way you did. Perhaps I am testing you."

If that was so, she was failing to keep her word in ways he could never imagine. Closing her eyes, she pictured him holding the reins in one hand while the other found its way beneath her skirt, between her thighs, working its way through the opening in her undergarment to her flesh. He would find her shamefully wet.

She ought to order him to let her down, but he would more than likely take her to the pile of hay at the back of the shed and finish what she had started in her mind.

Not trusting herself to speak, she held as still as the amble of the horse allowed, staring into the dark as he rode past the edge of the village and up the hill on the narrow, hidden trail, most of it through the wild growth on the side of the slope facing the sea, circling around until he came to the back gate in the villa's protective stone wall. Dismounting, he helped her to the ground and they walked to the back of the terrace.

"The men will return to the fields tomorrow," he said. It was the first time either of them had spoken since leaving the shed. "I will understand if you are not there."

Slipping out of the cape, she thrust it into his hands. "I'll be at work by dawn."

She had not planned any such thing. He drove her to extremes.

Hurrying up the stairs, the gun in her pocket, the dead lantern in her hand, she reached a conclusion that she had to hold to, regardless of what he said or did. She had to find a way to break their agreement. She could pay him for his work, though it would take much of the gold she had hoarded. His departure would be worth it. She could put no price on peace of mind.

No longer could she deny her growing obsession with him. Standing at the foot of the terrace steps, she had wanted to take his hand and lead him to her room. What would have happened there was something she would be thinking about all night.

Her physical passion wasn't the worst of the situation. Her obsession went beyond her body's needs. Disguised in a swirling cape, he most certainly could have been the one to guide her through the night to what could have been her doom. Already she had realized he made too many decisions, assumed too much control of far more than the toiling in the fields. On this night he had done something much worse, something unthinkable only a few weeks ago.

He had found a place in her heart.

Maria had been right: He was a danger to her. But the woman could not have imagined how much.

Chapter Fourteen

When Kate went into the field the next morning, the three men were already at work. With a nod toward the other two, she went straight for Michelangelo. According to Robert, she wasn't supposed to do more than acknowledge the man's presence. Too bad.

Thumbing back her hat, she stood in the worker's path. He could do little else but stop.

"I'm sorry about what happened to you," she said in her best Italian, speaking slowly to make sure he understood. "And I'm sorry I can't pay you more for what you've been through."

He gave her a quizzical look, but she hurried on.

"If there is anything I can do to make up for what happened, if it's in my power I will do it."

He shifted from foot to foot and looked down

214

without a response. Though he was no taller than she, there was massive strength in his shoulders, his arms, his stout legs. She shuddered to think that all that power, which he demonstrated daily in his work, had been felled by one sharp blow to his head.

"And thank you for returning," she said to the more wiry Leonardo, who was equally ill at ease and reluctant to look at her, though he stood only a few feet away.

As she spoke to the men, Robert watched from his vantage point on a higher terraced row. He made no attempt to interfere. He did not have to. His presence provided all the interference she could take.

She put on her gloves with a vicious tug. So much for her social skills and attempts to be a good employer. They were Robert's men and she was a Donati, two facts she could not overcome, though a single word of response would have been welcome.

At the top of a tall tree at Robert's back, a falcon perched, looking for his breakfast, a hapless field mouse or rabbit. She felt a kinship for the rodents. She felt like somebody's prey.

Despite her aching muscles, she spent that day and all of the succeeding week working from dawn until dusk in the fields, hacking limbs, pulling weeds, planting tender shoots very much like those that had been destroyed. She conferred with Robert when necessary, each of them choosing by unspoken agreement to speak Italian. It seemed the right language for the emerging vineyard and olive grove.

Her plan for dealing with him had been simple: Hard work would drive out all thoughts other than the task at hand. Or so she told herself. She was wrong.

Avoiding looking at him as he strode the furrows, reached his muscled arms into the limbs of the trees or cupped his hands around a tender bud proved as difficult as pulling up the most stubborn weed. She had to break their agreement. Tomorrow, she told herself each and every day, more than once. Tomorrow. It became her litany.

In the meantime, she hacked at weeds and stole sideways glances at him. If her two artist workers saw any sign of tension between the contessa and her unlikely partner, they gave no indication.

Every day, too, she waited for more trouble. None came, except, of course, for the unsettling view of the half-naked man who had stoked her desires.

Nighttime was when she was most foolish. Successfully avoiding a confrontation with Maria, she asked Alfiero to begin serving her dinner on the terrace instead of in her room. Bathing and dressing in one of the Boston gowns, the rest of which she had rescued from Pietro's room, she carefully brushed her unbound hair and hurried down to play with her food and sip at the wine and stare into the darkness that blanketed the land.

The terrace was bathed in the pale light from a pair of lamps hung on poles on either side of the lower stairs, making the darkness beyond impenetrable. If someone watched her from that void, she would not have been aware of it. Yet she always felt herself the object of a silent scrutiny, so strong she once called out Robert's name to let him know he should come up the stairs and into the light.

Receiving no response, she felt foolish. After a long day in the fields, her one-time lover was probably safe and secure in his bed, perhaps with a woman who was more accommodating than she. She could not imagine a man with his appetites sleeping alone.

The scrutiny must come from the four statues prancing atop the balustrade. She felt foolish to have thought otherwise. But feeling foolish did not make her rational. When, despite all her reasoning, she continued to sense unseen eyes focused on her, she told Alfiero she would again take her meals in her room.

At the beginning of the second week of the period in her life she now thought of as "After the Grotto," she walked out to work in the face of a strong wind blowing off the sea. The wind brought a welcome coolness and an even more welcome bank of dark clouds that promised rain. It whipped her clothes, lifting her skirt so that she had to grapple to keep it in place, molding the bodice against her breasts, tearing her hair from its anchoring knot at her nape.

No falcon greeted her this morning, but her artists were at work toward the top of the hill. Alone, Robert watched her approach. As with her, the wind tore at him, billowing his shirt sleeves, whipping his black hair in a swirl of air, the wildness of the weather echoed in his deep black eyes. Though she could barely keep herself upright, he stood straight and unmoved, legs apart, arms at his side as she drew near.

As always, he was magnificent. Her heart pounded with such ferocity she thought it might give its all in one final, pulsing frenzy, then suddenly stop altogether. She gripped her hat and gloves in one hand and foolishly tried to brush a tangle of hair from her face.

What would he do if she walked straight toward him and pressed her open mouth against his? Would he take her in his arms and carry her to the wild growth close to the land's end? In a howl of wind, would he lift her skirt and take her on the ground? Her stomach tightened at the picture that suddenly burned into her mind.

The Grotto

She took an unsteady step, and then another. The muscles of her thighs and hips constricted in the way they would if she matched his thrusts, there on the ground, with the thick brush and wind-bent trees thrashing about them.

Suddenly the wind died, one second roaring, the next still as death, plunging her into a quiet as deafening as the roar. She looked toward the sea to the clouds that were already beginning to disperse. Overhead the falcon came from wherever it had sought refuge and coasted with wings spread wide over the tops of the trees. Her heart slowed. But the churning inside her was not so quickly gone. Nor was the image in her mind, the picture of her and Robert in a lovers' embrace.

Ashamed, she stared at the ground. He had read her thoughts. Understanding had been there in his eyes. He had not only understood them, he shared them. He was a man of the earth; when it raged, so did he. And when the raging died, what happened then?

She drew close and dared look at him. The wildness remained for her to see.

"The storm plays with us," she said.

"We play with each other."

"It's not play." *Not for me.*

"You are right. It is not play."

Dropping her hat and gloves, she made a feeble attempt to tame her hair.

"Don't bother," he said. "I like you this way. You look as if you've just come from my bed."

He spoke frankly, and so would she. "If I had, would you be like the wind? Would you swirl around me for a frantic short while and then leave?"

"Whatever I answer, you would not believe me. Let us discover the truth, Contessa. Let us steal away for the day."

How sweetly he seduced, offering a day free of responsibility or conscience.

"Like children," she said.

"No, not like children. Like the man and woman we are."

He chose the wrong words. She did not know the kind of woman she was. Certainly she was given to momentary weakness. More than that she was afraid to find out.

Shoving her hat over as much of the tangled hair as she could and thrusting her hands in her gloves, she made a wide sweep around him.

"The storm could return," he said to her back. "Such things happen."

The storm that had threatened to sweep over the land? Or the other one, the tempest that had raged inside the two of them?

"I'll take my chances," she said, keeping a tenuous hold on her equilibrium. "I'm not so far from shelter."

"I have a bad feeling about today."

That stopped her, and she glanced over her shoulder.

"What about? Do you fear I'll reject you? It's a foolish fear. I already have."

She spoke lightly, teasing him, hoping he would tease her in return. He did not do it very often, but it was not completely beyond him.

There was nothing teasing in his expression. A sense of dread shivered through her, such was the power he had over her.

"I don't know what might happen," he said. "It's been a week since your fall."

She fought for lightness. "So it's time for something else bad to occur? Is the curse on a timetable? If so, you really ought to let me know so I can prepare myself."

She turned from him and in a few unsteady strides was at the olive tree where he usually left her digging tools. He was trying to frighten her, getting back at her for her refusal to spend the day with him. Yes, that was it. He was confirming his control.

With these thoughts humming in her mind, she reached toward the ground and heard an ominous hiss. Instinctively, she jerked back and fell against a solid chest. A strong arm wrapped around her middle and dragged her up and away from the sound at the same instant a snake slithered out of the cavity at the base of the tree. Black flat head, uneven stripe down its back, variegated markings on its side—she got only the quickest glance before Robert vented a terrifying word.

"Viper."

Its poison was the stuff of legend but all too real, and Kate knew genuine fright. Disturbed from its slumber, the snake wound its way toward them, tongue whipping from between its open jaws.

Like a thunderbolt, the falcon dropped from the sky, wings tucked tightly in its vertical stoop, and for one terrifying moment she thought the bird directed its attack at her. At the last moment it veered, toes spread as it landed on the snake. The back talon of each foot gashed into its prey and its hooked bill lashed at the viper's slender body, severing its head in a single blow.

As quickly as it had appeared, the falcon spread its wings and took to the sky, swooping toward its aerie high in the hill overlooking the villa that bore its name, the body of its prey dangling lifeless from its claws.

Kate stared in horrified fascination at the flight of the bird, then dropped her gaze to the detached head of the viper lying close to her feet.

"Its fangs still hold poison," Robert said, tightening his hold on her, pressing her hard against him. "Dead it may be, but it can still kill."

He turned her in his arms and she buried her

face in the folds of his shirt, listening to his heart. She imagined he trembled as much as she.

"You saved my life," she whispered when she could get control of her voice.

"And took a few years off mine."

She heard the pounding of heavy shoes as the two workers ran down the hill.

"Signore Vela," they said, almost in unison.

"I didn't know they could talk," she said, unwilling as yet to move from the security of Robert's arms. Maybe if she stood there long enough, the wind would return and blow away her memory of the past few minutes.

But no. She pushed away. At first he resisted, then eased his hold, and she turned to smile at the men, brushing her wind-tossed hair from her eyes.

"Signore Vela was very brave." She nodded toward the snake's head. "And I have a new respect for our falcon."

At the sight of the head, Leonardo jumped back and Michelangelo leaned close to get a better look.

Needing to prove herself, Kate leaned beside him. "A viper, according to Roberto."

"*Si,* a viper."

"I thought the head would be bigger because of the poison."

"The head is large enough. I have seen a man die from one bite. The death is not easy."

Leonardo came between them, shovel in hand.

223

Relieved, she stepped away and watched as the snake's head was scooped up in a mound of dirt. Without another word, the two workers trudged back up the hill.

"They talk, but they don't say much, do they?"

"Only what is necessary," Roberto said. He was watching her with a new expression, one that bordered on amusement or puzzlement, she could not decide which.

"Other women would have run screaming. You did not."

"I had you."

"That has not always been sufficient reason to quell hysteria."

"You rescue damsels from vipers very often?"

"There are other dangers, Caterina."

His voice was deep, thick. He was moving fast toward reactions far warmer than puzzlement or amusement. So was she. There seemed to be only two things they shared, a great capacity for hard labor and undeniable lust. Maybe one was linked with the other. She did not know, except that the former let her keep her pride.

She glanced toward the east. "The sun is rising fast. We'd best get to work."

"No."

She sighed in exasperation. "I thought we had that settled. You have no reason to worry. There's no danger. . . ." Her voice trailed off for a moment. "Maybe there was, but not now."

"You're giving me gray hairs."

She looked at his mane of black hair whipped by the frenzy of the wind.

"They don't show."

"That depends on where you're looking."

Here was where she needed a quick response, to show he did not intimidate or embarrass her with such remarks. But all she could think of was where those gray hairs might be.

"Look," she said brightly, the best she could manage, "I know you're shaken by what happened. So am I. But I can't run and hide every time I'm faced with a problem. This is my land and I must work it as best I can."

To her own ears she sounded reasonable. One look at Robert's expression told her he did not agree.

"If there is anything on this earth that I know as well as you, it is that the Villa Falcone belongs to you."

Was she supposed to be ashamed of the fact? She had earned the title to this last piece of Donati property in ways he would never know.

"Are you going to return to the villa?" he asked.

"Of course not. There's no reason for me to."

He scooped her into his arms as quickly as Leonardo had scooped up the snake and started across the field.

Several responses occurred to her, when she got over her surprise. She could fight him, she could argue with him or she could hold herself as stiff as possible. After a moment's consideration, she chose the latter, since the first two would do her little good.

He did not break stride until he had passed through the gate, walked through the weed-choked gardens, and reached the bottom of the lower terrace steps. Somewhere outside the stone wall she abandoned stiffness and simply rested in his arms. His response was to hold her close, close enough for her to realize a curious fact: the nearer they got to the villa, the more tense he became, his muscles tightening, his breath shallow, his lips in a flat, taut line. She would have liked to think the tension sprang from his not wanting to let her go, but in her heart she knew the truth lay elsewhere.

"Can you stand?" he asked brusquely when he finally halted.

"Of course," she said in a like manner. "I can work, too. I hesitate to point it out, however, since it gives you gray hairs. Somewhere."

He shook his head in disgust and set her on her feet. A moment of awkwardness passed between them.

"What am I supposed to do now?" she asked. "I never was good at knitting."

"Think of ways to bedevil me. You're adept at that."

She studied him, from his black hair to his dusty brown boots and all the points in between. "You're holding up well enough."

And so he was. The effects of wind and temper only served to make him look better than ever, something she had not thought possible. He looked so good her mouth went dry. She did not know whether she was swaying toward him or he toward her, but they were definitely drawing closer to one another. His breath might be shallow, but hers was nonexistent.

"Oh," she said, making a feeble attempt at lightness. "This morning I forgot the food. I guess with the storm and all, it completely slipped my mind. Please come inside and I'll get the basket for you."

"No. This is as close as I get."

"You've said that before. If you're worried about tracking in dirt, don't be."

"I am not worried about any such thing. I am not worried at all. One day I will enter the Villa Falcone, but it will not be like this."

He seemed to be speaking to himself more than to her. She was reminded of her suspicion that when he was a boy something had happened to him at the villa, something other than hard work in the

227

grove and vineyard, something so bad it had driven him away to the sea. She wanted to soothe him, to touch his face and stroke the cares away. But her comfort would not be welcome.

"Like what?" she asked, pretending ignorance of any consideration other than the moment.

He ignored the question. "Go inside, Contessa. Lock your door. Protect yourself as best you can. Protect your silken body, which grows more luscious every day. You have become a temptress, do you not know this?"

He cupped her face in his strong brown hands, his eyes a fearsome sight, dark and wild and unyielding. But when he slanted his lips across hers, it was with a gentleness that swelled her heart. Then he kissed her eyes and backed away.

"I once promised not to harm you, Caterina Donati, but I do not know if that is possible now."

Chapter Fifteen

Kate stood on the terrace a long while after Robert had disappeared beyond the stone wall, feeling both desolate and enheartened, though the two did not go together. It was no wonder she was pulled in two directions. She had known him in ways only a woman can know a man. Yet she did not know him at all.

She looked beyond the terraced rows of trees and vines to the high far hills with their hidden aerie and the row of tall, slender cypress trees. For the first time in her life she felt a fierce, protective love for something she owned, for her land. The smell of the air coming off the water, the taste of grit in her mouth after a sudden wind swirl, the feel of new life when she handled the tender shoots—she was obsessed with it all. Everything she had lost in life and everything she had gained came together in this remote villa atop a sun-drenched Tuscan hill.

No longer did she hope for success to ensure her own survival. She wanted the land to prosper for its own sake, to yield its wealth to the town, to become what it was meant to be.

She admitted another, more basic truth. There would be no prosperity without Robert Vela. Nor would there be happiness. She loved not only the land; she loved the man who had taught her the pleasures of being one with the soil, and more, the explosive sweetness that came with pleasures of the flesh.

She had not realized such a love existed in the world; she had known that no such feeling could exist for her. Yet here it was, fluttering in her heart, no less real because of its infancy, no less constant because it was not returned.

What sweet nothings did he whisper in her ear? That she should protect herself. That he might bring her harm. They were not the words a woman wanted to hear, but they were the words she must now consider. Did he know what was in her heart? Was she so obvious? The worst harm he could do would be to hold himself separate from her, to keep his secrets, to suffer in solitude his private pain.

Which did not mean he did not have any feelings

for her. He thought her body luscious. It was a laughable description, but she would not argue the issue with him. Let him desire her, if desire was all he could feel. His desire would not be in vain.

She turned to find Maria standing close behind her.

"Oh," she said with a jump, "you startled me."

"You think of him," the woman said.

It didn't take a seer to figure that one out. Maria must have seen him carry her from the fields, had probably heard what he had to say, had witnessed the kiss.

"I know, he is a danger."

"More now than ever before."

"You are wrong. Not an hour ago he saved my life. A viper came close to sinking its fangs into me and he pulled me away. That does not sound like someone who is dangerous."

Maria remained unblinking. "Has the contessa asked herself why there should be a viper in the place she was sure to place her hand? Does the contessa not know it is Roberto Vela himself who stores the tools at the base of that tree?"

Kate's heart jolted. "How did you know where the viper was resting?" She caught herself. "Oh, I forgot. You know things."

She tried to sound scornful, but the words came out weak. She had not asked herself any questions concerning Robert's intent. How could she, why should she, when he had been her salvation?

But Maria's words were like the bite of the viper. They shot poison to her heart. The woman was not totally to blame. Had not she herself once wondered why he was able to cushion her fall into the grotto? And now, today, when the snake was coiled around the tools used only by her, he was there to pull her to safety.

In his view such rescues might be a way to her heart, especially since his own heart was not involved.

What a vile creature she was to consider such things, only moments after admitting her love. Was she so fickle? So easily given to doubt?

She looked toward the hills and knew she could not accept Maria's view of him. No man bent on such evil could have kissed her as gently as he had only minutes before.

But he had done more than kiss her. His words came back to haunt her.

I once promised not to harm you, Caterina Donati, but I do not know if that is possible now.

The words stung more than they had when he had said them. If something bad happened, something unthinkable, would he then say he had tried to warn her?

More questions than answers, they were her real enemy. They destroyed the brief moment in which she had admitted her love. Destroyed the moment, but not the love itself. And that meant she must have faith in him. The snake had been an act of nature at its worst, the fall brought on by the mysterious caped figure whose identity she did not know.

And Maria was a superstitious woman of the country who fancied herself with supernatural powers that Kate did not believe existed in anyone.

She turned to face the woman. "I forgot to take the food basket with me this morning," she said.

Maria nodded, accepting the change in subject, as if they had been discussing nothing more important than where she chose to dine. "I have saved it for you."

"Let it be lunch for you and Alfiero. I won't be needing anything for myself."

"Alfiero prepares to ride into the village. This is his day to buy supplies. Even with the storm coming, he will not change his plan."

Kate suddenly became aware of the returning clouds and the cool breeze on her face, nothing like this morning's gale but still noticeable. How strange she could forget such an important matter like life-giving rain when Robert filled her thoughts.

"I'll go with him."

Her decision was immediate and irrevocable. Getting away from the villa seemed the best thing she could do, even if the townspeople refused to acknowledge her presence. Besides, she had not been there in weeks. Perhaps they had heard about her work and decided she was not such an ogre after all.

And maybe she had been chosen duchess of all Tuscany.

No, she would not ride into the village with any such hope. She would go there because she needed to get away, even from the place she so fiercely loved.

She hurried across the terrace toward the stairs. "Ask Alfiero to wait. I'll change clothes and be with him shortly."

She began unbuttoning her shirt as she took the steps quickly. At least, she thought, there would be no vipers slithering through the streets of Belmare.

Kate had been right not to get her hopes up about the villagers. They had not changed, not in any way she could tell. The ones who bothered to glance at her did so from windows and beside the road without a glimmer of friendship in their eyes. When she climbed down from the donkey cart at the edge of the piazza, the few who had been milling about moved desultorily away.

The only one who did not leave was the child Stella, who was throwing small pebbles into the dry blue-tiled fountain at the base of the leaping dolphin. Her mother was nowhere in sight. Kate dared approach her.

"*Buon giorno,*" she said with a smile. "That looks like fun."

The child looked down shyly.

"Is it difficult to do?"

Stella shook her head.

"Could I try?"

"Mama says you're not supposed to hit the dolphin."

"I'll try not to."

The child's small hand opened onto the rim of the fountain, depositing three small stones on the edge. She backed away, giving Kate adequate room.

"I've never done this before. Could you toss one for me so I'll know how it's done?"

Stella nodded gravely, then placed a pebble into the palm of her right hand.

"Sometimes I stand way back, but you better not since this is your first time."

"That sounds like good advice."

After careful consideration, the child chose a spot close to the target, settled her bare feet in place and pitched the rock. It rose in an arc and fell into the fountain, easily missing the raised dolphin in the center. At the moment she released the rock, a swirl of wind crossed the piazza, but her concentration was not affected.

Kate would have applauded, but that might appear as condescension. She settled for a nod and, "Very good. I hope I can do as well."

Placing herself beside Stella, she tossed a rock; it bounced on the rim and fell inside. "Does that count?"

With a twist of her mouth, Stella considered the issue. "It counts."

"What's the most rocks you've made without missing? I'm sorry. Maybe I should have asked first if you know your numbers."

Stella looked at her as if she had grown a second head. Hurriedly she began to count. Kate managed to stop her at twenty.

"How fine. I'll bet you're about twenty years old yourself to do that."

The child giggled. "I'm five. Twenty is old."

"When you get all your pebbles in the fountain without hitting the dolphin even once, do you get a prize?"

"We're too poor for such things."

Kate wanted to bite her tongue. When her childish accomplishments had been noticed, a none-too-often occurrence, she had been rewarded with a china-faced doll or a book. Never a hug, of course, or an encouraging word. And she had received these prizes only after great efforts on her part, like playing a long piano piece without error or memorizing a two-page poem. Nothing so mundane or as much fun as pitching rocks.

"Where is your mama?" Kate asked, wondering why she had not yet been accosted for approaching the child.

"Delivering laundry. Before the rain."

"You think it's going to rain?"

"Mama says so."

"What about your papa?"

"I don't have one."

"Neither do I."

"Is yours in heaven?"

"Yes," she answered, although she wasn't sure it was true. He had gone to church regularly, but he had not been a religious man.

"Mine's in Lucca. I don't know if it's as good as heaven. Mama says it's not. She says that since he left with that other woman, he's never—"

"Stella, get away from the contessa."

It was the command Kate had been waiting for, but still it came as a shock.

The child took it far more calmly. "I've got to go." She pulled a handful of rocks from the pocket of her worn and faded dress and set them on the edge of the fountain. "Here. You'll have to play alone."

With that pronouncement, she skipped to her mother's side and put her arms around her skirt.

The woman rested her hand on her daughter's head and glared at Kate.

"She means no harm." As if the haughty Contessa Donati might have been offended by the forwardness of a child.

"Neither do I. I have no children. It was a joy to talk with her." On impulse, Kate added, "You take in laundry?"

The wary expression in the woman's dark eyes was visible from across the piazza. "It's honorable work."

"And necessary, too. I can offer you a job at the villa. You can bring your daughter if you like. I will rarely be around since I'm usually out in the fields. I can't pay much, but I can give you a room if you need it and food for the two of you."

"We don't take charity."

"I'm not offering it. It's a large place, even with few living there, and there are always chores. You wouldn't happen to know anything about growing vegetables, would you?"

The woman started to speak, then drew back, her hold on her daughter tightening. "It's devil's work that you're offering. Do not speak to my child again."

She disappeared down one of the lanes leading into the piazza, leaving Kate to wonder what she had been referring to. In her mind she had meant helping with the cleaning and the washing and perhaps clearing the garden behind the terrace. Was it devil's work because once it was done it had to be done again? Somehow she did not believe that was what the woman meant.

The wind turned cold and she felt a sprinkle of rain. Looking up, she saw a black cloud directly overhead. She was not surprised. Black clouds had followed her most of her life. Glancing toward the produce stalls, she saw Alfiero bargaining with the woman who ran the place. Waving, she caught his eye and gestured that she would be inside the inn.

She barely made it to shelter before the deluge came. Shaking her skirt, she smoothed the droplets of moisture from her hair. Past the registration desk, she saw a dozen tables where a scattering of men were having coffee. Or grappa. Travelers, she supposed. In their suits they looked more prosperous than the village men.

On her last visit to Belmare, she had let Stefano Braggio order for her, then had practically begged for workers, exhorting anyone who would listen. She was not begging today. Her offer of work to Stella's mother had been a business proposition the woman could either accept or reject. She would make no additional offers today.

She took a table, but the waiter passed her without stopping.

"Signore," she called out, "I'll have a coffee,

please, and something to eat. A pastry, if you have one."

She couldn't afford such luxury, but he didn't know it. And she did have the money, even if she hoarded it for more essential purchases.

The waiter hesitated, wiped his hands on the white apron tied around his middle, then nodded and disappeared through a door at the side of a well-equipped bar. Maybe she should have ordered the grappa, to ward off the chill brought by the rain. One of these days she would really shake up the waiter and do just that.

The pastry more than satisfied, layers of thin dough wrapped around a filling of sweetened plums and mascarpone. It was, she decided, a suitable reward for a woman who had come close to the fangs of a viper and shortly afterwards had come to the conclusion she was in love.

That her love was not returned—or worse, that the man might have a dark and deadly purpose in staying so close to her—were matters she refused to consider. Such thoughts did not go with a celebration. Her one regret was that she could not share her treat with the child who had brought her a moment of pure delight.

Staring through the open double doors of the inn, she watched the rain. It was fast and furious and brief. Like her time with Robert in the grotto.

When the waiter came to collect payment, she

gave him extra money. "Do you know Stella, the little girl who plays in the piazza?"

He smiled briefly, then returned to his dour mien, as if she had caught him doing something wrong.

"The next time you see her, give her one of those pastries. Tell her it's a prize for throwing pebbles without hitting the dolphin. Don't let her know it comes from me or her mother won't let her have it. Tell her it's from you or the inn or somebody, one of the guests who saw her at play. If you can't lie, don't say anything at all. Just give it to her."

"I can lie, Contessa Donati."

She could have sworn that, if only briefly, he looked upon her with a friendly eye, he a citizen of the village. It was another reason to celebrate.

She went outside to find the very dignified Alfiero sitting high in the loaded donkey cart, presenting as incongruous a picture as she had ever seen. She couldn't laugh at him, but she could smile inwardly.

After all that had happened this morning, after all the talk of even worse possibilities, she had no idea why she was in such a good mood. She was in love without being loved in return, there was great doubt she could manage to scrape by until actually making a profit from her land, and even if she did, evidence suggested she might not live long enough to enjoy the success.

Otherwise, her life was going very well. Even the black cloud had moved on, leaving everything dripping and glistening in the reborn sun.

"The day has turned out to be beautiful," she said. "Go on. I'll walk back home."

"The contessa should not walk."

"Didn't Pietro's mother?"

Alfiero shuddered. "Never."

"But I am not she."

"No, Contessa. She was rarely well."

"Please, really, I want you to leave. I'm used to working, and on this day I've been far too idle. Besides, I have to walk off the food I just ate."

With great reluctance he snapped the reins over the back of an equally reluctant donkey and the cart creaked its way to the road that led to the villa.

Kate started to follow, then remembered a shorter way, the path Robert had taken when he returned her to the villa. After the grotto. Could she find it again? It became a challenge too enticing to resist.

It took her a quarter of an hour to follow the winding streets and locate the thick grove of trees and shrubs and the shed where Robert sheltered his horse. The animal stood in the back of the small enclosure, his eyes wary in a shaft of light. She took a moment to speak to him.

"Don't worry, you won't have to carry me up today."

The horse bobbed his head and whinnied.

A twig snapped behind her and she whirled around, expecting to see Robert staring at her in disapproval. Instead she was watched by a woman she had never seen before.

The woman was beautiful, not yet thirty, but with her hands on her hips and her sandaled feet spread wide, she bore an air of worldly knowledge that Kate had not yet achieved. Her hair was black and lustrous, her eyes equally dark and deep set. Her features, set in an almost round face, were large, especially her mouth, but they went with her voluptuous figure.

She was a woman Pietro would have liked very much. But Kate doubted she would have put up with the conte for very long. Though she was shorter than Kate by several inches, she had a stature that came not from height. There was a strength about her, a fieriness that came from within. She smoldered. Kate could find no other way to put it.

"I'm sorry," Kate said. "Does this place belong to you?"

"It is not the place that I mind, Contessa Donati. You are foolish to come out here alone."

Fiery or not, the woman went too far. Kate had suffered enough warnings for one day. She wanted no more.

"I can protect myself," she said and meant it.

An unpleasant smile played on the woman's full lips. "Accidents happen. No one can always be prepared, not even a contessa."

Kate's Yankee bluntness took control. "Are you threatening me?"

"I am warning you of what you should already know."

"I've never seen you before. What do you know about me?"

"You should never have returned."

"And why is that? Because the people don't want me? That is foolish of them. I mean no harm. I have offered them help."

But the woman seemed not to hear her.

"I have said all I can. You must leave."

Her skirt flared when she swirled, showing a length of slender calf and an equally slender ankle. Silently she disappeared into the woods.

She was, Kate thought, very much like Maria, though the two were nothing alike physically.

This was too much. In all of Belmare, she had met only two people who approved of what she did, even momentarily—the waiter at the inn because she had bought a child a pastry and the child herself. It didn't seem like much on which to build a life.

With an exclamation of disgust, she started up the narrow, twisted path that led up the hill and eventually to the stone wall of the villa. If vipers awaited, so be it. She would deal with them as they came. They would have to take care of themselves.

But it wasn't a snake that met her halfway up the hill. Robert blocked her way. A very angry Robert.

"Is this how you protect yourself?"

She held up a hand. "Don't say anything. Just let me by. I'm perfectly all right."

"No, you're not. I used to think you a sensible woman. I have changed my mind."

It was the proverbial last straw. Something exploded within her, something far more powerful than indignation.

"I'm not going to argue with you. You're right; I have no sense. Otherwise I would never do this."

Without another word, she threw herself at him, wrapped her arms around his neck and kissed him with both lips and tongue.

Chapter Sixteen

Robert learned submission fast. He opened his mouth and let her tongue invade. She danced inside his mouth, sucking up his juices, clutching at his shoulders as if she might spin off the earth.

At that moment she wanted to be anywhere but in this square of Tuscany, and only Robert could take her away.

Eventually she had to come up for air.

"You taste sweet," he said, once again using English. It had become their language for making love.

"Mascarpone," she whispered against his lips, not quite removed from reality.

"Cheese? I think not."

"Be quiet," she said with urgency and began to tug his shirt from his trousers.

He grabbed her wrist to stop her. With her free hand she brushed her fingers close to what was already a very hard erection.

He moaned. She decided it was an acceptable sound. Then he did the same to her, thrusting fingers between her legs, finding the place that already weeped for him.

She, too, moaned. There could be only one ending to this encounter. Her body demanded it, and so did his.

She pushed away from him with such suddenness that in his surprise he let her go. Taking his hand, she pulled him off the trail, thrashing through the brush, the residue from the storm showering down on them like fresh rain. As if she knew where she was going, she burst through a wall of hedge and thick trees into a clearing, its floor a bed of grass and leaves, its ceiling a canopy of intertwining branches that had kept out most of the storm.

She turned to him. Moisture was caught in his dark hair, and his eyes held the focused light of a wild animal. This time when she pulled at his shirt and worked at the buttons, he made no attempt to stop her. She tugged it halfway off his shoulders, pinning his arms to his sides, and bent to lick his nipples. His moan became a growl. If he meant to frighten her, he chose the wrong way. She kissed the contours of his chest and worked her way to the hollow of his throat, where her tongue got to work again.

She could not tell him she loved him, but she would show him in the only way she knew how.

Her body pulsed uncontrollably, just from the taste of his skin. Tugging him to the ground, pushing him to his back, she worked at her own clothes, frantic in her need to disrobe. When she was naked, she sat astride him and rubbed the pulsing against his trousers, against the hardness she longed to feel inside her.

She did not want to think, did not want to ask questions or consider what her actions meant. She wanted release from the pressures building inside her. And there was only one way to get it . . . after she let them build a little more. She was torturing herself, but she was also torturing him. She felt it in the thrust of his hips and she saw it in his mad, searing eyes.

As easily as she had pushed him to the ground, he did the same to her, then backed away long enough to take off his clothes. Cupping her breasts, she worked at the stiff peaks with her fingers, taunting him as he was taunting her with the steady exposure of his flesh. The hairs were darkly clustered around his erection. If body parts could speak, his called to her. She reached out to enfold him. He allowed her only one quick touch, then lay back down and pulled her on top of him, his hardness against her belly.

His hands smoothed the grass and leaves clinging to her backside, moving quickly at first, then slowly, stroking across her shoulders, down her spine, nestling in the small of her back before holding her buttocks tight.

"Your skin was made for satin sheets," he said.

He was trying to regain control.

"I've had satin sheets. I'd rather have the grass."

Bracing her hands on the ground above his shoulders, she lifted her upper body and ground her stomach against his sex. He strained to suckle her breasts. Smiling at the power surging through her, she slowly leaned toward him to give him the access he craved and watched his tongue work its magic.

He wanted her on top? So be it. He had placed her exactly where she wanted to be. Spreading her legs, pressing her thighs against his narrow hips, she rubbed herself against his shaft until he was as wet as she.

He dropped his head back and rewarded her with another groan.

"Is this another snake I feel?" she asked.

"It has a bite."

Kneeling, she took his shaft in her hands and played it against her private parts. His strong hands spanned her waist, then eased down so that his thumbs could circle in her pubic hair.

"Careful or it will spit at you," he said.

"Then I'll have to smother it."

She rose to her knees just high enough to ease him inside her. Hand in glove, pistol in holster, the fit was tight and smooth. She knew not how he felt, but for her he had come home.

The torture was exquisite as she lifted and lowered herself, letting him almost free, then sucking him back into her body, time and again until she could stand it no longer. With a shout, he spread his hands across her bottom and held her in place. In a few quick thrusts he took her to that deep, dark place with its sudden explosion of light.

Rapture came in waves that pounded against every sensibility, every sense. She tasted him, she smelled him, she heard his cry, even as the waves rippled through her, binding her to him in a way he could not know. Couldn't he hear her heart pounding *I love you, I love you?*

When rationality returned, she prayed he did not know of her heart's cry. For what could he tell her in return?

I warned you I would harm you.

But love was not harm. It was something he would not understand. As little as she knew of men, instinct told her this was so.

Slowly their breathing grew steady, the cries, the moans as distant as the storm clouds that had moved beyond the village into the hills, even now dropping their precious treasure onto the parched fields of the villa.

Sweat made their bodies slick. She rolled from him and sat on her heels, half facing him, afraid to let him gaze directly into her eyes, equally afraid of turning her back and letting him think her cowardly.

Now came the most difficult moment, now when she could think. Falling in love with him, unexpected though it was, had been far easier than keeping it to herself.

But, oh, how she wanted to tell him, to let him know that what had passed between them was for her far more than physical release.

She took a deep breath. "I would prefer you did not say a word."

He so seldom did what she asked. This time was different. His only response was to sit beside her and pick the grass from her hair. He smoothed the long strands over her shoulders until the ends reached the tips of her breasts. His eyes followed his hands.

Then he turned her head toward him and slanted his lips across hers, kissing her as gently as he had done when he returned her to the villa. Had it been only this morning? It seemed a lifetime ago.

When he kissed her eyes, invisible fingers clutched at her stomach. Everything he did was tearing at her, making her wish she could make love with him all over again. Somehow a second time would be wrong, here in the woods. This was a scene for savage sex, and the fever was gone. No longer did she feel wild. She wanted tenderness and, if she could have found them, even satin sheets.

What would it be like to look upon his brown body lying on an ivory bedcovering? It was an image she would take to bed with her each night.

She eased free of his hands and stood, maintaining the silence she had asked of him. Shaking out her clothes, she dressed quickly. He did the same. She had no idea what he was thinking. Was he wondering what had come over her? Did he imagine she was thanking him for saving her this morning? Did he suppose something had happened on her trip to town to drive her to a frenzy, to the sexual madness that had played to its conclusion in these woods?

Yes to everything, but more, much more.

She knew he would not keep silent long. She wanted to have an answer when he finally questioned her, an answer that was not a lie yet was not quite the truth.

When they were both as presentable as the past half hour would allow, she studied the impenetrable wall of woods surrounding them. She saw no way out of the clearing. She could barely remember how she had gotten them inside the circle, such had been Robert's effect on her.

As was growing his habit, he lifted her into his arms and found the way, shielding her with his body from the grasping boughs. When they reached the trail, he did not put her down.

"Mud," he said with a nod toward the upward path.

"You can't carry me the entire way."

"You don't weigh much."

"Didn't you say I was voluptuous?"

"Luscious. I said you were luscious. You don't become voluptuous until you're naked and everything swells."

"That doesn't sound very appealing."

Heat flared in his eyes. "It is, Kate. Believe me, it is."

She decided to take him at his word. If he said she was appealing, then that was exactly what she was.

Her task over the duration of the journey was as difficult as his. She had to keep from remembering all the things she had done. Not that she regretted any of them. But that didn't mean they weren't embarrassing. When he looked at her, did he see her naked, the way she saw him? Did she actually swell? Surely he exaggerated. Only parts of her did.

Would she have another chance to show him her

voluptuous side? Oh, yes, she thought with a shiver of abandon, though she did not know how or where that would be. And she wouldn't need threats from a more naturally voluptuous beauty with hatred in her eyes to throw herself into her lover's arms.

The next day Kate turned shy. After a dawn delivery of the food basket to the two workers, Robert being blessedly late for a change, she hastily retreated and looked for work far from anything resembling an olive tree.

She found it behind the villa, on the far side of her property away from the sea, in a partially barren field she had visited once years ago. The hilly field lay beyond the stable, where a team of matched carriage horses had once been kept, along with several mounts for riding, an overly elaborate stable that now held only one hard-worked donkey too unworthy for even the creditors to claim.

Close to the stable, chickens had once run wild, and on the downside of a slope had been a row of rabbit hutches and a grassy area where cattle and goats had grazed. Farther still from the house, hidden in a grove of trees, lay a small, ramshackle hut she had not known existed. Its presence did not surprise her. At Pietro's insistence, she had done little exploring, the stable being the outermost boundary of her wandering. Walking about wasn't suitable for his contessa, he claimed, a strangely conservative attitude when she considered the other practices he expected of his wife.

Perhaps the hut had been the residence of one of the servants, a stable hand or the keeper of the Donati family's small herd. Like so much of the villa, it was overrun with untended growth.

She put off thoughts of the hut until later. For the moment, she had a new goal, constructing a coop that could contain not only chickens but geese as well. She would use as her guide the structures she remembered from the country outside Boston. If she got good at carpentry and could get hold of some wire, she might also build a hutch or two. Her primarily vegetarian diet was beautifully prepared, but on occasion she would like some variety. And every day or so she would like to take thick slices of meat out to the men.

Armed with tools she'd found in the storage shed, she invaded the stable, ignored the incurious donkey and searched for wood. She found it in the form of a broken-down stall. Dragging the slats into the shade at the side of the stable, she proceeded to pull out nails and set the best ones aside for reuse, then take a rough measurement of the wood she would need. But always her attention kept wandering to the hut.

Thirst gave her the excuse she needed to quit work. She had brought a small wrapper of bread, cheese and slices of last night's eggplant, but nothing to wash down her noontime repast. Perhaps there was a well close by, like the one between the olive grove and the vineyard. With the food set aside on a wooden plank, she went to investigate.

The way was dry, yesterday's storm having skirted around this part of the villa. As she approached the hut, a warm wind stirred the trees, the resultant soughing sound ghostlike in the shadows, a warning for her to stay away. What foolishness, she told herself. Crunching over dead leaves and grass, pushing her way through overgrown shrubbery, she found windows on the walls flanking the stone fireplace, but they were too grimy to allow her much of a view inside. Still, she wiped at the cleaner of the two windows, cupped her hands to shut out the sunlight and peered into the one room.

Furniture, she could definitely make out at least one chair—

"Why not try the door?"

Kate jumped.

"Robert," she said, hand over her heart. "Don't creep up on me like that." He stood in shadow, only a few feet to her left. She took a deep breath, daring to look at him from the corner of her eye. "I thought you were out pulling weeds. What are you doing here?"

"Wondering the same thing about you."

Straightening, she stepped away from the window. "I was looking for water."

"I should have guessed."

She ignored the sarcasm. "I've never been out here before. I didn't know this place was here."

"So I ask again, why not try the door?"

"How do you know I haven't? Don't bother to answer. You've been watching me."

"I never know what you're going to do."

Neither did she. It was one of the few things they had in common.

With as much dignity as she could summon, she began to tromp once again around the perimeter of the cabin, stopping at the front, with its low overhang of roof and tangled vines covering the once-whitewashed walls. The door itself was free of growth.

"It would appear someone has been here before us," Robert said.

Again she jumped. He hadn't made a sound walking through the leaves, and she had not realized he was so close.

She studied the vine-free door and the pathway leading to it. He was right, they were not the first in recent days to come this way. Had a stranger invaded her land, or was the visitor someone she knew? Neither possibility gave her comfort.

The knob turned in her hand, and the door

creaked slowly open. She stared into the dimness of the hut's interior, feeling curiously like an intruder though she held the deed to everything at the villa. She waited for Robert to comment on her hesitation, but he held his silence.

Though he stood behind her, she felt a stillness about him that gave her pause. She looked at him. He was staring beyond her into the gloom of the hut, his expression as rigid as his stance. He had forgotten her existence, and she felt an ocean away from him. Whatever he saw in that darkness was something she would never see. His spirits, his ghosts—they were not hers to find.

Whoever the recent visitor had been, it was not Robert. He had not walked this way in years. He did not want to be here now. But he had come. Because of her.

A chill shivered through her and she rubbed her arms. She would very much have liked to take his hand, but he did not offer it and she walked inside alone. No dancing couple greeted her, no pair of naked lovers, as they had within the villa bedchamber, nothing but a rickety table and two straight-backed chairs in front of the stone fireplace, and a white iron bed, much like the one in her room.

The lone cover on the bed was rumpled, and the dust on the floor and table had been disturbed. Ashes lay in the fireplace, evidence of a recent fire. The only things left untouched were the cobwebs that hung from the open beams of the ceiling. It was an abode not only for ghosts, but also for some very real human being. Alfiero? Maria? She doubted it, but as soon as she returned to the villa she would ask.

Perhaps even Michelangelo or Leonardo had used the bed for a night or two. She was about to put the idea to Robert when he spoke from his post by the doorway.

"Donati men have long used this place for their trysts."

She knew he did not mean the servants. He meant Pietro and his father Renaldo before him, and on back for as many generations as the cabin had existed.

"There are no more Donatis. Who could be using it now?"

He did not respond.

"Either one of the workers might have slept here."

"No. They would have asked."

She studied the rumpled bed and the plain table and chairs.

"It doesn't look very romantic," she said.

She felt foolish even saying the words. The only Donati man she had known was devoid of romanticism. He had lacked the knowledge of its very existence.

Her remark got a reaction from him, though it

wasn't anything she wanted him to say.

"Sex isn't romantic. I thought you knew that."

His harshness stunned her. With only a brief comment, he made her ashamed of yesterday in the woods. She had vowed not to feel that way, but as always, Robert changed her plans.

"I knew," she said, sounding far more defensive than she would have chosen. She knew something else, too, and she turned to face him. With Robert, aggression was usually the best way to protect herself. "Something happened here. A long time ago. What was it?"

His eyes were shuttered. "Nothing to concern you."

"Why do you always lie to me?"

"I don't lie. I tell you what you need to know."

Kate felt a sudden anger. He did not sound smug so much as distant. She could take anything rather than his pulling away.

"You speak as though I were a child. But I'm not, and you damn well ought to know it."

Without considering the consequences, she unbuttoned her shirt.

His lips tightened. "Don't."

If she had not known such a thing was impossible, she would have thought him afraid. Ignoring the order, she tossed the shirt aside, letting him see that her breasts had swelled to voluptuousness.

"You said this was a trysting place for Donatis.

Surely that includes me. It's a little dirty, but then, so is what we do. It's certainly not ro—"

With only two steps, he loomed before her and jerked her into his arms, the shuttered look gone as his eyes burned into hers, his hands biting into the flesh of her shoulders.

"You won't stop, will you?"

She flung back her head and stared up at him. "All you have to do is leave. I'm not holding you here."

"There you are wrong, Caterina." He looked at her fullness, then back into her eyes. "You have no idea how wrong."

His lips claimed hers in an act of complete possession. His tongue ground against her teeth, then thrust deeper, filling her mouth, rendering her desperate for him to fill every cavity in the same commanding way. Backing her against the wall, he broke the kiss and unfastened her skirt and underdrawers, letting them drop to the ground, leaving her naked except for stockings and shoes. His movements were frantic, as though lust were a demon he must exorcise. He had to know the same demon invaded her.

With fingers equally frantic, she tried to unfasten his trousers. She was too slow. He took over. She rubbed her hardened nipples against his rough shirt as he freed his erection and stroked it against her pubic hair.

Her knees gave way. He lifted her into his arms, and as if she had done so a thousand times, she wrapped her legs around him while he lowered her onto his sex. His thrusts were hard, rhythmic, accurate. He rubbed where she needed to be rubbed.

This was no time for erotic strokes, or explorations with hands and lips. Theirs was a shared and primitive need, a wildness that could be tamed in only one way.

It was over within seconds, the spiraling tremors, the lost breath and pounding pulse. When the climax came, she cried into his shoulder, and he clutched her hard enough for bones to break, though the explosions left her impervious to pain, and the only injury lay within her broken heart.

How she could reach heaven and hell at the same time, she did not know. Robert took her to both. How could she love such a man? The question was impossible to answer. But love him she did. More than life itself.

If she couldn't get the romance she needed to feed her hungry soul, she would take the sex, every time a chance presented itself. She was more than just a fallen woman. She was a woman obsessed.

He seemed to hold her forever, though she knew the span of time was no more than a dozen heartbeats. She eased her feet to the floor, and his seed spilled down the insides of her thighs.

He saw it. He must have known the dampness

would be there, must have seen it, in the grotto and certainly yesterday in the woods. This day was proving different, in ways she could not begin to understand, beginning and ending with the expression on his face. Again, he looked afraid. No, worse, desolate, as if he stared at something he could scarcely comprehend.

She would have preferred he stab her with his knife.

"My God, what have I done? Not here, never here."

"We had sex," she managed, sounding firm when she wanted to grab her clothes and run. It was a reaction that had ended their moment of passion at least once before.

He straightened, seemed to get control.

"If there's a child . . ."

A fist squeezed her heart, but she held back the threatening tears.

"If there's a child, what?"

She could see the battle within him. As good as he was at keeping his thoughts from her, he could not keep this one to himself. He must offer her honor, no matter the cost.

He brushed a lock of hair from her face. Tenderly. In other circumstances she would be joyous. But not now. She backed away so that he could not touch her again.

"I would behave as a man should. As I want to. I would—"

"No!"

She covered her ears. She could see the words forming on his lips, the offer to marry her and give her child a name. And when he found out the truth about her, she would have to free him from his promise. The relief in his eyes when he heard would be her final undoing.

"Please, Robert, don't say anything more. Not just yet."

While he watched, she quickly dressed, covering the evidence of what had passed between them. He did not blink or look away. Either reaction would have been welcome. And uncharacteristic. As always, Robert watched.

When they were both ready to leave, she faced him. She needed a deep breath before she could speak.

"Don't worry. I am not carrying your child. Not if the curse holds true for me."

His penetrating stare made going on difficult, but she had no choice, not after what he had almost said.

"I'm going to tell you something I've never told anyone. Early in my marriage, I lost a baby." Her voice quavered. She willed it to strengthen. "Pietro never knew I was with child. I barely knew myself.

Later, I told myself there would be other children. But it never happened."

He looked as if he might respond. But she was not done.

"Isn't it the curse of Donati contessas that they bear only one infant?" She managed a faint, rueful smile. "I had my one time."

There, it was said, the words she could scarcely allow herself to consider. Her greatest fear was that he would show her pity. If so, he would destroy her. Pity was a poor substitute for love.

"Kate—"

"You don't have to say anything. I just didn't want you to worry needlessly."

Or make promises you would regret.

"It's a time for trading secrets," she said, hurrying on. "I told you mine. You tell me yours. Never before have you worried about consequences, not in the grotto, not yesterday in the woods. Why do you hate this cabin so much? What happened here that sets it apart?"

Slowly he drew his gaze from her and glanced around the room, as if viewing it for the last time, then gestured toward the door. "Outside." She did not argue. The walls were closing in on them both.

He led her to a shady spot at the edge of the grove, where the wind blew and the grass rustled under her feet. It was like returning to the real world. She had not realized it while inside, but the hut had an aura of unreality to it. A love nest for the Donatis. For an afternoon it had become hers.

Robert did not look at her as he spoke. Nor did he look at the hut.

"I told you of a storm that filled the grotto and killed two men."

"And earlier, a woman."

He ignored her. "After the storm had passed, your late husband showed little concern at the loss. I came upon him here with one of the servant women. It was long before you met him, shortly after his own father died. I was a spindly boy and he a grown man, but when I realized he was hurting the woman, I took it upon myself to rescue her."

"He let you?"

"He tried to beat me."

"Tried? You must have beat him instead."

"I did what I had to do to stop him. And then I left. It was why I went to sea."

His story was one she could well believe, concerning Pietro and Robert both.

She pictured him naked. "I can't imagine you as spindly."

"At twelve I was mostly arms and legs. I grew up on the decks of prison ships that ran from Liverpool to Melbourne."

"That was your experience as a sailor?"

"For the first few years. The trading vessels came

later. I even sailed for a while under the flag of the Royal Navy."

A silence fell between them. He had told her much, but everything had been relayed to her without passion. She waited for him to go on. What drove him to bouts of agony? The hut, his years away from Tuscany, both held memories he kept to himself. She felt as if she had crawled inside him and could see the gaps.

The truth remained hidden, seething, a secret buried so deep, she wondered if he could ever let it out.

I tell you what you need to know. Had he not said these very words to her? She did not need to know what was in his heart.

From the stable came the bray of the donkey, and the moment of silence ended with such absurdity she almost laughed. His secrets were still his, she thought, blinking back tears, while hers had been laid bare. Except one, the secret of her love. It was the one truth she would carry to her grave.

"We need to get back to our chores," she said.

His eyes flicked to her. "Are you all right?"

Something in the way he asked brought his tension vaulting into her. The seething passion was not buried so deeply after all.

She tilted her chin at him. "Why wouldn't I be?"

He nodded once. "Of course. Why wouldn't you be?"

And then suddenly, loudly, the explosion came, the one that had been building in him for so long. "Damn you, Kate, for stopping me."

He grabbed her arms and shook her.

"And damn you for being what you are. What would you have answered if I had finished what I wanted to say? Would you have scorned me as beneath you except when we're making love? Have you become that kind of Donati? Are you like Pietro after all?"

The words lashed out. She did not know him. He frightened her, but he angered her more.

"How dare you say such a thing?"

"You cannot know what I dare." He ground his lips against hers, brutally.

He thrust her from him, but he did not let her go. The world spun crazily. Though his grip eased, she could feel the trembling of his hands against her arms.

"Always I do the wrong thing. Damn me and damn you. You haven't figured out what's going on, have you? I should have told you. And now I fear it is too late."

He dropped his hands. She swayed once, fighting for balance.

"Tell me now, Robert," she said, letting the tears come. "Tell me now."

But he hardly seemed to be listening, so lost was he in his own torment.

"Yesterday there was a woman on the trail," she said, breathlessly, desperately. "She warned me against you. My servants do the same. Why? What is there I should have figured out?"

For a moment she thought he was going to answer. Then from far away she heard the mournful clanging of the bell that hung beside the front gate of the villa. The bell that had mysteriously signaled her return. It sounded no more welcoming now than it had on that first day.

He looked toward the villa, then back to her. A curtain fell between them. Stepping away, he bowed and slipped into Italian. "You have callers, Contessa Donati. You must see to them."

Before she could manage a ragged breath he had disappeared through the trees, leaving her more alone than she had ever been in her life. The echo of the clanging hung in the air. It was the echo of a funeral bell.

She stared after him. The air moved in more closely than it had inside the hut. He had damned them both, though she knew not why. And then he had abandoned her to misery.

She must escape from this terrible place, find a refuge where she could think. Turning quickly, she hurried past the stable and on toward the villa, picking out the path generations of Donati men must have forged. She was keeping the family tradition alive, she thought bitterly, a contessa substituting for generations of randy contes. She understood herself no better than she knew the man she loved.

As she ran, she did not wipe the tears from her cheeks, nor did she brush her clothes free of the dirt from the floor of the hut. Her hair had become unbound, but she did not care. The bell must toll because of the wind. Who could be calling on her this afternoon?

Several people, she found out when she was within sight of the terrace. Company did indeed wait to greet her by the back steps, company both wanted and unwanted, every one a surprise.

Stefano Braggio, absent for weeks, had returned, no doubt to argue once again the reasons she ought to sell the villa. As always, he was impeccably dressed, handsome, his warm smile turning to puzzlement and then distress as he watched her approach.

She nodded, nervously smoothing her unkempt hair, belatedly brushing the tears from her cheeks, calling on the residues of inner strength not to scream and run. She even managed a smile for Stella and her mother, who stood in the shadows behind him. The sight of them brought the calmness she so desperately desired. Wanting to hug them both, she stepped into the role she had been given, the Contessa Donati, though a different kind of contessa than had ever carried the name.

Her guests needed only one look to figure out
that one for themselves.

"Thank you for coming," she said to the pair in
the shadows, as if her appearance were an everyday
thing. "And Stefano," she added as an after-
thought. "I hope you have all introduced your-
selves." She spoke innocently, though she doubted
the agent had done more than glance their way.

"Please, come inside," she said, gesturing to
everyone, her hand steady, the words directed to
the mother and child. "There is much to do before
settling you in for the night."

Chapter Seventeen

"Marry me."

Kate stared across the dining room table. Stefano Braggio, his eyes deep and dark and rich with sincerity, stared back.

Light from the massive candelabra to the right and left flickered around the room. She had grown used to sunlight and moonglow. Artificial illumination made everything it fell upon seem false.

Including Braggio's plea.

It was the wine talking, not her business agent. It had to be. Two proposals in one day. No, make that one and a half. If she tried to respond right away, she would become hysterical.

Instead, she reached for her glass. Braggio took her hand and held it between the two of his.

"Surely this does not come as a surprise."

"Actually, it does," she said, eyeing the wine with mounting desperation.

"Perhaps I have been too subtle."

She couldn't accuse him of subtlety now. It would have taken one of the gardening tools to free her hand from his.

"I don't know what to say."

"Try yes."

"But I don't love you."

Even to her own ears, it sounded a poor excuse. In any world to which she had been exposed, love seldom was a reason for a betrothal.

"I know you don't," he said with a sorrowful look. "But you hold me in high regard."

Not all that high, she could have told him. Instead she nodded, in the brief motion resorting to a gentle lie.

She tried a smile. "I used up my dowry on my first walk down the aisle."

He regarded her with sympathy, as though she were a child. Or a simpleminded woman.

"I am your business manager, Caterina. Please let me call you by your first name, though you are far above me in every way. I know your finances better than you know them yourself."

For all his concern and sincerity, he was beginning to annoy her, as he frequently did, especially when he turned pompous. He didn't know about the money she had brought with her in the hem of her mourning gown. It wouldn't support her forever. The dwindling sum scarcely could sustain her and the few servants she had gathered around her. But she wasn't destitute, as he believed.

And she had plans, shaky though they were at the moment. The possibility that after today Robert would not stand by her had been tearing at her since he left. She thrust the thought away before she burst into tears once again. Braggio would interpret them as a sign that she was touched by his offer, or that she was merely touched. No sane woman would turn him down.

"I am not wealthy as you have known wealth," he said, "but I can care for you far better than you can care for yourself." Loosening his grip, he turned her hand over and looked at her palm. "You've been blistered and burned. No lady should bear calluses like these."

Proud of those calluses, Kate pulled her hand away and joined it with its mate in her lap.

"I have not complained about the work I do here."

"It is one of your most endearing traits, my dear. Over the past few years you have been given many reasons to complain. I will not speak ill of the dead, but I cannot ignore what you have endured."

She heard the edge of pity in his voice. If he hoped to get her to consider his proposal, he was taking the wrong tack.

"You are very kind, Signore Braggio."

"Oh, to have you call me Stefano would be the fulfillment of one of my dreams."

She had not realized how much he was given to exaggeration. His dreams, indeed. Still, it seemed a simple enough request. "Stefano, then."

His eyes warmed. "It is not kindness that motivates me."

Oh, dear.

She pushed back from the table and stood. "You do take me by surprise."

He came around the table after her. She held up a defensive hand. Amazingly, he halted a few feet away from her.

She glanced down at the black gown of mourning she had worn for dinner. "This comes so soon."

His lips twitched. He must have known there had been no love between her and her late husband. He also knew she knew that he knew.

Kate's head ached. Today kept proving itself to be a very bad time for her, when all she had wanted to do was build a chicken coop.

"Am I so repulsive to you?"

She dropped her hand and stared at him.

"Oh, Stefano, you're not repulsive at all. You're . . . you're quite handsome, as a matter of fact. I've never understood why you did not take a wife long ago."

"How could I, *bellissima,* after I met you?"

He moved closer, and she found herself trapped against the table. They were close to the same height. He did not have to bend his head to kiss her. With a sigh, she gave in. The kiss was long and dry and left her wanting the wine all the more.

"I burn for you, Caterina."

For all the passion he put into the words, he might as well have been discussing the meal they had just finished. If Robert had kissed her, she would have dragged him to the floor by now.

She tried to smile at him. Instead, thinking of Robert, she burst into tears. He thrust a handkerchief into her hands. Dear Stefano, ever the efficient one. Turning from him, she grabbed the wineglass and downed its contents. Looking beyond the table, she saw Maria watching from the doorway leading to the kitchen. Kate felt her animosity, both unexplained and unexpected. It sent a shiver down her spine. It also dried her tears.

She set down the glass. "Let's go to the terrace, Stefano. The air is too close in here."

Without waiting for a reply, she hurried to the entryway and through the doors leading outside. The agent's footsteps were not far behind. She did not stop until she reached the balustrade with its statues of prancing boys. Lights flickered beside the statues, but the world beyond was dark and impenetrable.

Was Robert out there watching? Was he waiting

for her to figure out what was going on? She had tried, every spare second since he'd left her, but her efforts had only left her more confused. What he had said, what she had said, what they had done—none of it made sense. The trouble between them was her fault. He'd let her know that clearly enough. But how?

"I do not ask for an answer tonight," Stefano said.

With a start, she came back to the present, this time with more determination.

"I won't change my mind. I can't marry you. I have no plans to marry again."

"Don't speak too soon. There are many things for you to consider."

His voice had taken on a sharp edge.

She did not respond. She had told him all she had to say.

"There is talk in the village. About a man who has come to work for you. Stories of an ugly nature I cannot repeat to a lady such as yourself."

She gripped the sharp corner of the balustrade. "It's true I have a worker here. I have three. Are there rumors about all of them?"

"Only the one. A peasant who comes from the sea and claims to have worked Donati land when he was a boy. His name is not a known one, though there are those who say he has a familiar look about him."

How could that be? He was spindly when he left, all arms and legs, nothing like the man he had become.

Her heart twisted when she thought of Robert as a lad, defending the virtue of one of Pietro's victims, and she loved him all the more.

Training her eyes on the darkness, she kept her voice even.

"You must mean Roberto Vela. You have known the Donati family for a long while. Does the name sound familiar to you?"

"I have known two generations of contes and their contessas. Peasants were never the concern of my father or of me."

"Your interest was limited to the money they could bring to the family coffers."

"It was what your husband's family asked of mine. Do you find the situation offensive?"

She had truly irritated him. This would not do. He was what he was. At least, unlike Robert, she could figure him out.

She turned to face him. "I'm sorry, Stefano. It's late, and it's been a long day. You have given me time to consider your proposal. Let me do so."

He bowed. "That is all I ask. I have taken a room in the village inn. Expect a visit from me within the week." He hesitated. "I have vowed to protect you and your interests, Caterina, and this I will do as it is my duty. But I want more, as I have told you tonight. It is this more that is my dream."

He turned to leave. At least, she thought, he had not mentioned her disgraceful state when she came upon him and the others on the terrace. At least he had been gentlemanly enough to make no comment, then or now, that would add to her embarrassment.

Her relief came too soon. They were by the front door when he stopped and gave her a look of dark warning, so dark she did not want to hear what he would say.

"When I saw you this afternoon, I wanted to kill whoever it was who had brought you such pain. If it is this Vela, then you must rid yourself of him. For your own good, of course, but also for his and for mine. Catastrophe awaits us all on the path you have chosen, though I know not your particular way."

He took her hand and kissed it, then pressed it against his heart.

"Do not doubt my sincerity, Caterina. It would be a terrible mistake to underestimate what I wish to do for you."

She could do nothing but stare at him. He spoke not with pomposity but a fierceness she had not known he possessed. He was threatening her, or Robert, or them both. Always he spoke after careful thought. But not tonight. She wondered if he realized all he had said.

It was the spontaneity of his words that made him frightening. Kill? Surely he had not said kill. And the prediction of awaiting catastrophe—had he lost his mind, or had she?

Before she could respond, Alfiero appeared mysteriously with Stefano's hat and cloak and opened the massive front door. With a bow, the agent left, the darkness gone as if it had never been, the bland courtesy returned. She and Alfiero listened as the carriage that had brought him here rumbled around the driveway and through the gate. Then suddenly all was quiet, her first such moment since she had approached the hut.

It was not a pleasant silence. Her beloved villa had turned into an asylum for the insane. Namely, herself.

"Will there be anything else, Contessa? Perhaps a glass of brandy?"

He spoke calmly, reasonably, though he must have heard the agent's departing threat.

She took a moment to gather her wits. "I didn't know we had any. Thank you for the suggestion, but no." Then, more brightly, as if she wasn't trembling inside, "Have my two new residents settled in for the night?"

"As you suggested, they were put in a room not far from the kitchen."

She could tell by his voice that he was not pleased by the presence of the new arrivals. Especially the child. Oh, but she was pleased. They made her life seem almost normal. When they were near, especially Stella, she could forget she walked a line that was close to tragedy.

Stefano had been right in one thing: The path she walked was one that led to catastrophe, though she knew not the form it would take, nor how soon it would strike.

"We need to work on your room."

Stella nodded at Kate. For the past half hour it was all she had done. In the early morning Kate had found the child in the kitchen finishing a breakfast of fruit and bread. Bianca, her mother, had taken the basket of food out to the field. Cowardly Kate had not wanted to face Robert. She didn't know how to behave around him, didn't know what to say.

She wasn't doing too well with Stella, either.

Here they were in the drab room assigned by Alfiero last night, a hard mattress without headboard for a bed, no rugs or curtains, only one chair and a bedside table without a lamp.

How neglected the mother and child must have felt, going to bed in the dark after what had probably been a spartan supper. When Kate brought up the subject to Alfiero, he had said with a sniff that it was better than they were used to in town. Maybe so. Maybe not. The fact remained that she hated the room.

"Will you help me?"

Stella traced the dust on the floor with the edge of her sandal.

"Mama says I'm to stay out of the way."

"You won't be in the way."

The child's brow furrowed.

"I have a secret place I want to show you."

The furrows went away. "I have a secret place, too. For the rocks."

"Oh, yes, the ones you throw in the fountain. I don't know what's in this one. Lots of things, I suspect. I asked Alfiero about it once, but he didn't say much. It's close to where we are right now."

It was two doors away, as a matter of fact, in the wing that housed the servants' quarters. Finding it locked, she had to seek out Alfiero to get the key. He passed it over with curious reluctance. When she opened the door to a jumble of boxes and crates and mismatched furniture, she understood why.

Rolling up the sleeves of her shirt, grateful she had not worn any of her more formal clothes, she breathed deeply of the clean air in the hallway and went inside, Stella close at her heels.

"We're looking for tables, chairs, rugs, curtains, bedcovers, definitely a lamp, even pictures to hang on the wall. Let me know if you see anything you like."

Over the next couple of hours, she and Stella went through the crates, found a few treasures, coughed on the dust. At the end of the session, she had in the hallway mismatched bedcovers and linens, a pair of velvet draperies that would add an incongruous elegance to the chamber, even a braided rug that a servant of long ago must have made by hand. No furniture, but she would get the table and chairs from the hut, even the headboard, since she was unlikely to go inside the place again. And if she did, she certainly would not use the bed.

She would have to ask Alfiero for a lamp.

Other than the draperies, and she was still uncertain about them, she found nothing that could be considered decorative. At that moment, as if her gaze had been guided to it, she saw the edge of what appeared to be a picture frame behind a wardrobe she had decided was too massive for the small room. Why she hadn't seen it before, she did not know.

She had to wend her way carefully around and past the clutter to get to it. Somehow it had become wedged between the wardrobe and the wall. It took several hard tugs to free it. Stella watched the struggle with wide eyes.

When it finally popped out, Kate staggered backwards, sitting down hard on a brassbound leather trunk that held tablecloths and napkins from a more opulent time. She stared in disappointment at her treasure. It was a picture frame, all right, but that's all it was. The picture itself had been removed.

Recently. A small strip of canvas caught on one of the nails appeared freshly torn, and the entire frame was without dust. It should have been draped in cobwebs, as was the wardrobe behind which it had been shoved. Clean as it was, it could have been put there yesterday.

She studied it. The missing picture had been about two feet wide and three feet high, but the heavy frame added to the dimensions, its gilded wood intricately carved and splashed with dark patches of color, red primarily, in contrast with the gold.

Holding the frame tightly, she closed her eyes. Her hands tingled, as if the wood moved beneath them, as if it put out heat. She had seen this frame before, hanging on a villa wall, but no matter how hard she concentrated, she could not remember where. The blurred memory stirred unpleasant feelings inside her, as did the tingling and the heat.

"You don't like it?"

She jumped, then saw Stella standing close beside her. Immediately the strange sensations subsided, and she was left with only the uncomfortable weightiness of the frame itself.

"It's very nice," she said, "but it would look a little strange hanging on the wall without a picture inside it, don't you think?"

Stella shrugged. "I've never had anything on my wall."

"Then you should have something. Oh, I know. The draperies will have to be cut down to the size of the window. We'll put some of that velvet in the frame. Later, if you want, we'll see about getting a real picture."

The child beamed. Kate's heart turned to mush.

"Now, let's see about having everything cleaned and ready for use. We'll need help bringing in the furniture I want. But we'll get it. When we're done, if you really help, I'll show you a special treat."

Over the next few days, when she wasn't in the fields or turning the dirt in the vegetable garden, Bianca helped Kate wash and scrub and carry furniture from the hut to the small room. Michelangelo—from Bianca she learned his name was Salvatore—helped with the latter, and Kate was saved from having to go inside.

Bianca proved a superior seamstress, and the draperies and framed swatch of cloth were soon in place, much to Stella's delight.

The only things regretful about the entire proceedings were the way Bianca kept shaking her head, unable to believe a contessa could behave in such a way, and the disapproving stares she got from Alfiero. She ignored them both, grateful that Stefano Braggio did not return to add his disapproval to that of the others.

And, of course, there was the picture frame, which continued to trouble her. Alfiero claimed he knew nothing about it. She did not bother to ask Maria, having decided that the woman's powers of seeing were no more than circumstances and talk.

Always, at the back of her mind, was the image of Robert as she had last seen him, angry with her, with himself. But why? Because she could not bear a child?

During the day she could not bring that image to the fore. At night it came to her, when her defenses were at their weakest, when she could go over all their times together, each memory twisting in her mind until she thought she would go mad.

Thank goodness for the day. When the room was finished, she showed Stella the special treat she had promised. First they gathered a bucket of rocks from the soil behind the terrace, then she led the child to the villa's east wing, having first explored all the rooms without finding a single uninvited ghost.

Passing through one of the rooms, they emerged into the courtyard, with its dolphin fountain identical to the one in the village.

"We can practice tossing rocks," she said to the

smiling child. "If you have friends in town, maybe they can join you sometime. This can be your own special playground."

Stella's grin was the only thanks she needed.

But the visit from friends was not to be.

The next day started innocently enough, with Kate trying her hand at pruning the few rose plants that had survived and Bianca having returned to the vegetable garden. At her mother's request, Stella worked beside her. Kate heard her laughter from time to time. Then came a squeal.

"Contessa Donati, come and look."

Throwing down her clippers, she hurried down to see what had thrilled the child. In a corner of the stone wall, beneath some thick brush at the far edge of the garden, Stella had uncovered a nest of baby rabbits, three of them, little more than furry brown balls of softness.

"Don't touch them," Bianca ordered. "The mother will return and find your scent on them. She will have nothing to do with them."

But the warning came too late. Stella was already cuddling one of the babies next to her cheek. With a shrug, Bianca turned her back on her daughter and took up her hoe once again.

Kate was halfway across the garden, ignorant of any danger, when she heard the rustle of wings. She looked up to see the falcon in full swoop, talons spread as it dropped from the sky, its aim for the garden, for the rabbit, for the child.

Stella saw the danger. She stood transfixed, the rabbit clutched tightly to her breast.

With a scream, Kate ran across the furrows. From the corner of her eye she saw the blurred figure of a man. He shouted, but she could not make out the warning. In her terror, she was beyond comprehension. Under the shadow of the rapidly descending raptor, she threw herself on top of Stella and waited for the claws.

Chapter Eighteen

Everything happened in an instant, a deafening roar, a woman's scream, Kate hitting the ground with Stella cushioned against her. Worst was the wait, the horrible wait, for the beak, the claws, the attack of the predator bird.

She felt nothing but the trembling of the child, then strong hands lifting her to her feet. Slowly, the breath knocked from her, she comprehended that the danger had passed. Bianca took her sobbing daughter into her arms, raining kisses on her face, frantic mother's hands searching her for injury.

Kate's comfort came from Robert. Enfolding her, he held her against his chest until her trembling stopped. She struggled to breathe, to stop the roar and the panic, her heart pounding until she thought it might shatter.

"Don't cry, Mama. The rabbit's all right."

Stella's soft, reassuring voice penetrated the terror. Kate's legs collapsed beneath her. Only Robert's embrace gave her the strength to remain upright.

She clung to his arms, his muscles taut and hard beneath the rough texture of his shirt. She managed to look up at him. His face was gaunt, cheeks dark and unshaven, lines of tension carved beside the stark black eyes and tightly held mouth. He had never looked more beautiful. She wanted to smooth the lines with a kiss.

"You were here," she said, having enough presence of mind to use Italian. She spoke as if his arrival was the most amazing thing that had occurred.

"I was here."

What a wonderfully deep, rich voice he had, the most reassuring voice in the world. Just the sound of it eased her breathing and eased her heart. It also cleared her mind.

"You had a gun."

"I've been carrying one lately."

An absurd thought occurred: Was the gun to fend off her amorous approaches? She held back a laugh; it would have been closer to hysteria.

When she could focus her attention beyond him,

she looked around for traces of the falcon.

Robert read her mind.

"I fired a warning shot. He's gone."

"Gone. Not dead."

"No, not dead."

This time she did manage a smile.

"Good. I don't think I can take any more bad luck."

"You risked your life for the child."

He embarrassed her.

"It wasn't anything I thought about."

"You wouldn't have to."

For a moment, with his lips hovering close to hers, his eyes still lit by a lingering fury, she thought he was going to kiss her. Then something—a thought, a remembrance—took hold of him, and she could feel the urge pass, like heat from a dying fire.

"Are you all right?" he asked. "Can you stand on your own?"

"I'm all right." But she wasn't. She wanted him to go on holding her, letting her share his strength.

He took her by the shoulders and held her far enough away so that he might look into her eyes.

"I'm having a hard time letting you go."

Then don't.

Instead: "I had the breath knocked out of me for a few seconds, but I'm all right."

He dropped his hands. She turned from him to

look at Bianca, still kneeling and holding her daughter.

"I didn't know falcons would attack a human like that." Kate's voice broke, but she went on. "The rabbit, yes. But not the child."

"It was . . . unusual."

"La maledetta," she said, little above a whisper. "The curse. It's supposed to affect only the family, isn't it?" She rubbed her arms. "I guess no one should get close to me."

"I don't believe in curses."

One simple statement and he forced her back to the way things really were between them, not gentle, supportive, comforting, but something else entirely different. She looked at him, stared into his unrevealing eyes. Was he thinking about the hut? Was he still convinced she might be carrying his child? Was the possibility still terrible for him?

Hurriedly she looked away to hide the pain, not being nearly so good as he at hiding her feelings.

"Neither did I," she said. "Especially this one. But that was a lifetime ago, before I felt its power."

Whatever he was going to say was lost in excited chatter as Salvatore and Carlos, once familiar to her as Michelangelo and Leonardo, came running through the gate.

"The gunshot," Salvatore said. "What is wrong?" He looked at the mother and child with far more warmth than came from friendly concern.

"The falcon," Carlos threw in. "We saw him descend, then flap away." He glanced toward the distant hills. "It is the curse."

"Si," Salvatore said and went to kneel beside Bianca.

"Maybe not," Robert said. "But it would be best, Salvatore, if you escort the woman and child to the villa. They will want to rest."

He did not have to tell the man twice.

It took a brief discussion with Stella to convince her that at least for the time being the rabbit would be better left behind with the two others. With Carlos trailing close behind, they slowly made their way out of the garden, moving in the direction of the terrace, leaving Robert and Kate standing atop the loose soil Bianca had recently turned. Overhead the sky was a brilliant blue, free of clouds and raptors.

She stepped away from him and nervously smoothed back her hair. Being alone in his presence was not the pleasure it once had been.

"It all happened so fast," she said. "One minute the child called out, then the attack. Who would have thought such a thing could happen?"

"Under normal circumstances, I do not believe it would."

"Tell me, Robert, what are normal circumstances? I no longer know."

But he did not hear her, his attention turned to

the nest beneath the thick brush in the corner of the garden. He went to investigate. She watched his long stride, then hurried after, stepping around the long-barreled gun he had dropped to the ground.

Kneeling, he picked up one of the rabbits from a hollowed out space beneath the brush, holding the vulnerable animal tenderly, the way he held the young shoots of tree and vine.

The tenderness did not go unnoticed. Kate smiled. "Bianca said the mother will not care for them now that a human has touched them."

"A human touched these animals long before the child."

"What are you talking about? Who?"

"A good question, Caterina. Who?"

Settling the bundle of fur in the cavity beside the others, he stood. "They'll be all right where they are for now, but Bianca is right. They will have to be cared for."

"Away from here." Kate shuddered. "The falcon might return."

"A corner of the terrace. A box filled with straw. That should be protection enough."

"And food and water. I'm certain Stella can be convinced to take over for the absent mother."

That seemed to settle the issue of the rabbits. Yet the matter was nowhere near over.

"Who touched them, Robert? What is going on?"

"You have a right to know. This is no natural nest. No mother would place them close to where people worked. These animals were purposely moved here."

A cold realization took hold of her. "Like bait. For the falcon."

She looked at him for confirmation, but the enigmatic expression he had perfected returned to his eyes.

"Go inside, Kate. Get Salvatore to set up the nest."

"What are you going to do?"

"We will talk later."

He dismissed her far too easily.

"Will we? What about? I'm stupid, remember. I haven't figured out what is going on. Are you going to tell me?"

"You are not stupid. Never that. Your problem is your goodness. It keeps getting in your way."

He touched her cheek, then dropped his hand as though she burned him.

"Inside," he said. "Go there now. It is the only place you are safe."

Scooping up the gun, he made for the back gate at the opposite edge of the garden. She didn't watch him. She had done that the last time he walked away from her.

Neither would she do as he ordered. She had business in the village, specifically at the Belmare inn, business far too important for a cowardly retreat to the sanctuary of her room.

She took a moment to look at the cowering rabbits. She must not be like them, weak, dependent, afraid. She loved Robert with all her heart. Because of that love, and despite it, there was something she had to do.

Inside the villa, in the large room off the entryway that had once been used to welcome guests, the workers, the mother and Kate all settled their attention on the child. She proved easily distracted from the near tragedy by plans for the rabbit nest on the terrace, bombarding the two men with questions about when the nest could be set up, what food she could put out and what she should put the water in.

Bianca took some convincing that the falcon would not come down to the terrace to threaten her daughter again, not if a protective shelter was erected over the nest. The gunshot, Kate assured her, had probably frightened the bird all the way to Florence.

"You came here despite many doubts whether helping me was good or bad. I cannot ever again let you doubt that decision, Bianca."

"Please, Contessa Donati, do not add to my

guilt." The mother's round, dark eyes filled with tears. "I came to the Villa Falcone for my own purposes. I needed work and a chance to care for *mia figlia*. I tried to forget I was helping you as well. But you risked your own safety for the safety of Stella. This I will tell to all who hate the Donatis."

It was a long speech for the woman, and she turned from Kate in embarrassment. Salvatore quickly moved to her side and wrapped a supporting arm around her shoulders. At the same moment Alfiero and Maria entered the room with trays of food and drink, the former straight-backed and formal, as if he served the grand duke, the latter setting her tray down and retreating as quickly as she had entered.

She's guilty of something, Kate thought, then brushed the thought aside. Too many unfortunate occurrences were making her suspect anything and anyone as sources of her troubles.

When mother and child were settled and the two men put to work, Kate changed from work clothes into a black mourning gown, thrust her hair ruthlessly into a back knot, slammed on the dowdiest bonnet she could find and practically ran down the side path to the village, the narrow way Robert had shown her. He would not be pleased she was using it today.

Too bad.

She passed no one, saw no one, not until she

arrived at the village. As she hurried through the twisting hillside streets, making her way to the piazza, she got the stares she expected and the curious glances. She also got the silence.

Stefano Braggio was sitting at one of the tables outside the inn, coolly handsome and clean shaven, sipping a glass of grappa. He stood at her approach, nothing in his demeanor suggesting the fervor he had shown when last they met. Kate might have believed she'd dreamed his proposal, except the memory was far too keen.

As was the threat to kill Robert.

"I'll take one of those," she said as she took a chair beside him and gestured for him to sit. It had become a day for fulfilling promises made to herself. Dealing with Stefano headed the list.

He started to protest, then signaled to the waiter to bring two more glasses of the potent liqueur. Neither spoke until she had taken her first sip. It burned, it choked, it brought tears to her eyes. The second went down smoother.

"I've come to give you a final answer," she said when she could get the words out.

"This is too soon," he said, still calm. "We spoke only yesterday."

"I do not wish to give you false hope. I cannot marry you, Stefano, though you honor me by the offer. No other man is involved in this matter." She turned to the lie she had worked out in advance, the best kind, one mixed with the truth. "Yesterday you saw me under great distress. I had just come from the small trysting place used by my husband and his father and countless Donati men before them."

When she thought about the hut and all that had taken place within its walls, the break in her voice came naturally. "Pietro took servant girls there while his bride slept alone."

Stefano's eyes narrowed. She sipped at the grappa.

"I did not think the dalliances of Conte Donati brought you pain."

"I am very good at hiding what I feel. My pride and my heart were both injured. It is true Pietro and I did not love one another, but I had hopes that through the years affection between us would grow."

"You wound me, Caterina."

She looked gratefully at the grappa and spoke another lie, this one purer in its falsity. "It is my greatest regret in all of this."

When she looked up at him, his expression was as bland as if she had commented on the weather. Why did she get the feeling he was seething inside?

And why was she regretting her lies? She knew the answer; they did not come easily to her. In addition to explaining her disheveled appearance when she came up on the terrace and drawing his ire away from Robert, she had also been trying to spare her agent's feelings. Somehow she had done the opposite.

She started to touch his hand, then remembered the way he'd behaved less than twenty-four hours before. The agent was a volatile man. Who among the male gender was not?

"I am sorry, Stefano, truly sorry that I have offended you. I never encouraged or expected your affection. I came to the Villa Falcone intending to live a solitary life, and that is what I shall do. I hope for your continued support. I will need it in the future, no matter how my endeavors in the fields work out."

When she stood, she realized others were watching, villagers, both men and women, not many, most of them scattered about the two stalls that flanked the piazza. But their number was enough to unnerve her all the more. If only they could be friendly stares that followed her. She was not so strong that she could forever ignore the distance separating her from the people she wished to help, the people she needed to help her.

Whether it was the grappa that made her dizzy or the sense of isolation in the midst of people, she did not know. She steadied herself, nodded a goodbye and headed out toward what she thought was the path that had brought her to the village. She had gone no more than a quarter mile before realizing she had thought wrong.

Disoriented—she really ought to have chosen coffee to drink—she took one turn and another. The village was small. How could she have gotten so lost?

The sound of angry voices coming from around the corner of a shuttered house brought her to a halt. She recognized the man immediately, and suspected who the woman might be. Peering around the corner, she saw Robert standing in the street, in low and heated conversation with the woman who had warned her on the trail about her association with him. The woman's hand rested on his arm, the look in her dark eyes one of anger, defiance and undeniable passion.

He made no attempt to move the hand. Instead, he looked down at the black-haired beauty with equal anger. And yes, with passion, though not of the loving kind.

So intent were they in their argument, they did not see her. Hastily she ducked back behind the stucco wall, heart pounding, stomach knotted. She ought to run, or announce herself. Honor dictated one or the other. But honor had fled. She could not move.

The heated Italian came at her in spurts. She caught only isolated phrases. Clearly Robert was angry at the woman for something she had done.

Something she just as vehemently denied. Kate also gleaned the woman's name: Elena. Robert used it more than once.

He was supposed to know no one in the village. Or so he had told her. But he knew the beautiful Elena. From the touch of her hand on his arm, from the fiery light in their matching black eyes, he knew her well.

Kate stumbled backward, covering her mouth to stifle a cry. No longer did she wish to hear anything that was said, nor see what passed between the two of them.

At last silence. The woman Elena passed the corner and continued on down the passageway. Without thinking, not knowing her own purpose, Kate hurried after her, looking back up the street without seeing a sign of Robert. Elena turned a corner and for a moment disappeared. Kate quickened her step, followed, and almost stumbled into the woman, who stood in the middle of the street, waiting, her eyes as fiery as ever.

"Contessa Donati, we meet again."

"Who are you?" Kate asked, little trying to keep the anguish from her voice.

"Elena Sacchi. The name has little importance to the contessa."

"But who are you?"

Elena's eyes took on a wily cast. "Who am I to

Roberto, is that not what the contessa means? Ask yourself who are you to Roberto."

"I know who I am," Kate said, hating herself for responding. "He and I are in business together."

"If this is what you believe, you lie to yourself. No woman can know him and not fall under his spell. I warned you once to beware of him. You did not heed my words. I make them stronger now. Roberto Vela—is this not what he calls himself?— is the true curse of the Donatis. He will be your doom."

"You make no sense. Who is he? Who are you?"

"These are questions you must answer for yourself. A toiler in the fields, he says, a peasant, and so he is. But he is much, much more. When you learn this, you will also learn all that you need to know about me."

She turned to leave, then paused for one last taunt.

"Ask him about Lucia Torelli. Ask him about the grotto. It is there you will find his secrets. It is there you will learn his true identity."

Chapter Nineteen

Kate began to move down the narrow, slanted passageway, her feet moving without direction, stepping carelessly, almost shuffling, as if they were no part of her. She was vaguely aware of villagers standing on the crossing streets, of open windows where occasionally a woman or a child stared out.

If the stares were kinder than they had been on her first few journeys through Belmare, she did not notice. And she did not care. Without willing herself to do so, she moved closer to the sea, coming at last to the narrow, rocky beach that marked the coastline of the small town. Empty fishing boats, anchored offshore, bobbed in the gentle waves, the sea's shining surface glossed by the light of the afternoon sun.

It wasn't until she was scrambling over huge

boulders at the base of an almost perpendicular cliff that she realized her destination: the grotto, the place where Elena Sacchi claimed she would find the truth.

No more than fifty yards from where the beach gave way to the line of tumbled boulders, she found the entrance to the watery cave. From her vantage point it looked like a gaping hole in the cliff, as if an ancient god had thrust his angry fist into the impenetrable rock, giving the sea access into the land itself.

Stepping carefully over the wet rocks, she moved inexorably toward the opening. The bright sun lit the interior, revealing the narrow ledge on one side of the grotto, a ledge that widened to the mossy surface where she and Robert had first made love.

She paused before entering. Except for the pounding of the waves and the cry of a low-flying sea bird, all was quiet. Then from far out on the water came the sound of distant thunder, like a roll of drums heralding her approach.

"Hello," she called out, feeling foolish as she did so. The only answer was the echo of her voice. A half-dozen steps inside and she heard the drip of water coming from the inky darkness where sunlight could not penetrate.

Reason and sensibility told her to leave. The Kate Cartwright who had first sailed to Italy would have done so. But not Kate Donati, the woman she had become. The new Kate's insistent heart forced her inside.

Why the insistence? She did not know, any more than she could ignore it.

What truths could rock and water possibly hold? What secrets should she have realized long ago? The only truth she understood was that Robert was slipping away from her. The pain was both bitter and absurd. He had never been hers, not even when their bodies were joined.

As the ledge beside the lapping water grew wider and the ceiling vaulted higher overhead, the light grew dim. Spying a lantern on the wall, she put it to use. Its light shaped a path into the void. She took one step and then another, her black gown of mourning heavy against her skin. Taking off the constricting bonnet, she tossed it aside and brushed tendrils of sweat-dampened hair from her face.

Her lungs tightened and she knew an unreasoning fear. Should she, like Robert, be carrying a weapon? The pistol she had found in her husband's wardrobe, the pistol she had carried the night she fell into Robert's arms, was now secured in a cabinet of the villa's *soggiorno*.

No gun would help her now. Only courage and a clear mind would serve. She had neither. Still, she moved away from the open sea and sky, each step taking her farther into a darkness so deep it swallowed the feeble lantern light. The sea had eaten twenty yards into the granite cliff, hollowing out the grotto.

Beyond the water's end lay a high, wide room, its walls slick with dripping moisture, its floor rough and equally damp. A few feet into the room she found a mattress and a blanket, and nearby the signs of a recent fire. She felt as if she had come uninvited upon someone's bedchamber.

Beyond the mattress she saw stacks of crates, tumbled one on the other much like the boulders along the Tuscan shore. Robert had told her the Donatis once stored the harvest from the vineyard within the grotto. Here was evidence he had spoken the truth.

But this could not be the truth Elena Sacchi had meant. The one Robert had wanted her to know. Perhaps she had missed something as she walked inside. The alcove with its steps to the surface, for certain. She had purposely not looked for it. The memory of her fall, and the terror, remained all too clear.

Confused, she turned to retrace her steps. Robert blocked her path.

"Oh," she cried. She pressed a hand against her pounding heart. "I didn't hear you."

"What are you doing here?"

They were not words of welcome, not the words of a man who came to soothe.

She lifted the lantern until the light fell on the hard lines of his face. His hair was ruffled, as if he had raked it with his hands a hundred times, and his bristled cheeks were sunken, altering the perfection she had always seen in him to something more human, more flawed and, yes, despite his harshness, more endearing.

Even as the warmth of love flooded through her, she felt another sensation, a tremor of fear. She had thought him formidable before, forbidding, but she'd seen nothing like the power of him now, this tall, strong man with the looks of a god and the sharpness of a devil in his eyes.

How dare he look so threatening? How dare he frighten her out of her wits?

"One of these days, Robert, you are going to greet me with a smile and a pleasant hello."

Turning from him, she waved the lantern toward the mattress and the dead fire. "What's all this? Have I found something I'm not supposed to?"

"I told you to stay at the villa."

It was not an answer. "So you did." Her moment of courage gave birth to another. "You really ought to try asking, Robert. And then explain why you are making the request."

His jaw tightened. His anger was a wall of heat.

He waved an impatient hand. "We don't have time for this—"

But she could not stop, not with her mind filled by the image of him and Elena Sacchi arguing in the village street, the woman's hand possessively on his arm.

"You really do not know how to talk to women, do you? We don't always have to be ordered about."

His demeanor altered, softening, as if he saw the irony of what she said.

"My failure is something you have shown me more than you can know."

"An admission I've done something right?"

More alteration, more softening. He did not move, yet she felt him reach out to her.

"You've done everything right. Except take care of yourself. You do not understand how fortunate you've been."

She almost laughed. Of all the words she might use to describe herself, fortunate was not among them.

"Danger," he added, "has been hovering over you since you arrived."

Danger struck the first time I saw you. But she knew his power over her was not what he meant. Despite the humid heat that pressed in on her, she shivered.

"What danger? Is this the something I'm supposed to understand?"

"Soon, Kate, I promise soon." This time he truly did reach for her, as if he would take her arm and guide her away from the grotto.

He was temptation. But too much had passed between them, and too little. She would have none of his help.

"You sleep here, don't you? The mattress, the fire. It's how you're able to get to the field so early."

The shuttered look was back in place, masking his eyes, his thoughts, as he withdrew from her.

"It was convenient."

"But uncomfortable. And dangerous, as you have been so quick to point out to me. I could have found a place for you at the villa."

"Yes, you could have found a place. If it worries you, I did not stay here every night."

She saw him in Elena Sacchi's arms, the two of them naked, lying on rumpled sheets stained with the evidence of his passion. The image carved itself into her mind.

She regarded him coolly, at a price he would never know.

"Sleep where you will. Here, if that is what you prefer. I give you permission."

That got him. His watchful eyes became those of a wolf in its lair, protective of its territory, alert to signs of weakness in its prey. But she was too lost in her own anger and pain to take heed of whatever possessed him.

"Permission?" he asked. His matching coolness should have warned her. It did not.

She waved the lantern. "An argument could be made that this is part of my inheritance. The crates at the back certainly belonged to the Donati family."

"Ah, yes, the Donati family." She could see the control evaporate from him, like moisture consumed by fire. "Everything has always belonged to them . . . the land, the wine, life itself and even death."

He spoke in a voice she had never heard, a thick rasp that came from his soul, as if the torment she had once seen in his eyes forced itself from his secret places into his words. Fear rolled through her, not for herself but for him.

He grabbed her shoulders and pulled her close. The lantern clattered to the damp rock floor. The light flickered, then held steady, drifting upward to cast shadows across his chiseled face. She wondered how she could ever have thought him soft.

"But not you, Caterina. Pietro never owned you, did he? You are mine."

Heaven help her, he spoke the truth.

"And what about you? Are you mine? Tell me the truth. It's long past time."

His eyes heated with anguish.

"It was not supposed to be this way. I did not mean to love you."

Her heart lurched.

"Do you? Is that what you're telling me now?"

His answer was to slant his lips across hers. "You have torn my world apart," he whispered into her parted lips.

"Is that so bad?" she managed in return, her pulse pounding with such ferocity, she could barely get out the words.

His answer was another kiss, this one long and deep. She felt its power in her blood, her marrow, her heart.

He broke the kiss to cup her face. "This is all I ever want to do. All I can think about." His hands left her face to trail down her throat and find her breasts, hard-tipped and full and waiting. "I think about these, too, Kate. How they feel and how they taste."

He spoke with a new intensity. Against all reason, she allowed hope to soar. Her questions, her quest in entering this unholy place melted under the heat of the molten hunger that began to flow through her, the familiar need for him that grew stronger each time he took her in his arms.

His hands moved on, to her waist, her hips, her buttocks, the urgency of his exploration searing through the folds of her skirt. When he held her tight against him, she understood how much his hunger matched her own.

Her body throbbed in deep places. Her fingers found his bristled cheeks, their rough texture as manly as his muscled arms, his sculpted chest, his long, strong legs. She wrapped her arms around his neck and kissed him as he had kissed her.

Surely he knew how she felt. Surely he knew she would not give him her body with such abandon without also giving him her heart. And if he truly did not know, if he did not understand—or worse, did not care—then she would have to live with that realization. He was her opiate. She could not give him up.

Suddenly all the misunderstandings between them, the secrets, the evasions became too much. If she had found strength and purpose here in this beautiful land, she had also found the need for honesty. She broke the kiss, but before she could reveal her own truth, he wrapped her in his arms and held her close.

"*Dio mio*, what am I doing?"

His were not the words of love she wanted. Her own declaration died in her throat. Stunned though she was, she struggled for a new kind of strength, a different kind of honesty.

"You are fondling me and kissing me," she said, wishing her voice were stronger. "Is there something else I'm not aware of?"

He eased her away from him. She expected anger. Instead, she saw understanding. It was the first time she had seen such a thing in his expression. It robbed her of breath.

"Are you trying to be brittle?" he asked, almost tenderly. "You don't do it very well."

He confused her. "I'm not trying to be anything. Other than what I am."

He rubbed a shaking hand over his face. "I wish to God I could say the same. You deserve better than this, Kate . . . Caterina. I never know which name to use. They are both so beautiful."

"Robert . . . Roberto. Or do you have another name?"

"*Stronzo.* Fool. I risk your life for a moment's stolen pleasure."

"Only a moment?" she asked, bitterly aware that his answer had been another evasion. "It's a good thing you told me. I might have thought you wanted more."

She could not wait for a response. Whatever he said would be no response at all.

Giving him a wide berth, she hurried toward the light at the entrance to the grotto. Dark clouds had begun to form against the horizon, and when she emerged into the open air a cool breeze brushed against her cheek. He took a moment to join her. Her eye was drawn to the pistol he carried in his hand.

Her heart froze. "What's going on?"

He thrust the weapon inside his shirt, anchoring it at his waistband.

"I told you, Kate, your life is in danger."

"Who threatens me? Don't I have a right to know?"

"I'm not certain of the answer. It's time I found out."

In the same way she had heard the whispers of the villa walls and the swish of dancing ghosts, she suddenly heard the explosion of a gun, saw its fire, smelled her lover's spilled blood, even as she cursed her imagination. In an instant she cared not about the truth, but only about Robert's safety.

She reached for him. "No," she said. "No. It's not important. I don't care."

He took her hand and held it tight.

"My life, Caterina, has been spent doing what I had to do. Today is no different. Tomorrow, if there is a tomorrow, perhaps the two of us can do as we wish."

They made the journey to the villa by horseback, riding up the trail that led to the back gate. Neither spoke. They had said so much, yet revealed so little, that Kate gave up on words.

He took her to the terrace but as always refused to come inside. A makeshift shelter had been erected in one corner, and as she stood at the bottom of the steps, Stella came outside slowly, balancing a shallow pan of water in her hands as she eased through the door, her mother close behind.

When the child saw Kate, she stopped. "The rabbits are thirsty," she explained with all the seriousness of a surgeon, then continued toward the shelter.

"They're lucky to have you as their caretaker," Kate said, and would have gone on except that she saw Bianca staring at Robert, as if she could not believe what she saw.

What now? Kate thought. Another terrible surprise? Did these two know each other as he and Elena did? The thought was alarming, but it did not last. There was nothing of passion in the mother's expression, only surprise. As if she felt Kate's eyes on her, she looked away and bent to help her daughter.

Kate had little time to speculate. The housekeeper Maria chose that moment to walk onto the terrace. One look at Robert and she came to a halt. The air was electric with more than the hint of a coming storm.

Robert had not given Bianca more than a glance, but he stared at the housekeeper, this time the surprise in *his* eyes.

"I should have known you would be here," he said.

"When I sensed you had returned, I had no choice."

A look of deep feeling passed between the two, so strong that Kate, reduced to onlooker, felt embarrassed to watch. More than embarrassed; she felt lost. What were these two to one another? Not lovers; it was not that kind of look. But something deep, something from long ago, something that had been kept from her.

The terrace's stone floor moved under her. Somehow she remained erect.

Robert's focus shifted to her.

"I promise to return and tell you what I should have told you in the beginning. In the meantime, you must promise me something. You must promise to stay here until that return."

"Where are you going?"

"I'm not sure." And then more harshly: "You haven't promised."

"You give me no choice."

She knew it was not what he wanted her to say, but before he could argue, Salvatore and Carlos came hurrying across the garden. Her face drained of color when she saw the gun in Salvatore's hand, the long-barreled weapon Robert had used to frighten the falcon away from the child. She could scarcely believe the scene had taken place only hours before.

"Is it time, Roberto?" Salvatore asked.

Robert removed the pistol from his waistband. "It is time."

"Then we are with you."

Carlos nodded in agreement.

They spoke as men do when they have business that does not involve what they consider the gentler sex. Kate fumed, even as she grew more terrified, feeling as far from gentle as she could get. But there was little she could do except welcome the warm promise in Robert's eyes as he gave her a final glance.

Without ceremony or further good-byes, the men were gone, leaving the women and the child. All but Kate hurried inside, as if separating themselves from the worry that came from not knowing what was happening. She would have liked to ask the two women about their strange reactions to seeing Robert. Later, when her heart quit pounding so wildly, she would think.

For now, she could do little but stand beside the balustrade, leaning against one of the statues of prancing boys, stricken with terror at what awaited Roberto, certain the stone image was laughing down at her.

Chapter Twenty

Jagged lightning lit the black clouds moving in from the sea. Within seconds thunder rolled over the Villa Falcone.

"Contessa Donati, the storm approaches."

Kate had not heard Alfiero's approach, but she was not surprised by his presence. Dear man, he could not hide his concern. But she could not leave the terrace, could not move from the place where she had last seen Robert.

A cold wind sculpted her gown against her body and whipped at her unbound hair, as if nature herself would blow Kate back to safety. She didn't want to be safe. She wanted to stay where she could see Robert walking across the dirt beds that once held riotous roses.

The few remaining plants bore only thorns. She

vowed after Robert returned she would make them bloom again.

"I'll come in shortly," she said without looking at Alfiero.

"The storm has brought evil to the villa."

Never had she heard him say such a thing, never heard such gravity in his voice. She glanced over her shoulder at him. In his far-too-formal suit of black he looked his old, bent self, ever ready to serve, but there was a new intensity lighting his faded eyes.

"Evil has been here since the moment I arrived," she said. "Is that not so?"

"I tried to warn you." He lowered his eyes as if to soften the rebuke. "Though it was not my place."

She shifted her attention from him to the distant fields on which she had toiled for so many weeks, fields invisible in the growing dark.

"There have been good times, too. This is my home. It is the only home I have. It has become the only home I want."

Even as she said the words, she felt a tightness in her stomach. On this late afternoon the villa and its grounds were not quite so fine as they had been yesterday, nor so comforting.

More lightning. More thunder. Alfiero moved to the door leading into the villa's entryway and held it open, a sentinel waiting for his charge to pass through.

He would not relent. It was her burden to find this trait of stubbornness in every man who affected her life. A few splats of rain darkened the stone surfaces around her. She turned to go inside, first making certain the protective canvas provided adequate shelter for the rabbits. Stella would ask about them when she came from her room, where her mother had taken her.

Kate was at the threshold when she heard a cry from the garden. She turned to see a hooded, cloaked figure hurrying up the terrace steps. As the figure grew close, the hood flew back and she recognized Elena Sacchi. Her cloak flapped in the wind, and her hair blew as wild as Kate's, black as the sky where Kate's was fair as the absent sun.

She halted halfway across the terrace. Kate took a deep breath, preparing herself for more bad news. The air was thick and smelled of the elements, promising the evil Alfiero had warned about.

To her surprise, he stepped between the two women.

"Get out of my way, *stronzo,*" Elena hissed.

"Leave," Alfiero said. "You are not wanted here."

Elena shoved the bent old man. Kate watched in horror as he stumbled backward. She caught him, then without thinking turned on his attacker.

Elena raised a hand, her nails long and sharp,

and brought them down to rake Kate's face.

But Kate had grown strong. She grabbed the woman's wrist. Never had she raised her hand to another human being. She did so now, twisting Elena's arm behind her and jerking upward until she heard a howl of pain.

Strong as she was, she was not used to such fighting. Just when she thought she had tamed the woman, Elena dug an elbow into her stomach and pulled free.

With a feral growl, she grabbed for Kate.

"Alto!"

The shouted order to stop came from inside the door, from the housekeeper Maria, who stood in the interior shadows. To Kate's amazement, Elena backed away, her wild eyes shifting to the housekeeper. Kate got a good look at the younger woman's face, twisted in fury, and saw madness.

Like the lightning, another truth struck. Here was the person who had led her on the late-night chase that culminated in her fall down the entrance to the grotto.

"Leave me be," Elena hissed. "It is time I did what must be done."

"No," said Maria, calm where the younger woman seethed. "You will not possess him this way."

. "I am finished doing what you wish. And you are

322

wrong. Already I possess him. He is in my blood and I am in his."

Elena's eyes grew wilder as she spoke, her voice piercing above the howling wind. With her black cape swirling and billowing, her black hair whipping in grotesque disarray, she seemed a banshee, come to warn of imminent death.

But it was not death in the usual sense. She cried of a death that would kill Kate's soul.

Fighting a growing panic, Kate called on all the training of her life. On this turbulent evening the toughness of her father must serve her in good stead.

"Who are you?" she said, and in a voice she cursed for its trembling, she asked the same of Maria, the woman who had lived beneath her roof these many weeks.

The women ignored her, their eyes focused on one another in a struggle she could not begin to understand.

"The portrait," said Elena. "Get it."

Maria shifted her attention to Kate, then back to Elena, as if considering which of the two she would support.

"*Si,*" she said, "for this, it is time."

"What portrait?" Kate demanded. "Time for what?"

No one answered.

All her strength, her toughness, seemed as nothing to this pair. Dread pressed in on her. The portrait, no matter its subject, would bring more pain, more testimony to a fate not of joy but of endurance.

The rain ceased, but thunder rolled overhead, even as the wind grew still. Like Kate, the world awaited what would be. In the quiet she could hear her heart.

"Let us go inside," said Alfiero, as if he spoke to his contessa and her guests about an approaching dinner. "I will get the portrait."

His calmness infected her. Gaining her own control, she felt as if she had wandered onto a stage where an unknown story played out with unrecognizable characters. And what was her part? She played the fool.

She looked at each of them. Their returning regard did not bring comfort: triumph from Elena, a seriousness close to pity from Alfiero and from Maria the enigmatic darkness she was used to when she stared into Robert's eyes.

Alfiero led the strange group into the *soggiorno,* then departed. Elena threw her cloak across a chair, revealing a skirt and low-cut blouse that accentuated her voluptuousness. She made no attempt to tame her wind-tossed hair. Instead, with hands on hips in a posture of insolence, she walked around the room, studying the faded rectangular shapes on the wall, the bare-topped tables and cabinets, the uncovered floor where once had lain expensive carpets from the Orient.

She sneered at everything she saw. "When I was a child, I dreamed of seeing this room." A grunt of disgust came from her throat. "I should have had better dreams."

It was the insolence more than any threats or claims that angered Kate. This was her home, her place of refuge. If it was to remain such, she could not allow it to be attacked.

She blocked Elena's path. "You once summoned me from the villa and led me to the entrance to the grotto. You tried to bring me harm."

Elena threw back her head in defiance. "I tried to bring you the truth. But you were too—"

"Basta, figlia!"

Stunned, Kate turned to Maria. "She's your daughter?" The words squeezed out of a tight throat, but they were lost in the spate of Italian the two women threw at one another.

Things were happening too fast—the arguing women, the threatening gestures, Kate trying helplessly to translate the crude, cruel epithets they threw at one another.

And then Alfiero standing in the entranceway, a scroll of canvas in his hand.

In an instant the argument between mother and daughter ceased. Elena lunged for him. "Give it to me," she rasped.

Alfiero held the scroll aloft and with one look quelled the rebellious woman. Kate had never been more proud of him.

"The portrait belongs to Contessa Donati."

Elena smirked. "So it does." She stepped aside to clear his path to Kate. But she could not hold her tongue.

"You have wondered, have you not, Contessa Donati, why Roberto returned to Tuscany. It was to claim land that was rightfully his."

"What land?" Kate asked, though she knew the answer even as she asked.

"The Villa Falcone." The name rolled smoothly off Elena's tongue. "Make no mistake: He will get it however he can. Even if he has to make love to the woman who has invaded his home. Even if"—her beautiful face twisted into a demonic smile—"he has to marry her."

Kate gripped the back of a chair. "You're lying."

She tried desperately to recall the warmth in Robert's eyes when he gave her a parting glance. Instead, she saw the turn of his back, his brusqueness, the gun in his hand.

"I warned you that he would be your doom," said Elena. "He marries you, then you die, and he is free to marry the woman he truly loves. Do you believe that on this evening he searches for someone who wishes you harm? He makes it seem that way. But he will meet with failure, or so he will say."

"No." Kate covered her ears, but Elena was not done.

"You come to harm and the blame is on your unknown enemy. After he has taken you as his wife. After he owns all that he wants. Your death leaves him free to marry the woman he truly loves. The woman he has always wanted."

Her smile of triumph said louder than words who that woman was.

Kate fought for sanity. "I don't believe you. How can he believe the villa belongs to him?"

Alfiero stepped close and placed the scrolled canvas in her shaking hand. Slowly she unfurled it, feeling the stares of everyone in the room. She looked down at the smears and dabs of paint, some of it now flaking, some poorly applied, but all of it adequate to form the features of a man.

Her heart stopped. She stared at the portrait of Pietro's father, the Conte Renaldo Donati. It was the portrait that had once hung over her husband's bed, the one that had disappeared from its frame, the frame she had found shoved behind heavy furniture amid the useless holdings crammed into one of the villa's many unoccupied rooms.

It was also a portrait of Robert Vela. The eyes, the chin, the set of the mouth—they were unmistakably his, though the portrait was of the late conte. Since the night of her marital consummation, she had carried her one glance at the portrait in the recesses of her mind.

It came back to her now in full force.

When she first saw Robert, standing among the villagers, she had thought he looked familiar, then had pushed the possibility from her mind. She should have thought on it longer.

"Roberto is a *bastardo,* is he not?" Elena said. "In many ways. He is your husband's brother, the last true heir of the Donatis, though his father did not know of him, nor would he have claimed him if he had. He waits for me now in our secret hiding place. We have been destined for one another since birth."

The woman's cruel words rolled over Kate like cutting blades. She looked to Alfiero, to Maria, for help. But there was no help for her. Elena Sacchi's words had the ring of truth. The portrait could not be denied. From the beginning, Robert had lied to her.

So much became clear. If Renaldo Donati was his father, then his mother must have been a servant in the villa. He had impregnated her in the tree-shaded hut beyond the stable, the place where Donati men took the women who were not their wives.

Within those walls Robert stared at his seed on her thighs and feared he had done the same to her, the sins of the father alive in his only surviving son. Thus had his almost-proposal of marriage been prompted. Thus his despair at her not having seen the truth of who he was.

It was a strange kind of honor he had presented. Why had he not told her himself? On this terrible evening he had sworn to do just that when he returned. But any explanation he gave would come too late.

Just as she had suspected the first time she saw him on Donati land, he was her executioner. He killed her will to live.

She turned from the stares of the others, all that she had been thinking proving too much to comprehend. A small, stubborn hope fluttered inside her. Perhaps she accused him too soon. She loved him—nothing could change that—and she must not be so quick to lose faith. She must hear from his own lips the why of all he had done. Surely, surely she would know if he spoke the truth.

Or was this latest reasoning born of desperation, without any basis in reality? She felt sick, close to losing whatever meal she had last eaten, her body limp, as if Robert's accuser had ripped her bones from her body, had shredded her muscles with words.

Deny what she could, there was no escaping one truth: Her lover was her husband's brother, in some cultures of the world her brother as well, though she doubted he had ever carried the Donati name. It was the sharpest knife of Elena Sacchi's arsenal. The pain was unbearable.

She turned to Alfiero.

"You knew who he was." Another truth stabbed at her. "You were the one who hid the portrait."

"This was my doing," said Maria.

"But he had seen it, from before if not this journey. He knew who Robert was."

Maria nodded, and at the same time Alfiero's eyes took on a great sadness. "The first time I saw him in the field," Alfiero said, "I knew."

"And you," Kate said to the housekeeper, "came to witness my destruction."

Maria did not flinch. "I came because I knew that with Roberto returning to Belmare, my daughter would do the same."

"Because they were destined for one another since birth. That was why you warned me against him, not for my well-being but for hers."

Maria did not answer. She did not have to.

For a moment the *soggiorno* was quiet. The walls creaked, but they did not speak to her. She would not have heard; the screaming in her head was too loud.

She needed to get out, away from lies and secrets and betrayal. Running from the room, she heard following footsteps. On the terrace, she turned to see the dim figure of Elena standing by the door.

The Grotto

The wind had renewed its assault, along with the rain, and the sky was dark as night, though the hour was still early evening.

"I will take you to him," the woman called out over the storm.

Behind her loomed Alfiero. She felt his will to follow as well, to stop her if he could.

"No!" she cried to them all.

"Go, then," said Elena, "and learn the truth."

Before she finished speaking, Kate had already turned and renewed her desperate flight. Within minutes rain soaked her, the drops streaming down her cheeks like tears. But she was beyond crying. Her heart had been torn from her. No simple show of emotion would suffice.

Across the muddied furrows and grassy slopes, more mud, past the gate, and she was making her way through the storm toward the thick jungle growth that lay to the west, topping the cliff that overlooked the sea.

Kate's destination was inevitable: the grated fissure that led to the grotto, the secret hiding place for two lovers who had been destined for one another since birth. The place that still held terror for her, a terror that could not keep her away.

In the dark storm that beat down on her, a force beyond her conscious mind chose her path, her steps taking her through the brush until she felt hard bars beneath the soles of her shoes.

With some difficulty she removed the grate. It was heavier than she had expected, but she had no trouble shoving it aside. The trouble came when she had to take her first step into the void.

A bolt of lightning lit the opening. In the accompanying thunder crash, she found the first ledge that formed the natural rock ladder she must descend. After the lightning, the darkness seemed all the more impenetrable, and the rain so fierce it stung her skin.

Despair had one benefit: It swallowed fear. She quickly if awkwardly scrambled into the darkness. When her feet at last found the solid rock floor of the grotto, only the echoing noise of the storm greeted her. Keeping her back pressed to the wall, she made her way to the lantern she had used once before and lit it. To her surprise and relief, the light flickered, then grew steady if not strong.

She held it aloft. Robert was not present, but she really hadn't expected him to be, despite Elena Sacchi's exultant declaration. But he would be there. She knew it, as surely as if she had the power of prescience that Maria claimed.

Ignoring the water that lapped high on the ledge, she made her way to the back of the grotto, where she gave in to exhaustion, collapsing on the mattress that sometimes served as Robert's bed. Setting the lantern aside, she sat and watched the encroaching sea.

Chapter Twenty-one

Water woke her.

She smelled it moving in, its briny damp closer than it should have been; the mattress was far removed from what was normally the edge of the sea's encroachment.

Sitting up quickly, she grew dizzy. Somehow, impossibly, she had fallen asleep. The lantern was out, the flint lost in the darkness. She sat in the dark, listening to the raging storm echoing within the rocky walls, and worse, to the lap of water, more horrifying because it could not be seen.

Kate refused to panic. Panic took time and energy, luxuries she did not have. She must concentrate on escape. Using the placement of the mattress as a point of reference, she estimated the direction and distance of the side wall. Crawling slowly, ignoring the cut of rock against her palms and knees, she moved along the course her calculations had determined, grateful she encountered no standing water.

When she reached the side of the grotto, she stood and stepped cautiously, feeling along the wall to maintain her balance, toward the alcove and the rocky set of ledges that led upward, through the tunnel to safety.

Two steps from where she had begun her slow progress she stepped into shallow water. Another two steps and the sea rose ankle deep.

Again she refused to panic. She could not begin to guess how long she had been asleep, but reason—what little she still held on to—told her the rise of the water was slow. She had time. She must move on.

When her hand met open air, she knew she had found the alcove, the steps, the tunnel. She wanted to shout with joy. She saved the shout for after the climb.

The sea-soaked hem of her skirt and her shoes felt leaden, but she could not let them hold her down. In her exhaustion she also could not risk climbing too rapidly, slipping and falling, finding herself unable to climb again. She forced herself to continue the gradual progress, sore fingers gripping each step as she lifted first one foot and then another in her agonizing ascent.

The Grotto

She dared one quick upward glance. The night sky proved as dark as the grotto, and she concentrated on letting her fingers serve as eyes.

After an eternity she felt the underside of the grate. She took a moment to lean her head against the tunnel wall and draw a deep, steadying breath. She had strength enough to push aside the heavy iron, to climb the few remaining steps and fall onto the rock-and-brush-strewn surface that topped the cliff. If she moved quickly. If she did not think too much.

She shoved at the grate, but it did not move. Again, and again the same result. Her fingers shook. She tried to thrust them through the bars, but something solid, something heavy stopped her. Frantic, she tried other openings, felt the barriers and knew them for what they were: boulders put where they could trap her inside the grotto, her only chance of escape closed to her, locking her in a tunnel that would fill as rapidly as the grotto itself when the storm floods came.

At last the panic came, raging as ferociously as the storm. She pounded against the bars, clawing at anything she could reach, shredding her fingers until the boulders became slick with blood and rain.

She screamed out for help but heard only the deluge. Her mind raced. She must not surrender. Perhaps a tool lay somewhere within the pile of broken crates, something she could use to lift the boulders and shove the grate aside. But that meant a return to the grotto, a search, and then a second climb. Impossible. She shook off her despair. Do it or die: such was her choice.

Down she went, the return trek more frantic than the ascent. She was scrambling in the backmost reaches of the grotto, shrouded in darkness, tossing aside empty, useless crates, when she heard a shout. Her imagination, she told herself. Trembling, she forced herself to hold still, though the sound and scent of unseen water tore at her senses.

Yes, a shout. It came from the top of the tunnel. She screamed in response, then stumbled through waves of the invading sea, now halfway to her knees, crying out in response, again and again, until the cries melded into a constant scream.

It was only when she was breathless that the screaming stopped. At the bottom of the tunnel she again heard the shout. Robert! Her spirit soared.

"Keep your place." His deep voice echoed down the tunnel. "I'm coming after you."

From behind her came a great crash of water. The sea had grown impatient and claimed the grotto as her own.

"I can't wait. I'm coming up."

The thought of Robert waiting for her worked like a rope pulling her to the surface. Muscles keening, fingers torn, she did not pause until she felt strong hands on her arms, pulling, tugging, lifting her through the narrow opening.

She trembled in the dark, pushing herself away from him, needing to let him know how things had been.

"I couldn't get out." At the moment it seemed the most remarkable part of the night. "Someone barred the way."

"You're safe now," Robert said.

He pulled her into his arms and held her tight. She could have stood like that forever. But she saw a light blinking through the rain and eased away from him. Alfiero stood close by, covered in a protective cloak, a lantern in his hand. Maria stood next to him in the circle of light, and behind her Elena.

Everything about the past few hours rushed in. For the first time since she'd caught sight of Robert in the village, she could not look at him. Her eyes were locked on the wildly beautiful woman who claimed to be his true love. How easy it was to believe such a passionate man could want a woman like her. Far too easy. Pietro's teaching, his denigration of his pale and scrawny wife, came back with all its terrible credibility.

"You put the rocks there, didn't you?" Kate demanded of Elena.

"Roberto moved them. He did not want such an ending. You are not yet his wife."

337

"Elena!" Robert's voice contained both warning and threat. "No more. You have done enough harm."

"Do not deny what is between us, *mi amore.*"

"Dio mio, woman, not now."

Elena tossed her head in defiance. *"Si,* now. No longer will I let you choose the time."

Robert turned from her, as if he would ignore whatever she had to say. Weak, Kate swayed and put a hand against his chest.

"No!" Elena pushed past Maria and went for her. "You cannot have him. He is mine."

Everything happened so quickly—Maria reaching out for her daughter, Robert pushing Kate aside, Elena thrown off stride as she stumbled on beyond them, regaining her balance at the edge of the open fissure.

"Stai attento!" Maria cried.

Elena gave no heed to her mother's warning. Her mad eyes were fixed on Robert.

"You must choose, Roberto. This *porca diavalo* or me."

With one step she slipped through the muddy entrance to the tunnel and fell from sight.

Maria screamed and threw herself at Robert. "Save her," she cried and pounded at his chest.

Robert took her hands to still them. Maria backed away and stared up at him, her stoic dignity returned. Unspoken words passed between them.

His eyes found Kate, the look in them suggesting much but telling nothing. He turned to Alfiero.

"Take care of her."

"No," Kate cried and ran to him. But he was quick. In the blink of an eye he dropped through the fissure and, like Elena, was gone.

"Robert!" she called out, his name echoing in the rain, but he gave no answer. She kneeled in the mud to follow. An arm circled her middle and forced her back from the fissure. She fought, but Alfiero was surprisingly strong.

Her struggles weakened into sobs. He loosened his hold and she found herself in the arms of the distraught mother.

"If you do what you wish," Maria said, "if you seek to find him, you will be lost. Roberto will expect you to be here when they return."

When they return. Somehow the words soothed. She pulled away, and the two women stood side by side, along with Alfiero, helpless as the remnants of the storm played out, waiting through the night for a reappearance that never came.

Kate stared into the *soggiorno* fire, numbed by a pain that could have no end. The possibility of Robert's duplicity, of his betrayal, no longer held importance to her. Nor did it matter that he had gone after Elena because of the bond between the two of them.

Kate would rather have seen him with a thousand other women, Elena included, than allow harm to come to him.

But that had not been his fate. Or hers.

Though she sat close to the hearth, beneath a blanket, her wet gown changed for a dry one, she felt a chill the fire could not reach. Her cleansed and doctored hands rested uselessly in her lap. They seemed no part of her. Nothing did except her leaden heart.

The light of early morning was breaking through the window when she became aware of Alfiero standing beside her chair, a tea tray in his hands.

"Maria suggested I bring you breakfast," he said.

She looked at the tray, then back to the fire as she nodded her thanks.

"How is Maria?" she asked.

"She is strong."

"Has she . . . seen anything?"

"Her special powers are useless, she says. What happens now is in God's hands."

"Tell her my prayers join with hers."

"Later, if the contessa will agree. This morning Maria does not wish to speak of what has taken place."

Kate understood. What could anyone say? They had waited hours, or so it had seemed, for Robert to emerge onto the clifftop with Elena in his arms. He had not done so and they had returned to the villa to await something equally terrifying, the death of hope.

Since their return, nothing had occurred that would slow that death.

"Do not despair, Contessa Donati. Roberto Torelli has returned from the sea once before."

"Is that his name? Torelli?"

"It was the name of his mother."

Through the fog that had descended upon her, she recalled something Elena had said.

"I was supposed to ask him about Lucia Torelli. I never did. I don't recall why." She wiped at her tired eyes with the back of her hand. "You said he had once returned from the sea."

"*Si*, Contessa. When—"

A pounding at the door stopped him. Kate's heart rose in her throat and she sat upright. "He wouldn't knock, would he?"

Alfiero was already moving swiftly from the room. She stood and tossed her blanket aside, then followed, stopping in the arched doorway between the *soggiorno* and the entryway, where she could see the villa's front doors.

He threw the doors open and Stefano Braggio stepped inside. She clutched the side of the doorway for support.

Pitching his coat and hat aside, Braggio hurried toward her. "Caterina, what is wrong?"

"Do you bring news?" Her voice was tight, squeezed from her throat.

"I came to make certain the storm brought no harm to you. Again I ask what is wrong."

Disappointment brought tears to her eyes, the first of many, she knew. She blinked them away and looked to Alfiero for help.

He did not fail her.

"Signore Vela, a partner of the contessa, has gone."

"Run away, you mean," Braggio said with a sneer.

"The contessa fears he is drowned."

"A woman is involved, is she not? Yes, I can see by the look you share that I am right." The sneer turned to satisfaction. "Dearest Caterina, I must tell you what I have learned about this Vela."

She wanted to cover her ears, to ward off accusations against a man who could not defend himself. But that would not stop Braggio.

"Whatever you have to say, I do not care to hear it. Leave. Your concern is not welcome."

The agent spied the tray and waved away her words.

"Some tea, that is what you need."

He tried to take Kate's arm. She pulled away and returned to her chair by the fire, using the blanket as a shield though her chill had given way to an uncomfortable heat.

Alfiero disappeared, then returned minutes later with a second cup. He poured, then bowed his way from the room.

Kate shot him a desperate glance, a plea for him to stay, but he did not see it. Ever the proper servant, even now, he kept his eyes lowered.

Braggio tried to hand her one of the cups of tea. She shook her head and he returned it to the tray, then proceeded to pace alongside her chair.

"After the death of Conte Donati, a fellow business agent approached me with an offer to buy the Villa Falcone."

Humor him, she thought, then send him on his way. What did she care what he said?

"You mentioned a possible sale a long while ago."

"I have learned the name of the man he represented. An Englishman by the name of Robert Vela. A very wealthy Englishman."

Hearing his name pained her, and for a moment she relived the last moment she'd seen him, standing tall in the rain, at once determined and vulnerable, his face gaunt, his haunted eyes only for her.

Somehow she rallied.

"A coincidence. That can't be Robert. He's a laborer. He works the land. You yourself scorned him for doing so."

"He has deceived us both, you most painfully, *bellissima*. Other questions were put to me by this agent. Questions about your inheritance and what would happen to the villa should you remarry."

His ramblings became too cruel. Kate could take no more. With a strength that surprised even her, she leapt to her feet, knocking over the tray and the untouched cups of tea. The porcelain shattered, and tea pooled in the floor's grouting.

"Get out," she ordered, her voice cold and harsh.

"The truth brings pain, I know," Braggio said silkily.

"Out."

Instead of retreating, he came close and put a hand on her arm. She jerked away and saw the meanness in his eyes, and more, a madness like Elena's, except that his was more controlled. She recognized it for what it was, the evil Alfiero had warned her about.

Braggio smiled. *"Per favore,* Caterina—"

"The contessa has asked you to leave."

He backed away at the interruption. Kate stared at the doorway, at the man who stood there, clothes torn and hanging loose on his tall frame, cheeks sunken and bristled, eyes piercingly strong. His right arm was caught up in a sling, the only sign of injury.

A cry of astonishment caught in her throat. Robert had returned.

Chapter Twenty-two

Braggio stumbled back from the doorway. "What are you doing here?" he rasped. "You are dead."

"You're a little slow this morning," Robert said. "I'm very much alive. And you're leaving. You heard the contessa. Out."

Kate started toward Robert, but Braggio gripped her wrist and jerked her against him.

"You told me he was dead," he hissed in her ear.

"Hurt her and I will kill you," said Robert.

Braggio stared at the sling. "No, you won't."

Robert started for him, but the agent was quick. He dragged Kate deeper into the room and bent to the floor. He came up with a jagged corner of porcelain and pressed the point against Kate's throat. Her blood roared in her ears.

"The contessa will be the one to die. It is she you will kill."

Robert's eyes hardened to obsidian. He lifted the sling a few inches. "The arm's broken. And I have no weapons. If you must hurt someone, hurt me."

"I have no intention of hurting anyone. Not if you tell the truth."

"Give up, Braggio. The man you hired to wreak havoc around here is already in the hands of the constable."

Braggio pushed the sharp point harder against Kate's throat. "You are lying."

Robert started forward, then checked himself. But his eyes were hard, and she saw the muscles working in his throat.

"Go easy with her. She's the only thing that's keeping me from you. And no, I'm not lying. I went after him yesterday. He was running, taking the trained falcon with him. But he served you well while he was here." Robert looked at Kate. "The broken step, the viper, even the rabbits, those were all his doing, most of it so he could put the falcon to use. And Salvatore, too. The attack on him, along with the destruction of the work we had done."

Kate tried to be calm. Each breath was a pain.

Braggio spat. "He is of little consequence. You do not speak of the truths the contessa needs to hear."

"I don't care, Robert," she managed.

Braggio tightened his hold on her. "Dearest Caterina, you will care more than you can imagine. Tell her, Vela. Admit you asked questions concerning her inheritance. Before you ever met."

Robert's eyes did not leave him. "I did."

"You asked about her remarriage. Tell her what you wanted to know."

"Whether she would retain title to the villa."

"Or, more to the point, would the title go to her new husband. Do you hear, Caterina?" He shook her. The porcelain bit her skin. "Answer."

She swallowed shallowly, afraid even to nod. "I hear."

She could see Robert's mind working behind his inscrutable black eyes, as if he was trying to tell her to be calm, that all would be well, the same message she was sending him.

"Did you not attempt to purchase the villa after Conte Donati's death?"

"I did," Robert said.

"But when I passed the offer on, Caterina, the poor fool, declined."

"It was a great deal of money. She surprised me." For a second he looked at her, and his eyes softened. "As she so often has."

"I didn't—"

Braggio's arm jerked against her, and her words were lost. He had not mentioned any specific offer,

Evelyn Rogers

only that he could sell her property if she let him.
It was something she would tell Robert, after she
was free.

"And why did you come to Belmare?"

"To meet the contessa. To marry her."

"It was to be your sacrifice."

Robert's jaw twitched. "So I thought."

He said things she did not want to hear. She
tried to think of other things, like the top drawer
of the bureau beside the hearth. She must pass the
message on to him.

"Only two more points, and then I am done."

Kate's heart stuttered. Done with what? The
questioning? And what then?

"First, you are the bastard son of Conte Renaldo
Donati, is that not so?"

"I am."

"As such, you have long coveted the villa."

"For as long as I can remember."

"It has been your life's dream."

The look in Robert's eyes as they shifted to her
took the sting from the weapon at her throat. "It
used to be."

"Lover's words," Braggio said contemptuously.
"How charming. But then, they should be. When
you left London, you also left a hundred broken
hearts."

"Not so many."

"But some."

"The hearts have healed by now."

"Spoken by a true Lothario."

Kate tried not to listen, tried not to take in everything that had been said. But for a moment an image of Robert among the society women of London burned in her mind. Darkly handsome Robert, wealthy Robert, strolling with the perfumed, powdered beauties of that sophisticated city. Beneath his polished veneer, he bore a hint of wildness calling out to be tamed. He would have been impossible to resist.

The bureau. She must concentrate on the bureau, on the top drawer, on the gun she had placed there after her first visit to the grotto.

Robert gave no sign he read her mind.

"Are you listening, Caterina?" Braggio bent his head to hers. "Which of us is truly worthy of you, a liar and profligate lover or a man who has devoted himself to only you?"

She felt his arm go lax. Remembering her struggle with Elena and the lesson she had learned, she dug an elbow sharply into his middle. He gasped and she whirled away, even as Robert threw himself across the room and crashed into him. The two men fell to the floor. Kate dashed to the bureau and threw open the drawer. The gun was gone.

She turned to the fight. As strong as Robert was, he had been through untold horrors the past hours. With his broken arm in a sling, he had trouble holding his own against the smaller man. They thrashed about on the broken cups and plates, bodies rolling across the spilled tea. She cried out at the pain he must be enduring.

At one point Robert rose to his knees and smashed his left fist into Braggio's face, but at the last second, freed by Robert's assault, Braggio twisted away, taking the blow against the side of his cheek. He scrambled to his feet. Robert twisted into Braggio's legs and came down once again.

Frantic, Kate darted around the men, searching for a weapon. In a room stripped of adornment by creditors, she saw nothing except the broken shards. She grabbed a wedge, razor sharp on two sides, but could not strike out, fearful of slashing the wrong man.

Robert got Braggio on his back. Like a bug, the agent flailed with fists and feet. A shoe caught Robert in the injured arm. He moaned and for a moment lost his hold. Braggio rose to his knees, caught his breath and stood.

Kate went for him, her weapon aimed at his face. He slapped her with the back of his hand. Her neck snapped and she fell away from him. He caught her by the wrist and jerked her toward the arched doorway. Robert staggered to his feet and came after them.

Suddenly the room exploded, and a bright red flower blossomed on Braggio's chest. He dropped

Kate's wrist and stared down in disbelief.

Time stopped. He looked up at her, his eyes wide and wounded, as if she had somehow hurt him. "Contessa—"

But he could say no more. He collapsed to the floor and was still.

Her head reeling from the explosion's echo, Kate looked beyond him into the entryway. She saw Alfiero, and beside him Maria, standing with arms limp at her sides, in one hand the pistol that Kate had put in the bureau for safekeeping.

Maria had eyes only for Robert.

"Elena did not return."

"No," Robert said. "I could not save her."

The mother did not flinch. "But you tried."

"A hundred times. After the water receded and carried me out of the grotto, I searched the shore."

She looked at the arm he cradled against his middle. "And the injury?"

"Waves washed me onto the rocks."

She nodded, as if what he said gave her satisfaction, and her attention turned to the man she had shot.

"I could not let him take the contessa. You have been my son. You wanted her. Elena should have understood."

She dropped the weapon. It fell with a clatter to the stone floor. Then she turned and walked away, disappearing through the door that led to the kitchen and on to her room.

Alfiero bent to inspect the fallen Braggio.

"He is dead." He looked up at his contessa. "I will attend to him."

Kate watched him remove his coat and lay it over the body. For a moment death overwhelmed her. She bowed her head, waiting until the feeling passed, then turned to Robert. Her eyes glittered up into his.

"You must let me see to that arm."

"It's not broken, only badly sprained."

"But you said—"

"I lied." He touched the small wound at her throat, so inconsequential that she had forgotten it. He leaned close and kissed it. "I love you."

Incredibly, she was able to smile. "Why do I believe you?"

"You want to. You love me, too."

She spared one last quick glance at Stefano Braggio and remembered Elena. But Robert filled her heart.

Sorrow and joy opened up within her, but it was the joy that lingered. Long ago she had journeyed to the Villa Falcone determined to stand on her own, alone. The need for self-reliance remained, and the sense of pride denied her much of her life. She would always feel that way.

But she never wanted to be alone again.

Embracing Robert, gingerly, making certain his injured arm was once again resting in its sling, she led him from the *soggiorno* and up the stairs to the privacy of her room. It was there she told him how she felt.

"I saw Pietro die."

Robert stood at the window of Kate's bedchamber, looking out on the fields where the two of them had worked so hard. He wore only the sling and a towel wrapped around his middle. It was the best she could come up with after shaving and bathing him.

Or so she had told him. She probably could have found something in one of the stored trunks. Looking at him from the bed, she knew she had made the right decision in leaving the trunks untouched.

He had let her do what she wanted. She had not hurried. He had not seemed to mind.

The constable had come and gone, and Stefano Braggio's body had been taken into town. She and Robert were both fed and rested, leaving nothing to do but make love and talk.

Robert was the one who chose talk, declaring that he still had confessions to make.

But she hadn't expected him to start out as he did.

"You'll have to say that again," was the best response she could manage.

"I left just as I told you, after the trouble with Pietro, and eventually made my home in England. It was there I heard he had come on hard times. I returned here to my homeland to buy the villa. My first night in Venice I tracked him down to a brothel, but he had already left when I got there."

"You found him on his walk home?"

Robert nodded. "He heard my footsteps. I believe he thought I was his father."

"Your father as well."

"Sometimes I almost forget that. He did not know of my existence. Until he looked at me, I hadn't realized how much I resembled Renaldo Donati. He stumbled and fell into the canal. I went in after him, but he had swallowed too much water."

As with Elena, it had been an unsuccessful attempt to prevent a drowning. The coincidence was unspoken, but she knew they were thinking the same thing.

He looked back at her. She hadn't done a very good job of shaving him and his face remained shadowed with bristles. She rather liked it that way.

"So I made the offer to you," he said. "Rather, my agent to yours."

"An offer I never got. But we've been over all this."

"Not enough. It's true I decided to marry you, if

that was the only way I could get what I wanted. I was not a good man."

"You were obsessed."

"Do not make excuses for me. I knew what I was doing. But from the moment I saw you in the carriage, taking the looks of hatred from the villagers, I knew matters would not be easy. I had heard you were a recluse, a simple American who had no business being a contessa. But I quickly learned the gossip was wrong."

"Not so wrong. I was very simple and completely out of place. I hated the title. The only thing I wanted was the land."

"And you worked to bring it back to life."

"You convinced two men to work with us when no one else would."

"They were well paid. I even gave them lodging at a small villa I bought south of the grotto."

"I keep forgetting you're wealthy. You are, aren't you?"

"Very. When I went to London, a captain under whom I had served gave me a bill of credit. I put it to good use. Does that bother you?"

"The fact that you're wealthy?" She thought it over and shook her head. "Not in the least. I'm not that simple. I also don't believe that captain gave you credit because of your seamanship. What did you do, save his life?"

Robert shrugged.

"That's what I thought," she said.

"Any other questions? Now's your chance."

"Why didn't the villagers recognize you as a Donati?"

"My father was not one to mingle with those he considered commoners. And remember, he died decades ago. Most of those who might see the resemblance have themselves died or left Belmare in search of work."

Kate sobered. "Maria called you her son."

"She raised me from birth. My mother—"

"Lucia Torelli."

Robert's eyes registered surprise.

She went on. "She was a servant in the villa, was she not?"

"A commoner."

"One who met with your father in the hut where we made love. I finally figured that out."

"That day with you was not my finest hour. And yet it was. I knew then that I loved you and could not ask you to be my wife."

"Strange reasoning."

"These are strange times."

A silence fell between them as they looked at one another. Kate forced herself to look away.

"You were talking about Maria."

"And about my entry into the world. I was born in the grotto. During a storm. My mother, disgraced and abandoned, went there when she knew

356

her time was due. Though she planned to take me with her into the sea, when the time came she could not do so. Maria found me."

"She knew you were there."

"She sees things."

"I will never doubt her again. Alfiero said she is doing all right."

"For someone who has lost her only true child. After she took me away from Belmare, she married briefly and gave birth to Elena. Right or wrong, she raised her to be my wife. No one knew I even existed, that Renaldo Donati had a second son. Not even the conte himself. No one except Maria Sacchi and then her daughter."

"Why the name Vela? Maria questioned it once, as if it was not really yours."

"I took it when I went to sea. It means sail, you know. It's mine as much as any name could be."

Kate fell silent. So much to take in, so much to think about and to feel.

And far, far too much death.

"Elena was very beautiful. She loved you very much."

"She didn't know me. We were both children when I left. She was obsessed with me. As I was obsessed with the Villa Falcone. But love has come only once to me—after I met you."

"So much you decided not to marry me."

He smiled. She could feel the atmosphere in the

room change, from a sense of loss and tragedy to something stronger, to the reemergence of hope.

"I was cruel to you, Caterina, in the grotto, the hut, too many times. I will spend the rest of my life making those times up to you."

She said nothing that would cause him to abandon the promise.

"You frightened me, did you not know?" he said. "The more I watched you—and I could do little else when you were near—you became something new to me, a promise of something good that had nothing to do with the villa."

She had to fight to keep from getting out of the bed and launching herself against him. Something told her to hold back.

"Now about that marriage." He dropped the towel. "I've changed my mind."

Kate's breath caught. It was a moment before she could speak.

"I can tell. Are you proposing?"

"Several things. But marriage most of all."

"I accept." She sat up straighter and let the covers drop to her waist, revealing her naked breasts. "The marriage, of course, but also the other things."

He gestured toward the sling. "You'll have to be in control."

"Now those, *mi amore,* are the words I've been waiting to hear." She raised a hand to hold him back. "You realize we've been speaking Italian for a long time. I guess it's our language now. The trouble is, there are some terms I don't know. The ones that have to do with making love."

"Are you asking for a lesson?"

He didn't wait for an answer. Instead, he slipped into the bed beside her and began whispering words that even in her advanced state of arousal made her blush.

It took a long while and many repetitions before she felt comfortable whispering them back to him.

Epilogue

Five years later

Kate lifted the wineglass to the light. "Good color." She twirled the glass and studied the way the wine moved down the sides. "Well-established legs. Good body."

Robert slipped up behind her and squeezed his arm around her waist.

"Ah, yes, and after two children, too."

She bent her head so that he might kiss her neck, then straightened and smoothed her skirt.

"Speaking of the children . . ."

"They've seen us like this before."

"I meant Stella and her friends."

They were standing on the terrace beside the round marble table. Close to the base of the back steps, three giggling girls ran down the rows of brilliant roses, playing a game of catch. Sitting on the top step, kicking her legs in impatience to join them, watched Lucia, the second born of the Vela children. Since she had only last week celebrated her second birthday, her cautious mother had decreed watching was all she could do for the next year.

The firstborn, Mario, who at four had not decided whether to play with girls or not, stood with his parents by the table, watching them sample the first pressing from the Donati vineyard.

"Are you going to taste it?" Robert said.

"I'm afraid to."

"Oil from the olives is excellent."

"Wine is different."

"You have become a true Italian."

The door to the villa opened, and they were joined by a very pregnant Bianca and her husband, Salvatore. His one-time working partner Carlos had moved on south to Rome with a promise to return, but he had not yet done so.

In her days of fear, Kate had wondered whether Bianca and Robert had been involved in a relationship. Only later had she found out that the woman's reaction to seeing him was because of his resemblance to his father, whom she had seen as a girl. Now her eyes were for Salvatore only.

Kate set down the glass. "We have people missing."

"I'll get them," Robert said. He went inside, then returned shortly with Alfiero and Maria.

Alfiero, Kate noted with pride, looked younger than he had five years ago when the two of them returned to Tuscany. Good food and rest and freedom from worry had taken years off him. With all the servants she and Robert had hired from the village, he really did not have much to do but give advice as to how the villa should be run.

Kate was proudest of the change in Maria. With Bianca taking over her chores as keeper of the house—at least until her new baby was born—Maria was free to care for Mario and Lucia, for Stella and the children of the other servants, who had been offered the choice of living down in the village or up on the hill.

Those with offspring chose the hill.

Maria oversaw them well. They liked to hear her stories of how her power had served her, though the events five years ago at the villa were never mentioned. She was the best at coming up with games and was the only one who could match Stella at tossing rocks into the dolphin fountain.

Thanks to Robert's largesse, the matching fountain in Belmare once again flowed with water. But the one in the villa contained only rocks. The courtyard frescoes that looked down on it were being repaired, the work having been postponed until the right artists could be found.

So much bounty. Kate kissed Robert's cheek. So much love.

Alfiero cleared his throat and gestured toward the garden, where workers from the fields had begun gathering. The success of the Donati vineyard, as it was still called, mattered as much to them as anyone.

Kate stepped away from her husband and handed the wineglass to Maria.

"Please, tell us if our vintage will be a success. We've blended Sangiovese grapes into what we hope will be the finest Chianti in Tuscany, but there's always the chance we'll end up with vinegar."

Maria took the glass in her still-strong hand, lifting it in a toast to the husband and wife. She took a sip, letting the wine rest for a moment on her palate.

"It's young," she said.

This much the Velas already knew, but neither spoke.

Another sip. "I'm getting a vision." Her face remained solemn, but she could not hide the twinkle in her eye.

"Life is good. So, too, is the wine."

A cheer went up. Robert celebrated by kissing

his wife, then ordering more glasses, more wine, a holiday, and food for everyone.

Success meant far more than the income it would bring. It meant a thriving village, people with purpose, and something else that most would not appreciate: the yield of the vineyard was the only place the old and once-honored name of Donati would survive.

Later, when the children were in bed and the celebrating done, Kate and Robert stood at the back of the terrace, between two of the statues of prancing boys, and gazed at the distant hills with their rows of tall cypress trees turned rosy in the dying light. Kate preferred the scene at daybreak, with the sun coming up behind them, but on this evening they had a peaceful look that matched the way she was feeling.

"We've got hawks and gulls and storks and countless other birds I can't begin to identify," she said. "But no falcons. Do you suppose they will ever return?"

"Will it worry you if they do?"

She turned to look at him.

"The curse was a myth, a dark story born of legend and coincidence. Nothing more. We've got two beautiful children to prove it."

She glanced back at the hills.

"No, their return will not worry me. As long as

I have you with me. You've taught me I can handle just about anything."

"Including me?"

"You most of all."

He yawned. "I'm getting sleepy."

"No, you're not."

"I concede. I'm not."

"But you want to go to bed."

"Am I so obvious?"

She looked down at the front of his trousers and nodded.

"After five years you would think I would have more restraint," he said.

"Restraint is not a trait I very much admire."

"That's one of the things about you that I love."

Her answer was to take his hand and lead him toward the door. She did not have to pull very hard.

Sometimes she felt guilty about possessing so much happiness, too greedy because she wanted the happiness to go on. But then she would think about the first part of her life, and the guilt would disappear.

Robert had suggested they take their children to America, to show them the land of their mother's birth.

Her response had been quick: "I didn't begin to live until I rode through the village and saw you for the first time. They know where I was born."

Upstairs in the airy room that had once been hers alone, the room she now shared with her husband, she had her own celebration. It involved no fancy dress, in fact, no dress at all, no food, not even wine, although that was a blasphemous idea considering the times.

All it took was two people who were very much in love, who had lost much and gained much, who understood that no matter how successful they were or would be, the greatest possession in life was love.

He rides out of the Yorkshire mist, a dark figure on a dark horse. Is he a living man or a nightmare vision, conjured up by her fearful imagination and her uncertain future? Voices swirl in her head:

> They say he's more than human.
>
> A man's life is in danger when he's around . . .
>
> And a woman's virtue.

Repelled yet fascinated, Lucinda finds herself swept into a whirlwind courtship. Yet even as his lips set fire to her heart, she cannot forget his words of warning on the night they met:

> Tread softly. Heed little that you see and hear.
>
> Then leave.
>
> For God's sake, leave.

Whether he is the lover of her dreams or the embodiment of all she fears, she senses he will always be her . . . devil in the dark.

___52407-4 $5.99 US/$6.99 CAN

Moonshadow

PENELOPE NERI

"Lillies-of-the-valley," he murmurs, "the sweet scent of innocence." Yet his kisses are anything but innocent as he feeds her deepest desires while honeysuckle and wild roses perfume the languid air.

"Steyning Hall. It is a cold place. And melancholy," he warns, "almost as if it is . . .waiting for someone. Perhaps your coming will change all that."

Wedded mere hours, Madeleine gazes up at the windows of the mansion, stained the color of blood by the dying sun. In the shifting moonshadows she hears voices calling, an infant wailing, and knows not whether to flee for her life or offer up her heart.

___52416-3 $5.99 US/$6.99 CAN

Dorchester Publishing Co., Inc.
P.O. Box 6640
Wayne, PA 19087-8640

THE SCARLETTI CURSE

CHRISTINE FEEHAN

Strange, twisted carvings adorn the *palazzo* of the great Scarletti family. But a still more fearful secret lurks within its storm-tossed turrets. For every bride who enters its forbidding walls is doomed to leave in a casket. Mystical and unfettered, Nicoletta has no terror of ancient curses and no fear of marriage . . . until she looks into the dark, mesmerizing eyes of *Don* Scarletti. She has sworn no man will command her, thinks her gift of healing sets her apart, but his is the right to choose among his people. And he has chosen her. Compelled by duty, drawn by desire, she gives her body into his keeping, and prays the powerful, tormented *don* will be her heart's destiny, and not her soul's demise.

___52421-X $5.99 US/$6.99 CAN

ACROSS A STARLIT SEA

REBECCA BRANDEWYNE

They were betrothed before she was born. She has no say in her future, no voice with which to protest the agreement made by her father that irrevocably binds her to Jarrett Chandler, a man whose hot blood and swift temper can make him as savage as their native Cornish moors . . . a man determined to claim what he's been promised. Unwilling to be a helpless pawn, Laura fights him in every way she knows. But even she has to admit that the tingling which courses through her body as Jarrett takes her in his iron embrace is not fueled solely by fear. Yet to succumb to the tortuous longings means she may have to forfeit the security of innocence and delve into desires that threaten to drown her in a sea of passion.

___52440-6 $5.99 US/$7.99 CAN

THE WOLF OF HASKELL HALL
COLLEEN SHANNON

With the coming of the moon, wild happenings disturb the seaswept peace of Haskell Hall. And for the newest heiress, deep longing mingles with still deeper fear. Never has she been so powerfully drawn to a man as she is to Ian Griffith, with his secretive amber eyes and tightly leashed sensuality. Awash in the seductive moonlight of his tower chamber, she bares herself to his fierce passions. But has she freed a tormented soul with her loving gift or loosed a demon who hunts unsuspecting women as his prey?

___52412-0 $5.99 US/$6.99 CAN

The Shadowing
Joan Overfield

Evil is the first word that comes to mind when Anne Garthwicke arrives at Castle MacCairn. Duty bound to help her father appraise the holdings, she has no choice but to stay. And her trepidation deepens after meeting the laird. Proud and powerful, he embodies all the wildness of the Scottish highlands and incites dreams of carnal passion such as Anne has never experienced. Achingly tender one moment and roughly forceful the next, Ruairdh MacCairn has a beast within straining to break loose. And according to legend, it is only a matter of time before the monster will escape. Anne already knows her heart is lost, but she can only hope that when the moment of fate arrives, her body won't be sacrificed as well.

___52458-9 $5.99 US/$7.99 CAN

Whispers of Goodbye

Karen White

I need you. I am so afraid. . . . As soon as she reads the words, Catherine sets off for Louisiana to help her sister. Upon entering the moss-draped woods surrounding the house, Cat finds herself immersed in a mystery as murky as the mighty Mississippi River. For Elizabeth has disappeared, and Cat suspects her sister's husband knows more than he is saying. His dark eyes tell her he has great sadness; his arms speak of much of warmth; and his lips have a language all their own. But not even a whisper of her sister. Drawn into a web of family secrets and ancient superstitions, Cat hardly knows what to fear most: the deadly cottonmouth snakes, the deceptively peaceful swamps, or the dashingly powerful man who can steal her breath and sear her heart.

Dorchester Publishing Co., Inc.
P.O. Box 6640
Wayne, PA 19087-8640

_52455-4
$5.99 US/$6.99 CAN